"Sorry about your dress," Max said,

apologizing once again.

"It doesn't matter." Lauren stared at him for a moment, silent, still. He'd felt awkward standing there with his fingers itching to touch her, his mouth wanting to kiss her. If she'd been any other woman he'd have done just that.

But she was *the* Lauren Remington and he was just Max Wilde.

She'd tilted her head and glanced over her shoulder at the open door leading into the mansion. Slowly, she'd looked back at him, the nervousness evident in her eyes, and asked, "Where are you going?"

"As far away from here as I can get. You know, it's not too late to run away with me."

"I wish I could go with you," she blurted out. "I wish . . ." She smiled, kissed him hastily, then turned around and ran, disappearing once more behind the marble walls that separated their worlds.

PATTI BERG

Born to Be Wild

AVON BOOKS
An Imprint of HarperCollinsPublishers

This is a work of fiction. Names, characters, places, and incidents are products of the author's imagination or are used fictitiously and are not to be construed as real. Any resemblance to actual events, locales, organizations, or persons, living or dead, is entirely coincidental.

AVON BOOKS
An Imprint of HarperCollins*Publishers*
10 East 53rd Street
New York, New York 10022-5299

Copyright © 2001 by Patti Berg
ISBN: 0-380-81682-2
www.avonromance.com

First Avon Books paperback printing: February 2001

Avon Trademark Reg. U.S. Pat. Off. and in Other Countries, Marca Registrada, Hecho en U.S.A.
HarperCollins® is a trademark of HarperCollins Publishers Inc.

Printed in the U.S.A.

10 9 8 7 6 5 4 3 2 1

To Bob,
for a million and one
wild and wonderful reasons.

 *One*

"*O*h, dear!"

Lauren Remington drew a fine line through Zippo's Delicatessen, the last caterer listed in the Palm Beach Yellow Pages. She couldn't possibly hire a deli—especially one called Zippo's—to prepare and serve the fine food for Betsy Endicott's wedding to Richard W. D. Stribling IV.

Henri's, the most in-demand purveyor of fine cuisine in Palm Beach, had been Betsy's choice. She'd wanted to serve her guests Henri's fabulous poached quail eggs with Beluga caviar, his medallions of grilled salmon with citrus dressing, and prawns with curry sauce and mango chutney. She'd wanted Henri's celebrated tall, dark, and handsome waiters, who never dressed in anything more common than Armani, strolling across the lawns as they attended each honored guest. Betsy had wanted her wedding to be the most marvelous event of the season.

Poor Betsy. She's in for a big disappointment, Lauren mused, drumming the end of her pen on the Yellow Pages.

Henri, sadly, had passed away yesterday morning, an act of God that no contract could overrule. This meant he would not be preparing the ultimate in canapés for Betsy's reception. As if that wasn't bad enough, Henri's entire staff, not to mention the best chefs for miles around, planned to attend his funeral, which, unfortunately, was scheduled for the same day and time as Betsy Endicott's wedding.

Lauren sighed. Who on earth could she possibly get to prepare the luscious feast that needed to be served in three days?

Staring at the blue ink running through Zippo's Delicatessen, she tried to imagine the hors d'oeuvres a place called Zippo's would concoct. Suddenly, visions of a six-foot-long submarine sandwich oozing with mayonnaise, American cheese, and salami came to mind. And then she imagined the garlic on everyone's breath!

She hastily scribbled a zigzag line through Zippo's, and spun around in the kitchen chair to face her butler. "This isn't going too well, is it, Charles?"

The only person she trusted enough to confide in about this dilemma came toward her, the soles of his wing tips silent on the gleaming black and white tiled kitchen floor. His face was totally devoid of expression, the look he usually wore when contemplating what to say. The tall, always slender, white-haired Englishman, who'd been part of her life for all but the first of her twenty-nine years, rarely spoke without careful consideration of his words, not even now, when she longed to hear him say that she'd only imagined the disastrous occurrences of the past few hours.

Crossing her legs, Lauren absently smoothed the ice-blue silk of her slacks over her knee as she watched Charles stir tea in a delicate Limoges cup. Steam from the Earl Grey whirled before him. It smelled delicious, but she had the feeling an entire box of rich, dark Godivas would be more comforting at the moment.

Charles set the saucer on the kitchen table and walked away, stopping when he reached the outside door. Lauren wondered if he planned to leave her alone, with this entire mess to straighten out on her own. She'd always—well, most of the time—valued his advice, and she needed it now. Thankfully he turned to face her.

Linking his hands behind the back of his crisp white jacket, Charles cleared his throat, which, Lauren knew from past experience, was not a good sign. "Pardon me for saying this, Miss Remington, but *no*, things are not going well."

"Those aren't the words I wanted to hear."

He cleared his throat again. "Have you considered contacting Miss Endicott and informing her that you've encountered a slight complication in her wedding plans?"

Lauren's eyes narrowed at the ludicrous suggestion. She'd failed at many things in her life, but she would not fail as a wedding planner!

"Betsy's wedding is three days away," she reminded Charles. "She's flying back from Paris today with her gown, and tomorrow the yacht and crew Dickie hired for their round-the-world honeymoon sails into port."

She pushed out of the chair and crossed the kitchen. Gripping the edge of the counter, she stared out the window at the swaying palms, at the lawn running down to the sandy beach, and across the dark blue ocean. Lauren remembered Betsy's happiness when she'd talked about getting married, remembered the wistful look in her eyes when she'd said, "Dickie really loves me." Lauren had mistakenly thought the same thing a time or two, but she would never burst Betsy's bubble. She wasn't that jaded by the misfortunes of love and matrimony to think that all marriages ended in divorce.

Besides, she truly believed that Dickie did love Betsy and that they were perfect for each other. And perfect people deserved an exquisite, flawless wedding.

She walked back to the table and sat down, resolved to succeed. "No, Charles, I'm not going to tell Betsy that the caterer died, *or* that I can't find a suitable replacement for the lavish event I talked her into letting me plan." She didn't add that Betsy had agreed to hire her in spite of her family's protests, which furthered Lauren's resolve. "Betsy is one of my dearest and oldest friends, and one way or another, I'll make sure her wedding goes without a hitch."

"I have every faith in you, Miss Remington."

Charles had never been good at telling lies. Still, she appreciated his effort.

"Do you have any cookies to go with this tea?" she asked, taking another sip of the Earl Grey as she turned toward the table once again. "Something chocolate would be lovely."

Determined to find a solution to the problem, she slid an index finger down the column of caterers to make sure she hadn't missed anyone, or crossed out one by accident. When that proved fruitless, she skimmed the list of other people she'd already contacted: chefs she knew, every country club she'd ever been a member of or visited, and cooks Charles had recommended. She'd come up empty-handed everywhere she'd turned because no one wanted to handle a wedding of this magnitude on such short notice. Obviously she had to look beyond the norm—but definitely not Zippo's.

She plucked a heavily-dipped-in-chocolate cookie from the plate Charles set before her and nibbled the edge as she watched Charles moving expertly around the kitchen. She'd never noticed how comfortable he seemed in this room. She wondered if he kept company with Mrs. Fisk, her cook, who, unfortunately, was on vacation in Tahiti. Could there be a possibility that Charles dabbled in the culinary arts, that he could prepare a meal as well as serve it?

Dunking her cookie in the tea, she studied the vast array of cookbooks filling a cabinet on the far side of the kitchen. Time and time again she'd watched Mrs. Fisk look up recipes and whip out seemingly effortless masterpieces. How hard, she wondered, could fixing canapés possibly be?

"I think I've come up with a solution to the problem," she announced to Charles.

"You have?"

"Of course. You and I will do the cooking."

Charles cocked his head toward her, and one of his bushy white eyebrows rose. "*You*, Miss Remington?"

"The *two* of us, Charles."

"But I don't cook, and, pardon me for saying this, but neither do you."

"I prepared a meal for you once when I was a teenager, and I believe you told me it was delicious."

Charles's eyes darted toward the black and white tiles on the floor. "I lied, Miss Remington."

She smiled, trying to disguise her hurt and to ease Charles's discomfort. The revelation that she couldn't cook shouldn't have come as much of a surprise, she realized, taking another bite of cookie. She stared at the blur of papers in front of her, remembering another time when she'd tried to please a man in that age-old-way: through his stomach.

She'd been a young bride of not quite twenty when she'd fixed a meal for her husband, hoping to give Chip a reason to stay home rather than run off to the track where he did nothing but lose money.

Chip, sadly, had preferred horses to her—and her cooking.

And then there was Leland Lancaster—husband number two—who'd preferred liquor to food, and sex with other women to making love to his wife. She hadn't bothered cooking for any man following her disastrous marriages to Chip and Leland. After all, the men she knew weren't interested in her homemaking skills, only in merging their old blue-blooded money with hers.

She'd learned far too late that neither one of her husbands was interested in a family life, a house full of children, or loving her, all the things she'd truly wanted, desires that were nothing more than elusive dreams.

But none of that mattered right now, she decided, shaking away the dregs of her past and her insecurities about her present and future. The important thing was finding someone who could create fabulous canapés. She would not let Betsy down on her special day.

Charles stepped toward the table, adding a few more cookies to the plate. "Are you sure you've called every caterer in the book, Miss Remington?"

"Every one. Even Bad Bubba's Barbecue."

Charles ran his own finger down the page, slowly looking at each entry. "I believe you might have missed one."

Lauren leaned close. "Where?"

"Right here." He tapped the page. "It's nearly hidden by the line you drew through Bad Bubba's."

Lauren scrutinized the entry for a moment, then laughed. "You don't really believe that a place called Born To Be Wild Catering could live up to the standards of Palm Beach society?"

"Might I remind you, Miss Remington, that you're beginning to sound like your mother."

Lauren gritted her teeth. She was not a snob—she had never been and never would be. On top of that, she was tired of doing things that pleased her mother, her father, her brother, her ex-husbands, or her friends.

She wanted to do things her own way, on her own terms. Her friends snickered about the choices she'd made in the last couple of years. They'd lambasted her for dumping Australian polo player Peter Leighton shortly before their wedding, and the tabloids were having a ball talking about her attempt to be a wedding planner.

The laughter hurt. They didn't know and they obviously didn't care how much succeeding at this venture meant to her. She'd failed at all the meaningful things in life, and she wanted desperately to change all that. Her business was just the first step in starting over; she wouldn't let pride get in the way.

Taking a deep breath, she stared at the phone number in the Yellow Pages and decided that desperate times called for desperate measures.

She grabbed the phone and punched in the number. Born To Be Wild might not sound like the perfect caterer for Betsy Endicott's high-society wedding, but Born To Be Wild appeared to be her only hope.

As she listened to the first ring at the other end of the line, she silently prayed for a miracle, for Born To Be Wild Catering to be available on Saturday and—she crossed her fingers—to be able to make something besides fried chicken or ribs.

The people of Palm Beach could laugh all they wanted at her attempts to be a businesswoman. She didn't give a fig for what they thought. All that mattered was her own self-esteem, which had been knocked for a loop a few times over the years.

She'd failed at two marriages, and would have failed at a third if she'd gone through with marrying that jerk Peter Leighton. The tabloids painted a picture of her as a flighty, not terribly bright fashion plate. But they were wrong—dead wrong! It didn't matter if she proved it to the people of the world or not. She had to prove it to herself.

Max Wilde lifted the wooden spoon to his mouth and tasted his newest concoction—sizzling pork ribs with pineapple and papaya hot and spicy barbecue sauce. Not bad, he had to admit. Helena Fabiano had asked for something special for her husband Luigi's seventy-fifth birthday party, because Luigi had grown tired of her raviolis and lasagna, and Max planned to go all out.

Tonight he'd test the menu for Saturday's

event on his kids. Ryan and Jamie never failed to tell him when a recipe sucked—their choice of words, not his. If he got even one set of thumbs down, he'd spend all night improving the recipe. He didn't know Luigi from Adam and he could have told Mrs. Fabiano that she'd have to select from the stock catering items, but that wasn't his style. Born To Be Wild Catering aimed to please. Besides, Mrs. Fabiano had tweaked his cheek when she'd asked for something special. How could he possibly turn her down?

"Hey, Max!"

Jed Trumbo's voice hit Max's ears long before his teenage assistant pushed through the swinging doors and swaggered into the kitchen. Before Max could stop him, Jed stuck his finger into the pot of steaming sauce. "Shiii . . ." The curse was stifled when Jed shoved his finger into his mouth.

"Lesson number thirty-two," Max said, turning off the burner. "Don't stick your finger in anything that's bubbling on top the stove. That's a sure sign it's hotter than hell."

Max turned the cold water on in the sink, grabbed Jed's hand, and shoved it under the faucet. "Hold it there for a minute and it'll feel better."

"You know, Max," Jed said, shaking his hand under the water, as if that would make the pain die down faster, "I'm not too good at this kitchen stuff. It's not that I don't like working with you, it's just that I'd be better off fixing engines or something."

Max knew full well that Jed knew how to fix

engines. He knew how to hot-wire them, too, which was what the kid had been doing when Max first laid eyes on him. Jed hadn't had a record when he'd tried to take off with Max's '68 Corvette, and Max was determined the kid never would.

He was a seventeen-year-old who'd been knocked around by his father, had dropped out of school, and was living on the streets—the same thing that could have happened to Max if his foster dad hadn't taken him in. So he'd found Jed a place to stay, had given him a job and attempted to be his mentor. After three weeks of trying to make things work, Max knew that Jed's mechanical skills far outweighed his abilities as a chef's assistant.

"Why don't you head over to the Hole and talk to Jazz or Gabe," Max suggested, pulling a tray of sweet potato biscuits from the oven. "See if they can help you find a new job."

"Does that mean I can't hang around here no more?"

"You can hang out here or the Hole whenever you want, as long you get another job, show up to work on time, and stay out of trouble." Max tossed Jed a towel. "Before you take off, could you call—"

"Oh, crap!" Jed blurted out. "There's some lady on the phone wantin' to talk to you about catering a wedding on Saturday. I told her you was busy, but she refused to take no for an answer."

Max bit back his irritation and slapped Jed on

the shoulder, knowing the kid needed encouragement more than harsh words. "I'll see you at the Hole later."

Jed didn't waste a minute getting out of the house, and before the back door slammed, Max grabbed the phone at the end of the kitchen counter. "This is Max."

He expected someone to yell. He thought for sure the woman at the other end of the line would ask him what the hell took him so long to get to the phone, but he didn't hear a word. Instead he heard the distinct sound of fingernails drumming against the mouthpiece.

"Sorry for the delay," he said. "I had an emergency in the kitchen."

"I know all about emergencies, Mr.—"

"Wilde." He liked the sound of her voice. Sultry. Sexy.

With his luck she was probably ninety-two years old!

"I have a definite emergency, Mr. Wilde," she said. "I have a wedding planned for Saturday and my caterer died."

"Henri?"

"Please don't tell me you're going to his funeral."

She sounded frantic . . . and a lot younger than ninety-two. "No, that day I'll be catering Luigi Fabiano's seventy-fifth birthday party."

"That's too bad," she said, followed by a very deep sigh. "May I ask what kind of food you're serving Mr. Fabiano?"

"Ribs."

"Oh." He couldn't mistake the despair in her voice.

"What's wrong?" he asked. "Don't you like ribs?"

"I love ribs. But that's not what I had in mind for this wedding."

"What did you have in mind?"

"Something a little more formal. Do you do anything exotic, like poached quail eggs?"

Max laughed at her question. He'd prepared quail eggs at the culinary academy and for too many uppity society shindigs when he worked with his foster dad. They were dainty and taste-less, a far cry from the spicy, finger-licking and mouth-watering fare he preferred. "Quail eggs were Henri's specialty," he said. "Mine's ribs."

"Oh, dear."

He leaned against the counter, thinking he could spend a good hour or two listening to this woman. He liked the little-girl sound in the way she said, "Oh, dear," the way she sighed deeply into the phone. Unfortunately, he didn't have an hour or two to converse with a stranger. He didn't have any time on Saturday, either, which meant he couldn't possibly help the lady with the sultry voice. "I'm sorry, ma'am, but I'm booked this weekend."

"I understand that, but as I mentioned, this is an emergency. I've got nearly two hundred guests coming. I hadn't wanted to serve ribs but . . . well . . ." She sighed again. "Are they good?"

The lady—if she was a lady—sounded awfully picky for a woman in need.

"They're the best in Florida. But like *I* mentioned, I'm busy on Saturday."

"I'll pay twice your normal amount."

"That sounds enticing, but I can't be in two places at the same time."

He heard her fingernails again, this time drumming on something other than the phone. A table maybe. A desk. Something expensive, considering her offer.

"Three times your normal amount."

"The money sounds good, but—"

"Four times, and that's my final offer." She was silent again, giving Max time to think it over. "Please."

He hated it when a woman said *please*. "Let me think about it, okay? Maybe there's a way I can swing both. I'll call you back in a couple of hours."

"I can't wait a couple of hours. I need an answer now. I'll even pay you up front if you're worried about the money."

"You don't even know what my ribs taste like."

"Look, Mr. Wilde, as long as your food is edible, I'll hire you. Of course, it would be nice to have something not quite as messy as ribs, something a little more elegant, but right now, I'll take anything. If you need references, I can give you a hundred different people to call. I always pay on time. Call my bank. Just tell them you're catering a wedding for Lauren Remington."

Lauren Remington? The Lauren Remington, the object of a foolish kid's affection? The woman whose dress he'd accidentally doused with a glass of champagne when he'd been a waiter at the rehearsal dinner before her first wedding? The woman who'd laughed at the incident, then followed him outside, where she'd kissed him and made him think that a tough, wrong-side-of-the-tracks guy like him could have a chance with a rich and beautiful socialite?

He rubbed his arm, where a tattoo served as a constant reminder of his folly, and laughed to himself. So, she was getting married . . . *again*. That shouldn't surprise him, not for someone as fickle as Lauren Remington.

"Did you hear me, Mr. Wilde? This really is urgent."

"I heard you," he said, annoyed that the woman who'd once bruised his ego had popped back into his life, and damn if she didn't have to do it right before another one of her weddings.

"Who's the lucky guy?" he asked, wondering what poor sucker had fallen for her this time around.

"You mean the groom?"

He laughed, as if there was more than one lucky guy in her life. "Yes, the groom."

"Dickie Stribling. Do you know him?"

A vision of Dickie Stribling hit Max between the eyes. "I know him." He'd waited on Mr. Stribling once or twice. He'd served half the people in Palm Beach, Florida, when he was younger, back in the days when everyone who was anyone hired his foster father's high-class French catering business.

Dickie Stribling wasn't a bad sort, if you could stomach the kind of guy who dressed in white shoes and pants, a navy blazer, and a gold-braided captain's hat. Dickie Stribling was rich beyond imagining, too, just the kind of man someone like Lauren Remington would go for.

"Dickie's such a lovely man and this wedding means the world to him," the woman continued. "So, will you *please* consider catering for me this Saturday? If not for me, then for Dickie."

Dickie's a gullible dope, Max thought. The woman sounded fond of him, not in love, which didn't seem like much of a basis for marriage, and now she wanted Max to make the day special! Considering the way Miss Palm Beach had humiliated him all those years ago and the fact that she'd probably humiliate Dickie somewhere down the road, he should have said no without any hesitation, but he plowed his fingers through his hair and said, "Hold on. Let me look at my schedule."

He knew full well he didn't have time to cater some fancy Palm Beach affair, especially a wedding for the oft-married Lauren Remington, but she'd said "Please" more than once, and she sounded desperate. Her breeding made her believe she could have anything she wanted, and damn if his upbringing didn't make it nearly impossible for him to turn down someone in need.

She wasn't exactly a charity case, but what the hell!

"All right," he said, hoping this wasn't a big mistake, that some asinine desire to see her again wasn't screwing with his brain, "it looks like I can work your wedding into my schedule."

"Oh, thank goodness. How soon can you come over so we can discuss the menu?"

Max looked at his watch. "How about one-forty-five?"

She was silent a moment, and he thought for sure he heard a sniffle on the other end of the phone before hearing her soft, sultry voice again. "That would be wonderful, Mr. Wilde. Thank you."

He hung up the phone and stared into the pot of hot and spicy barbecue sauce. It was as different from poached quail eggs as he was from Lauren Remington. He realized that now, but he hadn't given their differences much thought the first time he'd seen her.

His job that night was to serve champagne, to keep an eye on every crystal glass and to make sure they were never empty. But he'd forgotten all about the champagne when he caught a glimpse of the bride-to-be. The golden highlights in her light brown hair glistened in the candlelight, her smile glowed, and he'd thought she was the most incredibly beautiful creature he'd ever laid eyes on. Why she'd wanted to marry the man at her side made no sense to him. Chip Chasen was brash and arrogant and swilled one glass of champagne after another as he talked incessantly about his success at the track, comparing those wins to the conquest of his gorgeous bride.

Max had wanted to put a fist into the man's pretty face. But heading across the room, he found that the closer he got to Lauren, the less he thought about Chip. Stopping behind her chair, he tilted the bottle of Dom Perignon toward her glass and let his gaze roam over her shoulders, across her creamy skin and voluptuous cleavage. The champagne had just started to flow from the bottle when she turned her heavenly green eyes toward him. He was mesmerized, and he sure as hell wasn't paying attention to what he was doing as the bubbling wine spilled, and continued to spill, over the rim, right down the front of her fancy green dress.

Chip had yelled at him for his clumsiness, and Lauren had laughed in an effort to silence her husband-to-be. Max had apologized profusely, then made a bee-line out of the mansion, not stopping until he felt a gentle hand on his arm.

"Thank you," Lauren had said, her eyes suddenly warm, full of concern.

"What are you thanking me for?" he'd bit out in anger and embarrassment.

"For calming my nerves," she'd said softly. "For giving me a good reason to laugh." Her dress was soggy and she should have been enraged, but he saw only a hint of fear in her eyes, not fury.

"Sorry about your dress," he'd said, apologizing once again.

"It doesn't matter." She stared at him for a moment, silent, still. He'd felt awkward standing there with his fingers itching to touch her, his mouth wanting to kiss her. If she'd been any other girl he would have done just that, but she was *the* Lauren Remington and he was just Max Wilde.

She'd tilted her head and looked over her shoulder at the open door leading into the mansion. Slowly, she'd looked back at him, the nervousness still evident in her eyes, and asked, "Where are you going?"

"As far away from here as I can get."

"I wish I could go with you," she'd blurted out. "I wish—" She'd smiled weakly, kissed him hastily on the cheek, then turned around and ran, disappearing once more behind the marble walls that separated their worlds.

All night long he'd thought about her words, her trepidation. He'd spent an entire evening working up the courage to rescue her from the marriage she'd seemed to dread, and then he'd shown up at her mansion the next morning, just in time to see her walking down the steps, a picture of perfection in shimmering white.

Marching up the drive, he'd thrust a fistful of orchids toward her. "It's not too late to run away with me."

The color seemed to drain from her face as her gaze trailed from the orchids, to the curious people gathering around her, to his eyes. A hesitant smile touched her lips. "Why would I want to run away? I'm getting married today . . . and . . . and I've never been happier."

"But—" A big hand clamped down on his shoulder, dragging him away from Lauren as she lifted the hem of her gown and climbed into the limo.

He'd made a fool of himself, and she'd punched a hole in his self-esteem. She'd probably made fools of a lot of men. Fortunately he'd gotten over that day a long time ago—or at least he thought he had. Thinking about it now made him remember the humiliation he'd felt with so many laughing eyes staring at him as her limousine drove away.

He didn't want to like the woman whose name and picture he'd seen plastered on the front of the tabloids too many times to count, but in spite of the blow to his ego, he couldn't forget the anxiety that had been in her eyes that night. And he'd definitely heard the desperation in her voice over the phone today.

He cursed the sense of chivalry that had made him want to help her again. He also cursed the ridiculous urge he had to see her, because he had the uncanny feeling that Miss Palm Beach was going to cause him endless amounts of grief.

 *Two*

*L*auren stood in the center of the living room studying the all-white arrangement of anthurium, ginger, and Dendrobium orchids sitting on top of the pink and white marble mantel. "It's perfect. Exactly what I want," she told Mr. Friedrichs.

"Are you positive you don't want a splash of color? A little pink to match your furniture's upholstery? A speck of yellow or purple?"

"Oh, no," Lauren said, walking across the room to look at the flowers from another angle. "I'm going with an all-white theme for Betsy Endicott's wedding." Her mother would never approve—naturally—of an all-white theme, but her mother wasn't around. Mr. Friedrichs didn't approve of all-white, either, but going with the same old mixed-color bouquets seemed terribly boring.

"Very well," Mr. Friedrichs said, flipping open his calendar and studying his notes. "I'll be here early Saturday morning to personally supervise the arrangement of all the flowers."

"The interior designer will be here as well," Lauren said. "She has yards and yards of white satin ribbon and lace for the chairs—"

"Ms. Templeton and I have already coordinated our efforts. Naturally, it will be much easier with both the wedding and reception held here in your home. We won't have the logistical difficulties that can sometimes occur when we divide our efforts between a church and a reception room." Mr. Friedrichs moved one of the anthurium stems about a quarter of an inch in the vase. "You can trust me implicitly, Miss Remington. Betsy Endicott's wedding will be perfect."

He might be a tad stiff, Lauren thought, but she'd never hire anyone but Friedrichs of Palm Beach to do the flowers. He was persnickety, but his tastes were impeccable and his work habits decisive and prompt. Nothing could ever go wrong using someone like Mr. Friedrichs.

Of course, she'd also felt that way about Henri.

She quickly gave Mr. Friedrichs the once-over. Thank goodness—for his sake and hers—he didn't look like heart-attack material. Not only that, but she imagined a thorough and precise man like Mr. Friedrichs would have an operating procedure for his employees to follow should he suddenly expire. He was not a man to leave anything to chance.

She looked at her watch. One-fifteen. Max Wilde should be arriving within half an hour . . . she hoped. If he was late for their appointment, she'd worry from now until Saturday that the food for the reception would be a bust.

As she walked Mr. Friedrichs to the door, he offered more assurances that there wouldn't be a single wilted flower in sight, but it wasn't wilted flowers that worried her. Wilted lettuce and barbecue sauce were uppermost on her mind.

"Excuse me, Miss Remington."

"Yes, Charles," she said, closing the door as Mr. Friedrichs climbed into his Mercedes.

"Your mother is on the phone."

"Oh, dear."

"Would you like me to tell her you're out?"

Charles knew her feelings all too well, bless his heart, but she hadn't talked with her mother in well over a week, and even though their conversations were usually one-sided, she loved her mother dearly and enjoyed hearing her voice.

She retreated to her garden room, a homey place brimming with orchids, palms, and ferns. This was the place where she'd hoped to read to her children, where she'd planned to rock them to sleep at night. Much to her dismay, the only things she'd nurtured in this room were the tropical plants she loved.

Thoughts of children and family had been on her mind a lot in the past few months, ever since she'd received the wonderful news that her sister-in-law Samantha was going to have twins. Her brother Jack had waited a long time to get married, and when he did, he went completely against convention and married someone Mother claimed was totally wrong for him. But Jack had never been happier.

Lauren wished she'd gone against convention a few times. She definitely wished she'd ignored her mother's dictates. If she had, maybe she'd be married to the most wonderful man in the world by now. Maybe she'd have a house full of children to love. She laughed to herself. Celeste, Lady Ashford, was not completely to blame for Lauren's poor choices in men, even though she'd shoved Chip, Leland, and even Peter in front of her daughter's eyes. No, Lauren knew she had to take responsibility for her own actions—the disastrous ones of the past and anything that happened in the future.

Making her mother understand that she wanted to take charge of her own life, however, had not been and never would be an easy task.

Sitting in her favorite, flared-back white wicker chair, she lifted the phone. "Hello, Mother."

"Hello, darling. I've just gotten off the telephone with Bunny Endicott and she tells me that Chef Henri passed away. It's absolutely dreadful, and she's worried sick that something will go wrong at Betsy's wedding."

"Everything's—"

"Yes, yes, I'm sure everything's fine, darling,

but you can't possibly expect any of us to forget what happened at Holly Rutherford's wedding."

Lauren cringed at the memory. "That was an accident."

"It was a fiasco, Lauren. You can't believe my embarrassment when the legs collapsed on that table and the wedding cake slid into the swimming pool. I still have nightmares about that moment, and every one of those horrid dreams is played out in slow motion."

"The tables aren't going to collapse at Betsy's wedding," Lauren said emphatically, and absently crossed her fingers, hoping her plans for Betsy's wedding wouldn't fall apart, as they had for Holly Rutherford. "The cake isn't going to go into the swimming pool because the table won't be set anywhere close to the pool. And you're forgetting, Mother, that I'm the one who was responsible for everything, not you."

"You are my daughter—everything you do is a reflection on me. It always has been, it always will be. I certainly hope when Betsy's wedding is over that you'll call off this crazy whim of yours to be a wedding planner."

"It's not a whim, Mother. It's a career. And one that I enjoy."

"Perhaps, but we can't always do what we enjoy. You should do what you do best, darling."

"And what is that?"

There was a moment of silence, as if Lady Ashford was striving to think of something her daughter did well. Lauren could offer a whole string of suggestions, such as pour tea, smile, and dress to perfection, but she needed more meaningful endeavors in her life.

"Gerald Harcourt is flying in for Betsy's wedding," Celeste said, abruptly changing the subject to men, one of Celeste's favorite topics. "He asks about you whenever I see him."

"He's just being polite."

"It's much more than that. He's been single for nearly a year now, and you've been divorced from Leland for, what is it, darling, six years?"

"Eight."

"Eight years of loneliness, except, of course, when you and Peter were together."

"I'm perfectly happy on my own."

Her mother laughed. "You can't fool me. I know you better than anyone."

If only that were true, Lauren thought, but her mother knew little about her, because she'd never been around long enough to learn what made her daughter tick.

"Well, darling, I really must go. Your stepfather and I are going to a reception for the prime minister this evening. I picked up a lovely Balenciaga gown in Paris early this week. If you were close by, I'd borrow that antique ruby necklace of yours, which would look absolutely divine with the new gown. Andrew, of course, feels a string of diamonds is sufficient, but what do men know?"

"Andrew has wonderful taste. You couldn't ask for a finer husband."

"No . . . I suppose I couldn't." Lauren heard the

hint of tension in her mother's voice and the reluctance of her words.

"Is everything all right, Mother?"

"Of course, darling. Now, please, don't forget what I said. Give up this foolish wedding planning business as soon as Betsy's wedding is over. And whatever you do, make sure nothing goes wrong on Saturday."

Lauren heard a kiss blown across thousands of miles—from London to Palm Beach—and then the dial tone. "I won't give up, Mother," she said out loud, before hanging up the phone, more determined than ever to succeed.

She looked up when Charles came into the room, his timing perfect, as always. "Mr. Wilde has arrived."

Lauren looked at her watch. One-forty-five, exactly. At least she didn't have to worry about Mr. Wilde's punctuality.

"You'll find him in the library," Charles added, and cleared his throat. "Would you like me to accompany you?"

She appreciated his concern, but sometimes Charles could be a bit overprotective. Her brother Jack was the same way, rarely realizing that she was an adult and more than capable of taking care of herself. "Thanks, Charles," she said, as she headed for the library, "but I'm sure I can handle Mr. Wilde on my own."

"Very well, Miss Remington."

The first thing that caught Lauren's eye when she entered the library was a jacket tossed over the back of a gilt-edged chair, its black leather a definite contrast to the chair's delicate floral fabric. A battered black leather briefcase sat beside it on the floor.

Mr. Wilde, however, was not in the room. The French doors leading to a patio overlooking the Atlantic Ocean were open, and a light breeze rippled the drapes. She moved toward the doors, stopping in her tracks when she saw the man outside. His hands rested on the balustrade, bracing his body as he looked toward the surf.

Oh, dear! She could understand why Charles had wanted to keep her company.

Mr. Wilde's hair was, well . . . wild, and black, and the wind whipped through each collar-length wave. With him leaning against the railing, his white T-shirt stretching smoothly across wide shoulders and a muscular back, she couldn't help but stare at his entire form, especially the rich bronze biceps that flexed beneath his sleeves.

He wore faded blue jeans that weren't quite tight enough to show off the strength of his legs, but she could easily imagine the power beneath the denim. She allowed her gaze to leisurely travel down the length of his Levi's, to the black leather of his boots—those distinctive heavy ones that bad boys on motorcycles wore.

She gave some thought to running for Charles, but Mr. Wilde turned around, and the moment she was hit by the intense glare of his dark brown eyes—eyes that looked vaguely familiar—all thoughts of running disappeared.

It had been an awfully long time since a man

had set her senses on fire, and she couldn't remember the mere gaze from a man *ever* making her so hot that she needed to fan herself. What had come over her was anyone's guess, because a man like Max Wilde should not be stirring up anything more for her than delicious canapés.

Getting a hold on her libidinous emotions, Lauren marched across the patio to shake his hand. "Good afternoon. I'm Lauren Remington."

"Max Wilde," he said, his voice a deep, rich, and engaging—okay, erotic!—baritone that vibrated through her body. His handshake was strong and businesslike, although his callused palm felt much more virile than the smooth hands she usually shook. And his face. Goodness, he did not look like a businessman at all! His nose had a slight bend, as if it had been broken in one too many fights. A scar slashed across his right cheekbone. A hint of a smile appeared beneath his neatly trimmed mustache and goatee, and it didn't require close inspection to see the gold rings in his ears.

Mother would have banished the man immediately. Lauren, however, found him intriguing and rather . . . feral. But where had she seen him before? Men like Max Wilde frequented biker bars and, more than likely, strip joints. Naturally she'd been to neither. She didn't hang around tattoo parlors, either, but Mr. Wilde obviously did. It was impossible to miss the colorful design emblazoned on his right biceps, or the fact that what looked like the tail fin of a fish swished when his muscle flexed.

"It's a mermaid," he offered, when her eyes lingered on the undulating green and gold figure.

"How . . . interesting." Her fingers itched to push his T-shirt sleeve out of the way so she could see the entire tattoo, so she could touch an inch or two of his hard, masculine bronze skin, but somehow she managed to refrain. After all, this was a business meeting, and tattoos, not to mention sexy men, were not on the agenda.

Gathering her wits about her and turning her gaze back to his far too intense brown eyes, she smiled politely. "So, Mr. Wilde—"

"Max."

Oh, dear, they were not going to get very far if he continually addressed her in short, terse phrases, especially ones delivered in that all-too-familiar voice that nearly rendered her speechless.

"Is something troubling you?" he asked.

She could tell him he looked familiar, but it would seem terribly rude of her not to remember why, so she chose not to comment on that at all. Instead, she decided she'd be better off getting down to business. "Actually, I was wondering if you'd brought some menus for me to look at?"

"Yeah," he said, more than a tinge of annoyance sounding in his voice, as if he'd wanted to discuss something other than business. "I've got menus, photos, references."

She would have responded, would have said something along the lines of "Lovely," but he didn't give her the chance to speak, he merely stalked past her. His stride was long, his boots clunked heavily on the marble floor, and a casual observer might have thought he was angry. Goodness knows why!

Turning on her high heels, she followed him into the library and couldn't help but notice that everything in the room was delicate—except Max Wilde. He was overpowering. Breathtaking, actually. A tall, handsome, and untamed version of Marlon Brando in his younger days, and if she wasn't careful he might notice just how much in awe she was of him. And if there was one good thing she'd learned from her mother, it was to not let people who work for you get the upper hand.

She surreptitiously took a deep, calming breath while watching him open his briefcase. His shirt sleeve moved up another inch. The muscle in his biceps flexed, and the green and gold scales covering the mermaid's tail seemed to shimmer in the light from the chandelier. Did the creature have blond hair? she wondered. Could the nymph be a brunette or redhead? Was she wearing a skimpy bra, or was she topless?

A portfolio thudded on the desktop, yanking her attention away from the tattoo, but not from the man who whipped the Louis XVI chair around as if it weighed only a few ounces, then straddled it.

She swallowed hard as her eyes focused on his legs, on the worn spot on the inner thigh of his jeans, on his well-defined pecs stretching the cotton of his shirt. She was far too young for hot flashes but she could feel heat creeping up her chest.

Oh, dear! What had she gotten herself into?

"So," she managed to croak out, "where do we begin?"

His gaze dipped to her chest, which had to be crimson by now, to the fingers of her right hand which were twisting the diamond bracelet on her left wrist. This was the first time in her life a man had ever made her nervous, and when a slight grin touched his face, she ruefully realized he knew just how neurotic she was.

Without taking his gaze off her, he flipped open the leather-bound book filled with colorful pictures of tables laden with food. "Are you planning a sit-down dinner or buffet?"

Finally! They were going to discuss business. "Hors d'oeuvres," she said, putting on her best businesswoman pose. "It's a mid-afternoon wedding and I'd like the appetizers to be on the lighter side."

"How about a vegetable platter with ranch dressing?"

"No, I don't think that will do at all."

"How about fried zucchini and mini barbecued ribs."

"I was thinking something a little more . . . elegant."

Max chuckled as he flipped through the pages in his book. Was he teasing? she wondered, trying to make her even more uncomfortable, or were all his menu choices . . . common?

"I imagine chicken wings and ham pinwheels are a no, too?" he asked, his eyes sparkling as if he found the entire thing humorous.

"Out. Definitely out," she said, trying hard to

stay calm when she was thrown so totally off balance by this man. "The cake is decorated with white orchids, the flowers are being shipped in from Hawaii to give the inside and outside of my home a tropical look, and the wedding gown was handmade by Yves Saint Laurent." He looked like he was going to laugh, but she wasn't finding this at all funny. It was time to get serious and take the upper hand. "I'm sorry, Mr. Wilde—"

"Max."

"I'm sure you're wonderful at barbecues, *Max*, and the next time I have one, you'll be the first caterer I'll call. But I was hoping you could prepare something special for Betsy Endicott."

"Who's Betsy Endicott?"

Goodness, the man was maddening. "I'm guessing you don't read the society pages."

"Never. So, tell me, who's Betsy Endicott?"

"The bride."

He frowned. "I thought *you* were the bride."

"*Me?* Why would I want to marry Dickie Stribling?"

"Why did you want to marry Chip Chasen?"

Obviously he read something if he knew that she'd once been married to Chip, but the fact that he was literate, that he knew at least part of her background, didn't give him reason to be so rude.

"Why I married Chip is none of your business. As for Betsy Endicott, she's an old and dear friend, I'm planning her wedding, and it has to be perfect."

Once again he stared at her. "You're right, who you marry or don't marry isn't my business.

What you serve at Betsy Endicott's wedding is, so I suggest something along the lines of bleu cheese en croute, pink gulf shrimp, and Caribbean brochettes."

The way he easily ticked off each delectable tidbit surprised her. "You've prepared Caribbean brochettes before?"

"I'm a chef, Miss Remington. I don't hang my diplomas on the wall and I don't brag about my accomplishments. Instead, I let the food I prepare speak for me, and I haven't had any complaints."

He shoved out of the chair and Lauren followed him outside to the patio. He leaned on the balustrade again. She'd never appreciated abrupt individuals, but he did have a distinct way of laying out his credentials—all of them, including his backside, which was rather impressive, too.

"You'll need two ice sculptures," he said, staring across the lawn as if he didn't see her standing beside him. "I've got a guy who can carve a perfect orchid."

"His name isn't Fritz, is it?"

He hit her with that brown-eyed frown again. "No. Why?"

"He did an ice carving for a party I had a couple of years ago. He was drunk and mistakenly added—in great detail—a man's private parts to the sculpture of two lovers."

A hint of a smile touched his lips—finally. "That must have livened up the party."

"I never had the chance to find out, but I did learn before the evening began that I'm very good with an ice pick."

That made him laugh, a nice laugh that soft-ened his blunt demeanor, but it lasted only a moment before he got back to business.

"I'll set up your dessert tables with an array of pastries, petit fours, cakes, and tarts. I could make them all with a tropical flavor, to stay with your decorating theme, but I think it would be best to throw in some Viennese desserts to satisfy the guests who crave chocolate and whipped cream."

"Henri was going to—"

"I'm not Henri," he reminded her much too abruptly.

"No, you're definitely not Henri," she admit-ted, "but you're proving to be nearly as difficult." She watched his eyebrow raise a notch, but he didn't disagree. "All I was going to say is, I never cared for Henri's light-on-the-sugar-cream-and-chocolate desserts, and I prefer your suggestion. *Now*, what about the canapés?" she asked, not giving him a chance to gloat over the fact that she liked his style much more than Henri's.

"Stuffed mushrooms with spiced beef are always a hit. We can serve pink gulf shrimp, petit Wellingtons—you know, your basic upper crust hors d'oeuvres."

Max Wilde could talk a good story. Still, she had to ask, "What about references?"

"I though you were desperate."

Of course she was desperate, but she wasn't foolhardy! Max Wilde might have stunning biceps and a mesmerizing pair of dark brown eyes, but those impressive credentials didn't mean he could cook.

"You're a businessman," she stated, smiling politely. "Surely you understand the importance of checking references before you hire someone, even when you're sure they're perfect for the job."

He stared at her as if he were sizing her up, as if she were the one needing references. Then, without another word, he marched back into the library. The man had an unnerving habit of bolting from place to place, but she stayed right on his heels, stopping only when he ripped a sheet of paper from his briefcase and thrust it in front of her. "References."

He seemed irritated, something she'd seen far too often in creative types, but she didn't have time to be bothered by his little snit. Taking the list from his hands, she scanned it quickly, troubled that she didn't see even one familiar name. She'd hoped he'd worked for someone she knew, even a minor acquaintance who could make her feel more comfortable about hiring a big brute—even a sexy one—to cater Betsy's wedding.

"Is there a problem?" he asked.

"Of course not. But, I'd like to call a few of these people."

He lifted the receiver from the phone on the desk and held it out for her to take. "Better do it now. Saturday's not that far away. If you plan to hire me, I've got a lot of work to do."

It seemed awkward making the phone calls in front of him, but she dialed the first number, carrying the cordless phone across the room, hoping for some semblance of privacy.

Luann Tugmore gave Max a glowing recommendation. Best ribs she'd ever tried. As an aside, she mentioned that Max looked awfully good when she and her girlfriends invited him to stay for a swim after their sorority party. From the dreamy way the woman talked, Lauren couldn't help but wonder if Luann Tugmore had tasted more than Max's barbecued ribs.

Jennie and Dirk Chelsea had hired Max to prepare a real Hawaiian luau. Naturally he'd outdone himself, fixing genuine poi, serving the tenderest and best tasting pork they'd ever had, not to mention the fact that he'd helped Jennie procure fresh plumeria leis for half the cost she'd been quoted by several florists in town. The happy lady couldn't recommend Max highly enough.

It seemed to Lauren that Max had a way with women—but she wasn't about to let him have his way with her. The endorsements were all for barbecues, and she felt the need to taste his other wares before giving him the job, no matter how needy she was.

"Great references," she admitted, no longer unnerved by his eyes, definitely not shaken by the way he leaned casually against the wall, watching her every move. "However—"

"There's not enough time for *howevers*," he interrupted, heading for the desk and shoving his portfolio into his briefcase. "I told you on the phone that I already had another party this Saturday. I've told you what I'm willing to do for you.

If you want my help, we can draw up a contract—at my regular prices, even though you offered me more—and I'll provide you with the best food you and your society friends have ever eaten."

The man was decidedly impatient. And maybe she was too picky.

"I'm sure you're quite capable," she said, "but—"

"If you need a day or two, or even a few hours to think about it, you're out of luck."

He grabbed his briefcase and headed for the library doors.

"Would you stop and be quiet for just one moment," she blurted out, but he didn't slow down. "All I wanted to say is that I'd like to taste some of your food before I sign on the dotted line."

"Fine. Let's go."

"Where?" she asked, running to catch up with him.

"My place." He came to a stop when he reached the sleek black motorcycle sitting in the middle of her circular drive.

"But—"

"No buts, Lauren." He grinned as he swung his leg over the seat—revealing, to her dismay, that worn spot on his jeans—and gripped the handlebars. "Hop on."

She stared at the machine, at the shiny chrome, at the shimmering, long-haired mermaid painted on the gas tank. She looked at Max's wild, wavy black hair; his all-too-masculine mustache and goatee; at the powerful muscles in his arms and his flat, undoubtedly hard stomach; and realized just how easy it would be for a not-too-worldly-wise-woman to fall under this man's spell.

She, however, was a seasoned veteran of the war with men, and she fully intended to keep her distance. "I couldn't possibly get on your motorcycle, Mr. Wilde—"

"*Max*." He patted the back of the seat. "I'm in a hurry, and like I said—"

"Yes, I know, you have a lot of work to do," she stated. "As a matter of fact, I do, too. So why don't you head back to your place, grab a few canapés, and bring them here so I can give them a try?"

"Why don't you just go with me and save us both a lot of time."

She didn't want to go with him. She definitely didn't want to get on the back of the motorcycle. But she did want to sample his hors d'oeuvres, and she knew full well that she needed a caterer desperately and that this brusque, presumptuous biker was the only chef she could find.

He was going out of his way to help her, too. What would it hurt to meet him halfway?

"All right. Just give me a moment to get my purse and car, and I'll follow you."

"I weave in and out of traffic. You'd never keep up with me." He smiled, satisfied, more than likely, because he thought he was going to get his way. "Come on," he said, coaxing her, his voice turning suddenly seductive. "The bike doesn't bite, and neither do I."

She had her doubts.

"Do you need some assistance, Miss Remington?" she heard Charles ask from the doorway.

"I'm not quite sure." She moved a bit closer to the big black machine Max was straddling. She had to be out of her mind to even consider riding on the back of the massive bike. Getting on a motorcycle—especially one driven by Max Wilde—had to be dangerous. Then, again, would living dangerously be all that bad?

Drawing in a deep breath, she called out to Charles over her shoulder. "I'm going with Mr. Wilde. Could you get my handbag, please. The silver Prada."

"You're sure?" Charles asked.

She looked at the big black motorcycle again. She looked at Max's boots planted on the driveway, scanned the length of his powerful legs, his flat stomach, and the muscles in his arms. The tail of the mermaid swished as his biceps flexed, and she allowed her gaze to trail slowly up his arm to the ring in his ear, to the mustache and goatee, to the grin on his face.

For one more moment she contemplated the utter foolishness of zooming off with a stranger whose mood changed from one tick of the clock to the next, then turned to Charles and said, "I'm sure."

Max chuckled, and she snapped back around to look at the smirk on his face.

"May I ask what's so funny?" she asked.

His eyes darted to her ice-blue silk pants suit, to the diamond solitaire at her throat. "Silk. Diamonds." He shook his head and chuckled again. "You've got to be the most well-dressed woman I've ever had riding behind me."

"Thank you," she said, gracious enough to keep a snide retort from sliding over her tongue. She would have changed into something more practical, but she didn't own leather pants. Besides, she doubted he would have given her time to change, considering the hurry he was in. And, to be quite honest, she was anxious to see how it felt to ride something so powerful.

She slid her hand over the leather seat, and her fingers rested mere inches from Max's jeans-clad bottom. "Are you sure there's room enough for two?"

Max eyed her up and down. The last man who'd done that was Peter, right before he took her to that snooty fat farm in the English countryside, insisting that she lose twenty extra pounds before their wedding. Peter's gaze had always been critical; Max's gaze was altogether different—hot-blooded and erotic, making her quiver inside.

"Climb on," he said, taking hold of her hand and clasping it against his stomach, obviously something one did for balance. "There's more than enough room."

Taking a deep breath, she swung her right leg over the seat and felt her body slide exceedingly close to his. Her breasts squashed against his back, her thighs grazed his thighs, and her heart thundered. Oh, dear!

He slipped his hand over her leg, taking liberties she hadn't expected.

"What do you think you're doing?" she asked, tugging his fingers from the back of her knee.

His hair blew in the breeze and tickled her nose as he glared at her over his shoulder. "Helping you put your foot on the peg."

A likely story. "Thank you, but I'm sure I can do that myself."

Shaking his head, no doubt annoyed—again—he gripped the handlebars as she lifted one silver spiked heel from the pavement and put it on the shiny chrome peg. Her strappy sandals, not to mention her ice-blue silk pantsuit, weren't exactly biker mama gear, but they'd have to do for now.

Her right foot found its way to the other peg, and she rested her hands on her thighs. She wasn't about to wrap her arms around the owner of Born To Be Wild Catering. That seemed far too personal, and this was a business trip, nothing more.

Peering over Max's shoulder, she could see him lift his helmet from its resting place between the handlebars. "Put this on," he said, turning halfway around in his seat and unceremoniously slipping the heavy helmet over her head.

"What about you?" she asked, her words muffled as he fastened the strap under her chin. "Isn't it against the law to ride without a helmet?"

"I'll take my chances."

The motorcycle jerked when he released the kickstand, and his thighs rubbed against hers. When he started the engine, she could feel the vibration between her legs, and it pulsed faster and stronger as he twisted the ends of the handlebars to rev the motor. She hated to admit it, but the sensations were sinfully delightful.

"Here's your handbag, Miss Remington," Charles shouted to her over the roar of the engine. "Is there anything else you'd like?"

"No, Charles," she said, latching on to the Prada, as if it were her only lifeline between craziness and sanity. She should be worrying about what seedy part of town Max Wilde planned to take her to. She should be wondering if he drove sensibly, or if he had a streak of Evel Knievel in him. She should be afraid that she'd never see her family or her home again. But at the moment, the only thing bothering her was the fact that a whole lot of her body was touching a whole lot of this brash and fascinating stranger.

"You have Mr. Wilde's phone number if you need to reach me," she shouted to Charles through her helmet.

"Very well, Miss Remington," he shouted back, then smiled slyly. "But I will do my best not to interrupt you."

Lauren knew quite well what Charles was insinuating by that statement. How could he possibly think she was interested in a man like Max Wilde? When she returned home, she'd inform him that she'd gone with Max Wilde *only* to expedite the arrangements for Betsy's wedding, and not to go jumping to conclusions.

Max revved the engine again. "Ready?" he asked, looking at her over his shoulder.

Smiling weakly, wondering one last time if she'd lost her mind, she slipped her arms around Max's waist, giving up on propriety for the sake of safety. "Ready," she answered, as bravely as possible.

The machine beneath them rumbled. Her heart beat wildly, and she could hear Max's laughter as the motorcycle streaked down the driveway. "Hold on tight," he hollered against the rush of wind. "You're in for the ride of your life."

 *Three*

"*W*hat is it that you don't understand about leaning with the bike when we go around a corner or take a curve?"

Oh, dear, did she have to listen to Max's lecture again? Lauren wondered, feeling a tad foolish standing in the shade of a palm on the corner of Cocoanut Row and Cocoanut Walk, wearing a not-quite-fashionable motorcycle helmet that afforded her only a small measure of anonymity.

They were far too close to the chamber of commerce and Flagler Museum for comfort, and she knew that many prying eyes must be lurking behind their windows.

Max, on the other hand, didn't seem to care where they were or who was listening. He just sat on his motorcycle, arms folded stiffly across his chest, with a scowl on his face, no doubt annoyed because they'd had a similar conversation at the corner of Ocean and Worth.

"There's nothing I don't understand," she explained for the umpteenth time, "but could you please keep your voice down so everyone in Palm Beach doesn't hear how disgruntled you are?"

"I'm not disgruntled, and I am keeping my voice down. You, however, didn't listen to a word I said earlier about leaning with the motorcycle, not against it."

"I did listen, but I can't quite grasp the concept of why I should take the chance of having all my skin painfully ripped to shreds, just because you get a thrill from leaning dangerously close to the ground. Really, Max, it's bound to be safer to lean in the other direction."

"Look, I already gave you the technical explanation, all the whys and wherefores of gravity and balance, so let me just tell you this. If you and I lean in opposing directions, I might lose control of the motorcycle and when that happens, both of us are going to take a dump, we're both going to lose skin, and I'll have a very expensive motorcycle that's in need of extensive repairs."

"So why don't we both lean in the same direction . . . and I don't mean toward the ground?"

He sighed, obviously perturbed. "Because leaning against the turn goes against the laws of physics."

"Physics was never one of my better courses in school. I just barely squeaked by with a D-minus, and my mother was so upset that she called the teacher, told him that she gave a lot of money to the school, and that I deserved at least a B or C. Unfortunately Mr. Broome wouldn't budge, so Mother pulled me out of that private school and sent me to another."

She was going to tell Max that changing schools hadn't made her any better in math or the sciences, but an all-too-familiar black Lamborghini, the one owned by her ex-husband Chip, cruised by at a very slow speed, making her forget anything vaguely resembling school. The darkly tinted driver's window lowered as Chip pulled the vehicle over to the curb.

A frown formed on his face as he studied her unconventional attire. "Good Lord, Lauren, what on earth are you doing here, and wearing a motorcycle helmet, no less?"

Lauren patted the shiny black fiberglass surrounding her head. "It's a new fashion statement. Hadn't you heard that riding a motorcycle is all the rage in Europe?"

His continued smirk said, loud and clear, that he didn't believe her, but she didn't see the need to justify what she was doing, especially to Chip. Slowly, his cool appraisal traveled to the motorcycle and to Max, who'd abandoned the bike and strolled confidently toward the car.

"I'm Max Wilde," he said, sticking out his hand.

Oh, dear! Chip was being his usual boorish self, inspecting Max's hand, obviously to make sure it was suitable to touch, before he shook it quickly. "Chip Chasen," he said, and continued to stare at Max. "Have we met? You look oddly familiar."

A semi-grin tilted Max's mouth, what you could see of it beneath the mustache. "We may have met at one or two parties in the past."

Why hadn't she thought of that? Obviously he'd catered other parties she'd attended and *that's* why he looked familiar to her.

"You have family in Palm Beach, then?" Chip asked. "Newport, perhaps?"

Max's grin deepened, and for the first time she noticed the dimple off to the right of his mustache. "*West* Palm Beach," he stated, definitely the wrong thing to utter in front of Chip, who considered anyone from West Palm Beach to be a second class citizen.

Chip frowned. "I see," he said, his snobbery so thick Lauren wanted to crawl inside the helmet and hide. As if Max had ceased to exist, Chip turned away and addressed Lauren.

"I had lunch with your mother in London last week. At the Ritz. She tells me you're giving up this wedding consultant—"

"I'm a wedding *planner*, not a consultant."

"Either way, she tells me you'll be dispensing with this nonsense right after Betsy Endicott's wedding."

"That's wishful thinking on Mother's part."

His eyes flicked toward Max again. "Does she know about your current . . . *hobby?*"

Lauren saw no need to point out that Max was a caterer, not a hobby—Mother wouldn't approve of Max in any capacity. Chip Chasen was her mother's idea of the perfect man. He was the embodiment of every negative cliché about the filthy rich, but at nineteen Lauren had been too naïve to notice.

She'd fallen in love with his sophisticated good looks and what she'd perceived as charm. He'd complimented her, he'd always wanted her by his side, and his close-knit family had embraced her and made her one of them.

She'd hoped they'd have children together and looked forward to having her own close-knit family, but after their honeymoon, Chip rarely shared her bed. He told her she hadn't done anything wrong, said he was perfectly content with what they shared in their marriage—which wasn't much, and she'd wanted so much more. When she realized she'd fallen out of love with him, when she was positive he'd never be a good husband or father, she'd asked for a divorce.

How they'd remained on speaking terms for the past ten years amazed most of Palm Beach society. He might have been a lousy husband, but deep, deep down under that handsome exterior was a lonely rich guy. There was no point in disliking him, it was impossible to avoid him, and he seldom bothered her.

But right now, Chip was an annoyance she didn't need.

"It was very sweet of you to stop and say hello," Lauren said, "but I'm sure you've got a horse race or something important to get to."

"Actually, I've just bought partnership in a colt named Satan's Triumph. His sire retired with earnings of over three million, and I fully believe Satan's Triumph will soon be winning one stake after another. I'm off to see him now."

"Well, give him my best," Lauren said, blowing Chip a goodbye kiss, wishing he'd hurry on his way.

"I'll do that." Chip laughed as he blew a kiss in return. "See you Saturday at Betsy's wedding," he said, his words fading as the Lamborghini whizzed away from the curb.

"Nice guy."

Lauren couldn't miss the cynicism in Max's voice as he swung a leg over his motorcycle.

"He has his good points," Lauren admitted. "He's very good at tennis, he does a mean fox trot, and—"

The grin forming on Max's face brought her rationalization to a halt. "What's so funny?"

"I always wondered why you married him. I should have known it had something to do with his tennis game and the fox trot."

"Those are *not* the reasons I married him," she said, swinging her leg over the motorcycle, wishing they would continue on their way. And then his words hit her. She tapped him on the shoulder and he tilted his head toward her.

"This is the second time you've brought up my marriage to Chip. Do you have some personal vendetta against him?"

"I just keep wondering why you married him when you wanted to run away the night before your wedding."

She laughed. "That's the most ridiculous thing

I've ever heard. I was in love with Chip. Yes, marrying him was a mistake, a foolish mistake," she admitted uncomfortably. "But I never wanted to . . . to . . ."

"To what?" he asked, his all-too-familiar intense brown eyes boring into her.

"Oh, dear."

The dimple next to his mouth deepened as his grin grew wider. "Something troubling you?"

She glared at him through the visor of the helmet, thankful that he couldn't see her embarrassment. "You're the man who poured champagne on my gown, aren't you?"

"Afraid so. I'm also the one who distinctly heard you say you wanted to run away—with me."

"I don't recall those being my exact words. I think I *wished* I could run away."

"Wished. Wanted," he quipped. "It's all the same thing."

She wondered why something so insignificant, something that had happened ten years ago, could make her feel so uncomfortable now. Then she realized it was because Max wanted her to feel uncomfortable. He wanted to make her feel miserable about that moment, and he was doing a darn good job of it.

"I was nineteen. I was nervous, scared half out of my wits," she explained. "Whether I wished it or wanted it doesn't matter. It was a crazy thing to say and I regretted it later. But *you*. You were older—"

"I'd just turned twenty."

"Old enough that you should have laughed it off."

"I did."

"You expect me to believe that? You've spent the past couple of hours stomping around my home as if you were annoyed with me. You've been terse, rude, and you've used your motorcycle as an instrument of torture. If you weren't acting out your aggressions for some silly little mistake I made ten years ago, if you weren't trying to get back at me for hurting your feelings, then what, pray tell, were you doing?"

His jaw tightened. So did his eyes. Suddenly he turned around and kick-started the engine.

She tapped him on the shoulder again, but he didn't look at her. Could he possibly be sulking? Had he really thought she would run away with him, when her comment had been nothing more than the verbal musing of a young, foolish, and very nervous girl?

Suddenly she remembered him showing up the next morning, his bravado when he'd said he'd come to take her away. Men could be so confident, so sure of themselves in every situation, while she was sure of so little.

The only thing she'd been sure of that morning was that she wouldn't end her marriage to Chip before it had begun. She'd been raised by a mother who considered divorce the rule rather than the exception and had a father who bounced from one blond bimbo to the next. She wanted a different kind of life—and she'd hoped to have it with Chip.

But Max hadn't known that. He'd only heard her say she wished she could run away with him, he'd believed her, and she'd hurt him. That bothered her terribly.

This time when she tapped his shoulder he jerked around.

Lifting the visor so he could see the concern in her eyes and not mistake her words for something being said just so she could get what she wanted from him, she said softly, "I did want to run away that night. I doubt you can understand this, but I was afraid I couldn't live up to Chip's expectations, afraid he didn't love me as much as I loved him. But . . . but running away frightened me, too."

"You don't owe me any explanations."

"Maybe not, but I do owe you an apology. I'm sorry if I hurt you."

He laughed. "Apology accepted. Now, can we get going? I've got other business to take care of."

She almost growled in annoyance. Typical man! He hadn't really accepted her heartfelt apology, he just didn't want to hash it over until they had the whole ridiculous incident cleared up. If this were a *real* relationship she'd insist they talk about it until they were both blue in the face, until he could laugh at it. But this was merely a business relationship. She'd said she was sorry, she'd meant it, and now she had to move on and just make sure he'd cater the wedding on Saturday.

"We are still going to your place, aren't we?"

"That's the plan."

"Good. Then let's get going." She flipped

down the visor and wrapped her arms around his waist as he revved the engine.

"So," he said, twisting around again and hitting her with his intense brown eyes, "are you going to lean with me, or against me?"

"With," she conceded, now that their discussion had gone full circle without resolving anything. "But could you please do me a favor and give me a warning when you're about to do something rash? That way I can close my eyes. I know that won't make it hurt any less when we crash, but at least I won't see the ground when I hit."

Max seemed to take a special delight in finding roads that twisted and turned, and hitting ruts had to be one of his favorite pastimes. It didn't take long for Lauren to tire of squeezing her eyes so tight they watered, and after their seventh or eighth death-defying feat, she found that leaning was far more exciting than she'd imagined.

She'd never admit it, of course, but Max would have to be deaf not to hear her laughter as they sped past cars and semis. She'd never admit, either, that she secretly wished she wasn't wearing a helmet, because she wanted to feel the wind whipping wildly about her face. She was a lady, however, and ladies didn't do such things.

All too soon the motorcycle slowed when Max turned onto a street lined with small, older homes in varying degrees of disrepair. The purple stucco house with screaming yellow trim was fairly interesting, as were the loud sounds pulsing from one of the many vehicles in the driveway, on the lawn, and lining the curbs. The house next door had wrought-iron bars on the doors and windows plus a high chain-link fence surrounding the entire yard. And then there was the vicious-looking dog running back and forth, barking up a storm.

She had the distinct impression that she wasn't in the best part of town.

"Excuse me, Max," she hollered through the helmet, tapping him on the shoulder as she leaned close. "Are you sure it's safe for us to be here?"

He merely tilted his head toward her, grinned, and waved to a bunch of guys heading the opposite direction in a low-riding, beat-up black Cadillac.

Perhaps she should close her eyes again, she thought, but Max took another turn without slowing down, and she forgot her worry when the giddy exhilaration tumbled through her stomach.

No sooner had they turned the corner than they entered a completely different world, where sprawling houses sat far back from the palm-lined lane. Their expansive lawns were neatly trimmed, with banana trees, ferns, and bird-of-paradise rimming each home.

Max waved at an old gentleman standing in one front yard watering his plants and, oh dear, he was doing it in the nude! Perhaps this wasn't the best of neighborhoods after all.

Her shocked but curious stare stayed fastened on the naked man until Max turned into the next driveway and came to a stop alongside what appeared to be the largest house on the block. The brick front had been painted white, the trim a dark forest green, and the sun glinted off the windows. Where the other homes had subdued, well-maintained landscaping, this yard was lush and wild. The banana trees, the ferns, and the bird-of-paradise seemed taller and fuller than any she'd ever seen. Pink, lavender, yellow, and white frangipani blossomed everywhere, and the garden was fragrant with the sweet scent of gardenia.

She'd never expected Max Wilde to live in a veritable Garden of Eden. Then again, she looked at the rings in his ears, the mustache and goatee, and the thick black wavy hair that nearly brushed the collar of his T-shirt, and couldn't picture him living anywhere but in an untamed jungle.

What different worlds they came from.

Max planted both boots on the pavement and steadied the bike as she scrambled off—far too fast. Her legs quivered, and she had the horrid feeling they were going to give out beneath her. But then she felt a pair of big, supportive hands clutch her arms.

"Next time you ride," Max said, grinning lightly, "try to relax."

That was impossible, especially now, with him touching her. "I was completely relaxed," she fibbed.

"You forget how close we were. I could feel every tense muscle in your body."

She hadn't forgotten how close they were. She'd felt the heat of his skin, the seams of his jeans against her thighs, his leather belt rubbing back and forth, up and down against her stomach, not to mention the hard planes of his back colliding with her breasts. Those were the things that had made her tense once she'd gotten over her fear of riding. Those were things best kept to herself. "Maybe I was a bit tense, but I didn't want to fall."

His fingers grazed over her arms, her shoulders, and his knuckles brushed lightly along her neck. Maybe he *had* put that long-ago incident out of his mind. Then, again, maybe he was teasing her, paying her back for what he had mistakenly thought she'd done to him. Either way, his touch made her feel dreadfully hot, made her wonder—with too much anticipation—what he planned to do next.

Releasing the chin strap, he slipped the helmet off her head. A hint of warmth softened his intense brown eyes. "In spite of what you might think, I wouldn't have let you fall."

All too quickly he let her go, and she thought she would crumble—a ridiculous thing to feel, especially with a man who didn't particularly like her.

She smoothed her silk top and pants, fluffed her hair, and pulled her wits together, repeating to herself again and again, "This is business, nothing more."

"You have a nice home," she said, following Max to the door and trying to sound calm, collected, and in control, as she took in the sights of his backyard grotto, where a free-form, boulder-rimmed swimming pool sat amidst a tangle of brightly flowering bougainvillea, plumeria, and fern. "It's a far cry from the neighborhood around the corner, although I must admit you've got a very interesting gentleman living next door."

"Mr. Hansen's ninety-three," he said, not bothering to look at her as he unlocked the door. "He lost his wife last year, his only son the year before that, and now he's slowly losing touch with reality."

Max said the words so matter-of-factly that if she hadn't been listening closely, she might have thought it was no big deal. But she could hear a trace of sadness in his voice, which seemed out of character for a motorcycle-riding brute who liked to torture women.

"Can anything be done to help him?" she asked. "Medicine? Therapy?"

"His doctors say no. In fact, they think he should be in a nursing home." Max chuckled, an unexpected sound that touched her heart. "Mr. Hansen won't have anything to do with being shut away. He loves his garden and his neighbors, and we take turns watching out for him. The neighborhood wouldn't be the same if he went away."

Max looked like a man who thrived on having fun, living hard, fast, and dangerous. He definitely didn't look like the caregiver type, but she was rapidly finding out that Max didn't fit any mold. He was the exact opposite of the men she was used to, who, more than likely, wouldn't watch out for a ninety-three-year-old neighbor.

Max wasn't at all what one would expect at first glance, and she wondered what other secrets hid behind his rough façade.

He held open the back door and she stepped into a laundry room piled sky-high with dirty gym clothes, jeans, underwear, towels, and sheets. This was what she expected from Max Wilde!

"Excuse the mess," he tossed over his shoulder, and kept on walking. As she stepped around laundry baskets and the occasional dirty sock, she thought how desperately he needed a housekeeper, or . . . a wife.

Of course, maybe he had a wife, a pretty, petite blond who worked as a receptionist in a dentist's office. Someone who looked good in tight black leather, someone who didn't worry about the laundry because she had a sexy, wild husband who preferred that she join him in more athletic adventures—indoors and out.

For some odd reason, that thought annoyed her.

From the chaos of the laundry they stepped into the orderliness of the kitchen, an impressive room of gleaming stainless steel, white walls, a terra cotta tile floor, and framed posters of souped-up choppers and hot rods. Pots and pans hung in clusters from the ceiling, as did wire baskets overflowing with tomatoes, apples, and bananas. On one wall was a massive stove, several oversized refrigerators littered with magnets and notes, a bank of ovens, homey touches like a red and black motorcycle cookie jar on the counter, and at the far end a sunroom blooming with plants.

"My cook would probably abandon me if she saw this kitchen," Lauren said, taking a seat on the barstool Max pulled out for her. "She convinced me to put in a third oven a few years ago, and not a week goes by that she doesn't come home with some new kind of gadget. I don't know one from another, of course, but Mrs. Fisk is absolutely wonderful in my kitchen, so I don't think I'll tell her about yours."

Max liked the way she chattered. Hell, he liked far too much about her, just as he had ten years ago, and that was a big mistake. Earlier today he'd told Jed that if you touch something hot you're gonna get burned. Practice what you preach! he told himself.

But he liked the soft and feminine sound of her voice, a like that didn't come anywhere close to resembling the lust he felt for her soft and feminine body. Tall, womanly, and gorgeous, she had generous curves that had felt damn good snuggled up against him as they'd ridden through the streets of her neighborhood and his. He'd even taken a few wrong turns so he could stretch out the exhilaration he'd felt with her arms wrapped tightly around his stomach, her breasts pressed against his back.

She was one hell of a woman, and maybe he'd been a little rude, stomping around like a man with a chip on his shoulder. There was just something about rich, snooty women that rubbed him the wrong way, even if this rich, snooty woman was incredibly charming.

But was she as charming as she seemed? Was she really sorry for leading on a naive kid ten years ago? Or was her apology simply a ruse to make sure he didn't back out on catering Betsy Endicott's uppity wedding? He'd had a mother who'd used her beauty as well as lies to get what she wanted, a mother who'd hopped from one man's bed to another and eventually abandoned her kids. He'd never once believed that all women were like that, but he could easily believe it of Lauren Remington, given her tendency to turn up in the tabloids and her history of marriage and divorce.

Maybe it was high time someone taught Lauren Remington a lesson or two about men. She needed to learn that she couldn't flash her pretty smile—or offer someone an armload of money—and get whatever she wanted. She needed him, and he was going to make her work hard for every speck of his help.

Turning his back on the pretty woman who was still chattering about her cook, and her butler, and her kitchen in that pink marble monstrosity where she lived, Max opened one of the refrigerator doors and rummaged around for a bowl of barbecue sauce. While he was looking, a smile touched his face. As much as he hated to admit it, educating Lauren was bound to be an education for him, too, one he had the sneaking suspicion he was going to enjoy—far too much.

"I had to draw the line at calling Zippo's," she was saying as he poured the sauce into a pan and put it on the stove to heat. "I mean, really, can you see a delicatessen catering Betsy Endicott's wedding?"

"No," he stated, considering the fact that Zippo's had been closed down by the health department a few months back.

"And then there was Bad Bubba's Barbecue." Her smile brightened. "I liked the sound of their name, but, pardon me for saying this, I was a little hesitant about hiring a company that specializes in barbecues."

"*I* specialize in barbecues."

"I didn't know that at the time, which is probably a good thing because if I had I wouldn't have called you. And if I hadn't called you, you'd still be stewing over what happened ten years ago."

"Think you're that unforgettable, do you?" he asked, stirring the sauce, cautiously testing its temperature with his fingertip.

"Well . . . no . . . but I would like to say once more that I *am* sorry and I hope we can move on."

He flicked off the fire as he stared into her eyes. "I've moved on."

She took a deep breath and he couldn't miss the rise and fall of her breasts under her sheer silk top. "I'm so glad to hear that, because I had the distinct feeling you planned to make my life miserable from now until Saturday."

Holding back his grin was difficult, but somehow he managed. "I wouldn't think of it." He pulled a teaspoon from one of the drawers, and asked, "Ever had ribs?"

"Mrs. Fisk makes them occasionally, and they're always on the menu at my brother's ranch in Wyoming. Of course Crosby, that's my brother's cook, doesn't have much of a flair for cooking. He's been at the ranch since the thirties, when my great-grandfather hired him to drive the chuck wagon on cattle drives. From what I hear he was a lousy cook back then and he hasn't improved with age, but he's the dearest old man."

"Like Mr. Hansen?" he asked, offering her a spoonful of the tangy sauce.

"I don't recall Crosby ever walking around naked," she said, taking the spoon, "but, just like your Mr. Hansen, the ranch wouldn't be the same without him."

Max watched the leisurely way she drew the spoon to her mouth, the way she slowly, gracefully placed it between her lips. His imagination ran wild, picturing her tongue swirling around the spoon, licking away the sauce. Slow. Real slow. His heart thundered in his chest until she finally withdrew the spotless spoon and smiled.

"Delicious." She licked her lips in the same slow way she'd licked the spoon, and he was beginning to wonder who was going to educate who. "Is this one of your special barbecue sauces?" she asked, dipping the spoon into the pan for more.

"Hot and spicy," he said. Hot and spicy—a hell of a lot like the woman sitting across from him.

"I've never tasted anything quite like it. Did you dream it up on your own?"

He nodded, once again watching her draw the spoon between her full luscious lips. God, the woman was going to drive him mad.

"You don't do *all* the cooking for Born To Be Wild, do you?"

"Depends. Occasionally I hire other chefs, and I've got a part-time staff that help with parties. This place will be a madhouse Friday and Saturday, with people running every which way washing fruits and vegetables, carving meats, preparing hors d'oeuvres."

"How soon will I get to try some of your creations?"

"You've already tried one."

"The sauce is wonderful, but you brought me here so I could sample some of the foods you'll be serving at Betsy Endicott's wedding. I really would like to try something more . . . cultured."

Spoiled, that's what Lauren Remington was. Rich, spoiled, and used to getting her way—but not with him. He braced his hands on the countertop and stared into her pretty green eyes. "The way I see it, someone as desperate as you should be a little more trusting. In fact, you should be happy with anything I choose to serve."

She folded her arms on the counter and leaned forward. When her eyes were leveled at his, she smiled sweetly. "If you're trying to frighten me, you're doing a lousy job. I've already got you figured out."

"You don't know the first thing about me."

"You may look big and bad on that motorcycle of yours, but I think you're a pushover. The way you talked about Mr. Hansen told me that you're a sucker for someone in need. Well, I may be rich, Mr. Wilde, but right now I'm pretty darn needy. I don't care how much it costs me, I don't care what I have to do, but one way or another you're going to fix something resembling Caribbean brochettes—not hot and spicy ribs—for Betsy's wedding on Saturday."

He couldn't help but grin as a thought came to mind. "All right, Miss Remington, you'll get your Caribbean brochettes, but I've got a couple of conditions."

Her eyes narrowed. "I'm sure that *one* condition would be enough. But, all right, what torture do you intend to impose upon me now?"

"First, that you trust me to provide the best food you've ever tasted, without trying it first."

"But—"

"That's condition one," he stated emphatically, interrupting her protest.

"I don't see why you can't whip up something for me to try."

"Because I don't just *whip* something up! I *create*, and right now I don't have time to create because I had to spend too much time teaching you the right and wrong way to lean on a motorcycle."

"Yes, that's true, but you *are* the one who insisted I ride with you—to save time, as I recall."

"A slight mistake in judgment," he said, although there'd been no mistake in how good her body had felt against his. "However," he continued, realizing Lauren's education was flying right out the door and she was taking the upper hand, "I don't make mistakes where food is concerned—and that goes for ribs as well as fine cuisine. So, are you going to accept condition number one, or do we call off the whole deal?"

He could see her gritting her teeth. "Fine," she stated flatly, "but I'm not used to doing business on trust alone."

"There's always a first time for everything." He moved a little closer, liking the scent of her perfume, liking her eyes, the curve of her blue-blooded nose. "Now, for condition two. I want you to dance with me at Betsy's wedding reception."

Her already frowning eyes narrowed even more, as if she were sizing him up, wondering what he was up to. "I'm afraid dancing with you is out of the question," she finally answered. "You're the caterer."

"And once upon a time I was a waiter. Obviously you weren't such a snob back then, because you contemplated running away with me."

"I'm not a snob, and, as I've mentioned before, my comment about running away with you was *my* slight mistake in judgment, one you obviously haven't moved away from."

"But I have, and now I want you to dance with me on Saturday."

"I can't."

"Caterers are hard to come by at the last moment."

"Is that a threat?"

"What do you think?"

"That you're all bluster."

When, he wondered, had sparring with a woman become such fun? "All right, so I have no intention of letting you down on Saturday, but that doesn't negate the fact that I want to dance with you. Consider it payment for me working doubly hard to ensure that your needs are taken care of."

He could see her jaw tightening. "You drive a hard bargain."

"Is that a yes?"

"What choice do I have?"

"None that I can see."

Without thinking, he smoothed a speck of barbecue sauce from her lower lip, shocked by the sparks that ricocheted through his body. If one small touch could affect him that way, what would dancing up close and personal do to him?

Had she felt the same shock? he wondered, as her eyes locked on his, looking surprised by his caress, maybe a little frightened. God, he didn't want to have feelings for her, not when he knew how the people of her world reacted to people from his, not when he knew too much about her past.

But it was impossible not to want her.

"Maybe we should substitute dancing for some other condition," she suggested.

Max shook his head. He'd rather give up condition number one.

"But people are going to talk," she said softly. "They're going to wonder why I'm dancing with you."

"And that bothers you?"

"I don't like gossip, especially when it's aimed at me."

"Then tell everyone the truth."

"What, that you forced me to dance with you?"

He moved even closer. Their eyes, their noses, their mouths were just inches apart. "If that's the truth."

She didn't move. In fact, it seemed as if she'd ceased to breathe as she stared into his face and, more than likely, tried to figure out the real reason why she'd agreed to dance with him. Hell, maybe Miss Palm Beach wanted him, too.

As if she couldn't look at him another moment, she pushed away from the counter and strolled across the kitchen, her high heels clicking on the tiles. She stopped in the center of the garden room where he grew his herbs and stared toward the flower-filled backyard. "I'm going to dance with you for one reason and one reason only—because I want you to cater Betsy's wedding." She faced him again, her arms folded assertively over her breasts. "If you have some crazy notion that I've agreed to dance with you because you're charming, think again. You've been difficult and demanding, something I wouldn't have stood for with any other employee—but as you reminded me earlier, I'm desperate. If you *had* been charming, I might have asked *you* to dance."

"And suffer the gossip?" he asked, moving toward her.

"I didn't say I'd ask you to dance at Betsy's wedding."

"Then where?" He stopped directly in front of her, meeting the tall, voluptuous beauty almost eye to eye. "Someplace private?" He grinned. "Someplace where we could be alone?"

"It doesn't matter, does it? We're going to dance at Betsy's wedding, I'm going to be the talk of the town, and you're going to have your revenge."

He curled a strand of hair behind her ear. "Is that what you think this is all about?"

"There couldn't possibly be any other reason." She looked startled by his touch. "You know, I really think we should change the subject."

"To what? Whether we're going to dance slow or fast?"

"Of course not. I'm here to discuss business, things like the menu, the cost, how many servers you're going to have, what kind of tuxedos they'll be wearing."

"Servers?"

"Yes, you know, the men who carry around silver platters laden with champagne and delicious food." Her eyes narrowed. "You do have waiters in your employ, don't you?"

"Of course I do, but—" He let out a frustrated breath, wondering how that detail had escaped his usual precise planning. "They're working at Mr. Fabiano's birthday party."

She threw up her hands and stalked into the kitchen. "What kind of caterer are you, that you didn't think about the importance of waiters for Betsy Endicott's wedding?"

That did it. "I'm the caterer who's going to save your butt."

She spun around. "Well, I'd like to know how you're going to do that when you don't have any waiters?"

"Improvise," he declared.

"*Improvise!* Are you mad? This is Betsy Endicott's wedding. You can't just grab people off a street corner, put them in a tux, and call them waiters."

"I can do better than that." He stormed across the room, grabbed her hand, and tugged her toward the kitchen door. "Come on, I know where I can find the waiters we need."

"You mean like a union hall, or something?" she asked, her high heels clicking rapidly behind him as he headed for his motorcycle.

"Or something." He chuckled, knowing full well that she wasn't going to like what he had in mind.

 *Four*

*N*ot even the grim alleyway Max zoomed through or the roar of the motorcycle's engine echoing against the warehouse walls could take Lauren's mind off the man she had her arms wrapped around.

He was rugged and dangerous and he turned her on as no other man had. Maybe because he didn't back down to her, didn't cater to her. Oh, she'd been told how to act, how to talk, how to walk and dress by many other people in her life, but this was completely different. Max was making her do things that went against the grain of everything she'd ever known.

And so far, she hadn't died. In fact, she was having an awfully good time—of course, she couldn't tell him that.

But she could sense there was something eating away at Max, something that made him waiver between despising her and enjoying her company. Whatever it was, it went much deeper than the incident between them years before.

Her sister-in-law Sam could probably pinpoint it in a moment. Sam was the wisest woman Lauren had ever known, a resourceful woman who'd lived on the streets, not to mention in her car, and had even masqueraded as Lauren's brother's fiancée to earn enough money to pay off a loan shark.

Lauren wished she had the same gumption. Wished she had just half of Sam's street smarts so she could figure out what was annoying Max. That shouldn't matter, of course, since he was only an employee, but it mattered more than she thought possible.

Max skillfully whipped the motorcycle around a Dumpster, and she let her thoughts roam from Max's aggravation to their upcoming dance. She had the nicest feeling that his movements on the dance floor would be slow and sensual, the sexy kind of dancing she'd dreamed of doing at sixteen, when she'd been forced to dance with boys like Frederick Hart and Mitchell Burke, who gracefully, placidly, and—oh yes—very boringly waltzed her around at one cotillion after another.

She seriously doubted that Max did the fox trot or would hold her lightly as Chip had done. Oh, no. A man like Max would probably place both his hands firmly on her bottom and hold her tightly against his hips, and then he'd move in the most erotic ways.

A wise woman would wipe that image from her mind, but she was feeling daring, not wise, and discreetly let her fingers roam over Max's hard, flat abs, watching the flex of muscle in his shoulders and arms. Sitting so close, she was becoming quite familiar with the contour of his upper body, with the form and fit of his T-shirt, and realized just how much she looked forward to their dance, to having her breasts press against his chest rather than his back, to look into his intense brown eyes rather than at his wild black hair.

Her fingers stilled when Max turned down a darkened alleyway littered with old newspapers and empty bottles. Suddenly she realized how ridiculous her thoughts had become. Once again she remembered that she and Max had a business arrangement, that he wore a goatee and hoop earrings, while she wore designer chic. Not that there was anything wrong with his look. Definitely not. It was new, different, and thoroughly . . . sensual, but his look served as a very visible reminder that their lifestyles were a million miles apart.

Max came to a sudden stop next to a circle of deserted motorcycles, cut the engine, and pulled off his helmet. His black wavy hair caught in the afternoon breeze whispering through the alley. It was wild and unruly and he was bold and brash and—oh, dear!—she really had to fight this strange attraction she felt for him.

Leaving this lonely alley seemed like a good place to start. "Is there some reason you're stopping here?" she asked, staying put on the back of the motorcycle even after Max swung his right leg over the gas tank and slid off the bike.

"You wanted waiters, right?"

She looked at the motorcycles around her, at the Dumpsters lining one wall, at the huge, graffiti-covered warehouses that surrounded them, and she laughed. "I suppose they're lined up on shelves inside, and you just walk down an aisle and pick out the ones you want."

He grinned. "Something like that."

He was teasing, of course. She knew full well that he couldn't find qualified waiters in a storage building on the outskirts of West Palm Beach. "Really, Max, where are we?"

"The Hole in the Wall."

The Hole in the Wall, she repeated to herself, then frowned. "This isn't a biker bar, is it?"

"A hangout," he corrected, as if his choice of words would give her a cozy feeling about the place. "I spend a lot of time here."

"That doesn't surprise me, but what are *we* doing here?"

"Taking care of business, just like I said. Are you going to stay out here or go inside?"

She had no way of knowing what kind of business he could have in an old, dilapidated warehouse, but she'd heard stories about bikers and what they did in their free time, things like drinking and carousing, not to mention having their way with women. She couldn't imagine Max mixed up in anything so disreputable, but that didn't mean the people he hung out with weren't a bit on the shady side.

"Well, what are you going to do?" he asked, combing his fingers through his hair, only to have it fall right back into its natural state of disarray.

She slipped off her helmet and looked at the big black door and the huge, racy motorcycles, with lightning bolts, fanged serpents, and fire-breathing dragons painted on their gas tanks. Thoughts of the men who rode them, and the knowledge that they'd be inside, helped to quickly make up her mind. "I believe I'll stay here, thank you."

Max shook his head as he walked to the door. "Suit yourself."

Even though Max had put down the kickstand, she settled the tiptoes of her silver spikes on the ground and hoped the bike wouldn't topple over. She was five-feet-ten-and-three-quarter-inches tall, she was packing a few too many pounds on her frame—or so her ex-fiancé had told her—but she still felt small on the massive Harley.

She slid from her perch to the scooped out part of the leather seat, where Max always sat, and put her hands on the grips. Suddenly she didn't feel so little. Riding along as a passenger she had no control, was totally at the mercy of the man at the helm. But sitting in the driver's seat was exciting, empowering.

"Feels good, doesn't it?"

The sound of Max's voice drew her gaze toward the door. She'd gotten so carried away by the thrill of the bike between her legs that she hadn't noticed he was still in the alley, that he'd been watching her movements. "A girl could get used to this."

A slow grin touched his lips. "Then keep it warm for me while I'm inside. I won't be long."

He opened the door and she heard a blast of music—a heavy guitar and the heavier beat of drums—before the weighty metal door slammed with a deep clank behind him, leaving her all alone.

The sense of power left her when she realized the only thing keeping her company was the sunlight bouncing off the chrome of half a dozen motorcycles. It was quiet now, lonely, and it seemed as if the walls were closing in on her.

Being alone was nothing new. She'd been alone many times as a child, when her mother would run off unexpectedly, leaving her behind for months at a time, with only Charles and her nanny for company. But she'd been on familiar ground then.

Right now she was out of her element, too far from the places where she felt at home. She should be shopping with friends and ducking into Café L'Europe for linguine and shrimp, a glass of wine, and good conversation, while a pianist played lightly in the background.

Instead she sat on a motorcycle outside a biker hangout, where God knows what was going on inside.

She looked at her watch. Four-thirty-two. If Max didn't come outside by four-forty, she was going in after him. She drummed her fingers on the gas tank, right next to the painted mermaid. The green and gold scales on her tail shimmered in the sunlight. Her light brown hair flowed about her as if she were swimming far below the ocean's surface, and delicate strands wisped over her chest like shredded silk, revealing hints of her firm, voluptuous breasts.

What was Max's fascination with mermaids? she wondered. How did he get interested in motorcycles, or becoming a chef?

Why did he have long hair? Why did he wear a beard and earrings?

Why was she thinking about him—again—and why on earth was he taking so long?

She twisted the rearview mirror to check her makeup, dug into her silver clutch, found her lipstick, and applied it sparingly. Last but certainly not least, she fluffed some life into her hair. Frederico, her stylist, would have a fit if he saw the damage the helmet had done to her coif.

"I'm as ready as I'll ever be," she whispered to herself as she climbed cautiously off the bike and smoothed the wrinkles in her silk trousers, but her words were drowned out by the roar of an engine echoing through the alley. Her eyes darted once more to the rearview mirror and caught sight of a red machine racing toward her, closer, closer, until it rumbled to a stop at her side. A muscle-bound man with a Fu Manchu stared at her, and she in turn gaped at his wide, hairless chest and the black leather vest that did little to hide his skin.

Oh, dear!

When he climbed off the motorcycle he towered over her, an impressive feat for most anybody, especially when she was wearing heels. He continued to stare as he removed his helmet, revealing a red bandana tied about his head and glittering diamond studs in his ears.

He folded burly arms over his brawny chest and smiled, flashing a set of amazingly straight, pearly-white teeth. "You must be a friend of Max's."

"An acquaintance," she answered, smiling weakly.

He stuck out his hand. Instantly, Lauren looked at his fingernails, wondering how much grease was beneath them, but they were clean, his cuticles trimmed, each nail rounded and white as if he'd just had a manicure. "I'm Vince Domingo," he said, "but my friends call me Bear."

Lauren hesitantly lifted her hand, and he clutched it in a viselike grip. "It's nice to meet you . . . *Bear*. I'm Lauren Remington," she said, trying to sound cordial in spite of her anxiety. "Do you hang out here, too?"

"Every chance I get, which isn't often enough." He pulled the bandana off his head—a totally bald head—and stuffed it into his helmet. "It's cooler inside than out here," he said, wiping a bead of perspiration from his temple. "Why don't you come in with me and have a drink. Meet some of the guys."

Maybe she didn't want to go inside after all.

"I told Max I'd wait out here, but thank you for the offer." She anxiously checked her watch. "He'll be out any moment now."

Bear's laugh rumbled through the alleyway, almost as loudly as his motorcycle's engine. "It's obvious you don't know Max all that well. If he gets caught up in a game or something, he won't be out for hours."

"A game?" So that's the business Max had to take care of. "I didn't realize there was gambling inside."

A wide grin spread across Bear's face. "Why don't I show you what's inside." He gripped her upper arm and ushered her toward the door. Part of her wanted to pull back, to tell him she had no intention of going inside, but she had the feeling no one ever said no to Bear.

How could she possibly have gotten herself into such a mess, when all she'd wanted to do was hire a caterer for Betsy Endicott's wedding? This entire day had gone all wrong. Now she was heading into a den of iniquity, and she seriously doubted that Max would come to her rescue, because he was probably enmeshed in a poker game, having a high old time with his gang.

Bear opened the door to the Hole in the Wall, and the heavy bass of the music vibrated straight through Lauren's body. Her legs were shaking when she touched her right foot down on the concrete floor, the same place her eyes were aimed, because she was afraid of what she might see if she looked around. She took a quick sniff of the air to see how badly it reeked of stale cigarettes, and noticed only the faint hint of sweat. Slowly her eyes drifted upward. At the far right end of the warehouse, at least a dozen kids were shooting hoops and dribbling balls. At the other end were vending machines filled with sodas, coffee, and snacks. And far across the room was a cluster of tables, where kids bent over opened schoolbooks.

Where were the men rolling dice? Where was the cock fight? Where were the brazen biker mamas with teased, bleached blond hair?

Why hadn't Max told her this was a hangout for kids? And why on earth had he let her think the worst?

"Not much gambling going on right now," Bear said, his bright white teeth gleaming through his wide-mouthed grin.

"So I see." Lauren felt a tinge of embarrassment rise in her cheeks. Obviously she'd prejudged Max, Bear, and everything connected with the Hole in the Wall. When would she ever learn not to judge a book by its cover?

A basketball rolled to a stop against her heels, and a cute, blond-headed boy nearly knocked her over as he raced to retrieve it. "Hey, Bear!" he hollered over the music, jumping up in the air to slap the burly biker a high-five.

The boys and girls scattered around the warehouse had hair in shades ranging from pink to green, and styles that ran the gamut of Mohawk to lacquered spikes. Their clothes were a mishmash she couldn't begin to describe. Yet this boy, who dribbled his ball in a circle around her, looked fairly neat, although the baggy shorts hung nearly to his knees and his oversized white T-shirt looked as if it might belong to his dad.

"Hello," she said, when he bounced the ball close to her toes.

"Hi," he said all too quickly, revealing a mouthful of silver braces. "You aren't gonna work here, are you?"

"Well . . . no."

"I didn't think so."

"Why?" Lauren asked. She knew she didn't have a clue about troubled kids and their needs, but was it all that obvious?

"Not too many people around here wear diamonds."

"If I come again, should I leave my jewelry at home?"

"Might be safer," he said, twirling the ball on the tip of his finger, obviously showing off. "Hey, Bear," he said, turning his attention away from her, "did you hear Rob got thrown in juvie last night?"

"Yeah, I heard." Lauren couldn't miss the disheartening tone in Bear's voice.

"Max says there's not much we can do," the boy said, tossing the ball to Bear.

"I don't mind helping someone who's screwed up once or twice," Bear commented, "but Rob pushed too far this time." He bounced the ball hard against the floor, then tossed it back to the boy. "Breaking into a house doesn't set too well with me."

It didn't set too well with Lauren, either. In fact, the entire conversation left her feeling completely dismayed.

"The kids here aren't . . . *delinquents*, are they?" she asked Bear, after the boy dribbled the ball to the far end of the warehouse.

"Some are, some aren't. Unfortunately we can't turn every kid into a model citizen."

"Is that what you do here? Rehabilitate problem kids?"

"If that's what's needed. Sometimes we help the older ones find a job, or give them one ourselves, just to keep them off the street. Jed, over there," he said, pointing to a skinny young man in greasy overalls, who was tinkering on what looked like a pile of motorcycle parts, "was working for Max until this morning. Turns out he's a lousy chef's assistant, but great with engines, and it just so happens I had a bike that I wanted rebuilt."

"What about the younger kids?"

"Most of them have only one parent, one who's either not the best role model or who is too busy trying to pay the rent to pay enough attention to them. They need help with schoolwork, need someone to listen to their problems, and sometimes they just need a place where they can hang out, especially when things aren't going well at home. That's what we're here for."

"I had no idea." She looked around the warehouse, spotting Max talking to a couple of kids. One of his boots rested on the edge of a bench, and he hunched over a boy's shoulder, pointing something out in a book. "Is Max as involved in all of this as you are?"

Bear laughed. "It was his idea, not to mention his money, that got it started."

Oh, dear! She looked at Max again and for a moment thought she saw him dressed in shining armor. Half an hour ago she thought he was one step away from being a hoodlum. She really should be careful about judging people she knew so little about.

Turning her curiosity toward the blond-headed boy shooting hoops, she asked, "Who's the boy with the basketball?"

"You mean Max hasn't introduced you?"

"No. Should he?"

Bear scratched his head. "I thought you and Max were friends."

"We're business acquaintances, that's all."

"Then I guess there wasn't much reason for him to tell you about his son."

"You mean the boy with the basketball?"

"Yeah. That's Ryan."

Those were the last words she'd expected to hear. Max hadn't even hinted that he had a child, which made her wonder if there could also be a Mrs. Wilde that he hadn't told her about. Maybe a pretty blond in tight black leather? But, if he was married, why had he asked Lauren to dance?

"That's Jamie over there," she heard Bear say, as he pointed to a girl in baggy jeans, a pink T-shirt, and a Harley-Davidson baseball cap with a curly blond ponytail sticking out the back.

What else had Bear been saying about the girl

while she'd been mulling over the fact that Max had a child and maybe a wife? "Who's Jamie?" she asked, trying to catch up.

"Ryan's younger sister."

Oh, dear. Max had a daughter, too. "Does Max have other children besides Ryan and Jamie?"

"That's it . . . as far as I know." Bear grinned. "Maybe you should ask Max."

"Ask me what?"

Lauren turned at the sound of Max's voice.

"Lauren was wondering if you've got kids scattered all around the country—"

"That's not what I asked," Lauren stated, wishing she could slap the grins off both their faces. "I've met Ryan, Bear pointed Jamie out to me, and since I wasn't aware that you had *any* children, I just wondered if you had others."

"Not at the moment."

"You're expecting more?"

Max laughed. "Someday, maybe. You never can tell."

She hated his noncommittal answers. "Then you and your wife aren't sure you want to have more?" she brazenly asked, determined to end her doubts about Max's marital status, even though she knew she shouldn't have any interest in his personal life.

"I'm not married. Never have been."

She frowned in spite of her relief. "But what about Jamie and Ryan?"

"Foster kids," he stated, then turned to Bear, bringing the subject to an abrupt end.

"Rico's got an algebra test tomorrow that he

needs to ace if he wants to get something better than an F on his report card," Max said. "Algebra's your specialty, not mine. And Gina's threatening to run away from home again. I can't talk any sense into her."

"I'll see what I can do," Bear answered.

"I need some help, too," Max said. "Think you can dust off your tux and play bartender on Saturday?"

"What's happening on Saturday?"

"A Palm Beach wedding."

Had she heard the conversation correctly? Had Max really asked Bear to bartend at Betsy Endicott's society wedding? She put a hand on Max's arm. "Excuse me, but I need to talk with you a moment. In private."

"As soon as I finish here," he said, ignoring her as he turned back to Bear. "Can you do it?"

"I've got a rally on Saturday," Bear said. "A bunch of us are heading down to the Keys for the weekend." Bear seemed like a genuinely nice man. He did charity work and had a terrific smile, but he wasn't Lauren's ideal bartender, and relief flooded through her when he said he had other plans.

Unfortunately, it didn't seem like Max was going to give up. "You know that Indian you've been wanting to buy from me?" he asked, throwing a friendly arm across Bear's shoulders.

A slow, satisfied smile touched Bear's face. "The '29 Scout?"

"That's the one," Max stated. "Help me out on Saturday and I'll let you ride it occasionally."

Bear laughed. "You've got to come up with a better offer than that. You know how I hate to miss a rally." He pulled away from Max and headed across the warehouse.

"All right," Max called out, "you can have it two weeks out of every month. We'll make it a joint-custody arrangement, but that's my final offer."

Bear grinned at Max over his shoulder. "When and where?"

"I'll call you tomorrow with all the details."

"Make sure you have a set of keys for me on Saturday. I plan to take the Scout home after the wedding."

"Just make sure you brush up on your bartending skills. You screw up and the deal's off."

"I've never screwed up in my life," Bear threw back. A moment later he was sitting at one of the tables between a boy with a Mohawk and a girl whose head was shaved except for a waist-length ponytail.

And now that Max's business was settled with Bear, it was Lauren's turn to settle things with Max.

"What do you think you're doing?" she asked as softly as possible, not wanting anyone to hear her anger. "You can't have someone like Bear tend bar at Betsy's wedding?"

"Why not?"

"He looks like Mr. Clean, for heaven's sake."

"I'm surprised someone like you even knows what Mr. Clean looks like."

"I used to watch a lot of television, but that's

neither here nor there. Bear's not exactly what I had in mind when we discussed waiters."

"Should we go ask some of *your* friends to do it? Chip, perhaps?"

"You know we can't do that."

"Then we'll have to go with my friends." His mustache twitched just the slightest bit when he smiled. "So, what do you think of the Hole in the Wall?"

"I think it's a lovely place and I imagine you and your biker friends are doing an admirable job trying to point kids in the right direction. But I don't want to talk about the Hole in the Wall or the fact that you made me think it was a lowlife bar. I don't even want to talk about you being a foster parent or any of your other good deeds right now. I want to talk about bartenders and waiters, starting with Bear."

Max angrily folded his arms across his chest. "Bear tends bar on Saturday or you do without. It's your choice."

"You're not giving me very many options."

"I don't have time for options and neither do you."

She gritted her teeth and took a long, hard look at Bear. His smile was infectious. So was his laugh. In fact, he seemed like an intelligent, easy-to-like man. A sigh escaped when she knew she had to give in. "Okay, Bear can bartend, on one condition."

Max's eyes narrowed. "What condition?"

"That he not tell anyone he goes by the name Bear."

"That's reasonable."

"I'm glad you're finally seeing my point of view. Now, how does he look in a tuxedo?"

Lauren could easily see Max's jaw tighten in frustration.

"All right," she said, before he could hit her with a lecture, "how he looks in a tux isn't all that important, given the circumstances. So, now that we have the bartender issue straightened out, what do you plan to do about waiters?"

His brown eyes grew cold. He looked like a man who didn't want to hear another argument, but she had the feeling there would be plenty more before Saturday ended.

"The other waiters are already taken care of." She followed his gaze to the basketball court. "That's Gabe," he said, pointing to a short, balding man with a long curly gray ponytail. He had a pot belly and wore a black T-shirt that said "Gabe" on the front. The back proclaimed, "I'm the guy your mother warned you about!" "He's free on Saturday, and doesn't mind helping out."

"I'm afraid Gabe won't do," Lauren stated. He couldn't possibly work!

Max ignored her, pointing instead to a platinum-blond woman in a red tank top and skin-tight jeans. Her arms and even her chest were laden with tattoos. "That's Jazz. She and Gabe have worked for me before when I needed last-minute substitutes."

"I need more than last-minute substitutes for Betsy's wedding. I need *qualified* waiters. *Classy* waiters. And we'll definitely need more than two."

"Jamie and Ryan make four."

For one long moment she stared at him, speechless. She needed experienced waiters, not children, and definitely not Gabe and Jazz, who were just a little too nonconformist for a Palm Beach affair.

"I'm sure your friends—*and* your children— are lovely people. I'm sure they could wait tables at a barbecue without any trouble at all. But you seem to forget that I'm not having a barbecue on Saturday."

"You're the one who seems to have forgotten a thing or two."

"Such as?"

"I believe you told me you're not a snob. Well, maybe you aren't, but you sure have one hell of an elitist attitude."

"And you seem to have forgotten who's the employer and who's the employee around here."

Max hit her with an infuriated scowl. "I don't recall ever signing a contract, and I don't remember any money being exchanged. The way I see it, *Miss Remington*, you're once again in desperate need of a caterer, and *I* no longer have to figure out how to juggle two events at the same time."

"Very well, if that's the way you want it," she said, flatly, succinctly, making sure he knew that everything between them was over, because she refused to give in, especially after he called her a snob. She wanted to cry, of course, but she couldn't let him see her desperation. No doubt, he'd enjoy watching her suffer.

She threw back her shoulders. "Do you have a telephone I could use?"

"Why?"

"I need to call a taxi."

"Don't bother. I brought you here. I'll take you home." He started to march across the warehouse.

Lauren wasn't about to get on that motorcycle again—especially with Max Wilde. "I'd prefer a taxi."

Max stopped dead in his tracks, and she watched his shoulders tense. Slowly he turned around, a very nasty frown on his face. "In my entire life," he growled, through nearly clenched teeth, "I've never met such an obstinate, impossible, spoiled—"

"Three adjectives is enough, thank you," she interrupted, before he could call her a brat. "Now, if you don't mind, could you please show me to the phone."

"Fine!" He stormed across the warehouse, and it was all Lauren could do to keep up with his long-legged, angry pace. "Here," he snapped, shoving the receiver for the pay phone toward her.

"Would you mind holding it for a moment?"

If looks could kill, the one Max hit her with just then could have pulverized her instantaneously. Fortunately he took a deep breath, and relaxed against the dingy wall. In spite of his calmer stance, he continued to glare at her as she dug around in her purse for something smaller than a twenty.

Of all the times to be without change or her cell phone, this should not have been one of them.

"Here." Max sounded a tad disgruntled as he held a quarter out to her.

"Thank you." She offered him a small smile as she took the coin from his hand, shocked by the sudden jolt of electricity that zapped her when they touched. With shaky fingers, she dropped the coin into the slot, then tilted her head and smiled again.

"Do you have a phone book?"

"No."

"You don't by any chance know the phone number for the local taxi service?"

"No."

She looked at the cracked concrete floor rather than his icy brown eyes and wished she'd taken him up on his offer to drive her home. Now she was going to have to ask, and she could just imagine the satisfied smile he was going to hit her with.

Slowly her gaze drifted up. "Then I believe I'll accept your offer of a ride home."

It wasn't a smile he hit her with, but an irritatingly smug grin. "Yeah, I thought you would."

Max stomped across the warehouse, his boots echoing through the silence as her heels clicked rapidly behind. When had the music stopped blaring? she wondered. When had every eye in the place turned toward them? Goodness, they

must have put on an interesting show for everyone to see.

Slamming through the door, Max mounted his
motorcycle, barely giving her a chance to hop on
behind, and a few moments later the Harley
streaked out of the alley.

Lauren didn't touch him this time, resting her
hands nervously on her thighs instead, even
when they leaned into the turns. She wasn't worried about falling off or getting hurt. The only
thing bothering her now was the fact that Betsy
Endicott's wedding was going to go down in the
record books as the biggest disaster in Palm
Beach history.

Maybe she'd overreacted on the waiter issue.
Maybe she shouldn't have been so upset over
him calling her a snob, since she had been called
worse things.

Right now, however, none of that mattered.
She had to think of a way to make Max cater
Betsy's wedding, and she had to think of some-
thing fast.

But what?

When Max jerked to a halt in front of her pink
marble mansion, she slid slowly off the motorcycle and took her time removing the helmet before
Max extricated it from her hands.

"I realize we don't see eye to eye on a lot of
things," she said, stepping in front of the motorcycle to keep Max from driving away without at
least hearing her out.

"We don't see eye to eye on *anything*."

"Be that as it may, since we've already discussed the menu, *and* since I graciously gave in to you and your conditions, would you reconsider catering Betsy's wedding ... if I could find the waiters?"

He didn't take long coming up with an answer. He just shook his head slowly and very succinctly said, "No."

That wasn't the answer she'd expected. "Why?"

"Because you want too much," he said, all too seriously. "Because the food, the staff, and even the chef at Born To Be Wild could never live up to your high expectations."

"That's not true."

He turned the wheel and rolled the motorcycle so that she was standing right next to him again, so close she could almost feel the bitter chill of his eyes. "You've got a lot going for you," he said. "You're rich. You're beautiful. Hell, Lauren, there've been a few moments today when I found myself wanting something far more than a business relationship with you. But you know what? That high-and-mighty attitude of yours changed my mind."

His words hurt, but she couldn't give up under pressure. "We could still have a business relationship."

He shook his head, and she felt as if her entire world was going to crumble in on her.

"All right," she declared, "we can use your waiters."

"Too late. I'm going to concentrate all my efforts on Mr. Fabiano's birthday party."

He revved the engine.

She felt tears welling up behind her eyes, but held them back. "You're my last hope, Max. If you desert me, what will I do about Saturday?"

He laughed. "To be perfectly honest, I don't care about Betsy Endicott's highfalutin wedding. But—"

"But what?" she interrupted, feeling her lips begin to tremble.

"I'm not going to leave you high and dry."

A little bit of her hope was restored. "You're not?"

"No." He grinned. "There's a Costco in West Palm Beach. They've got frozen quiche and shrimp trays that aren't too bad. Why don't you give them a try?"

"But—"

"I don't have time for any more buts, Lauren."

"Please."

"Saying please worked the first time, but not anymore." All too soon the motorcycle thundered down the drive and onto the street, drowning out Lauren's last attempt to keep Max around.

She stared straight ahead until the roar of Max's engine died away, her mind muddled with all the horrid scenarios that this latest calamity could bring about. And then she thought of Betsy's happiness, and she threw back her shoulders.

If Max thought he'd won, if he thought he'd extinguished all her optimism that Betsy's wedding would be a success, he had another think coming. Palm Beach would experience the best wedding ever this coming Saturday, and when it was all over, Lauren planned to tell Max all about her victory—in spite of him!

 *Five*

A streak of white shot past Max's eyes, dragging his attention from the paperwork spread before him on the bar. The balled up pair of socks skidded across the tile counter and came to an abrupt halt when it hit the cookie jar.

"Stop throwing things at me!" Jamie cried out between bursts of laughter.

"They're your socks," Ryan yelled back. "Can't you wear them more than once before throwing them in the dirty clothes?"

Max grabbed the remote control, aimed it at the CD player, and turned the volume up on "Purple Haze," but Jimi Hendrix couldn't compete with the playful bickering between Jamie and Ryan. They spent nearly fifteen minutes every night arguing over who would do the dinner dishes and who would toss a load of clothes in the wash, and more often than not they tried to drag Max into the argument. But he stayed out of it, having realized long ago that the kids were bright enough to work out this ongoing problem on their own.

When the last resounding guitar chord vibrated through the room, Ryan retreated to the laundry, Jamie sulked toward the kitchen sink, and Max went back to work, poring over myriad dessert and entrée recipes as he fine-tuned a new catering menu for Born To Be Wild.

It was a good thing he and Lauren Remington had parted company this afternoon, he thought, as he scribbled a few minor changes to his recipe for Easy Ridin' Mud Pie. He kept his life simple and his work to a minimum, preferring to give Jamie and Ryan the bulk of his attention. The last thing he needed was a rich, spoiled, snobbish socialite, one who chewed men up and spit them out, imposing on his time.

Of course, she didn't need a man like him, either, not when he wanted her one minute and despised her the next. God, he'd come on to her right here in this kitchen, and not long after he'd been rude, abrupt, and downright mean. He'd known damn well how she'd react to having Bear, Gabe, and Jazz working as waiters.

He hadn't had any choice in whom he hired, because getting qualified help for a society affair—especially on short notice—wasn't an easy task. But he could have broken the news about whom he planned to hire sooner, explained to her that they'd all worked for his foster dad when they were younger and knew the ropes. But, no, he'd wanted to tease her, wanted her to suffer just the smallest bit for her elitist attitude, and the whole thing had backfired. If he'd caught Jamie or Ryan treating someone—anyone—that way, he'd have their hides.

But it maddened him to think how much he wanted her, when she wasn't the kind of woman he thought she should be.

Hell, now *he* sounded like a snob, looking down at someone he barely knew, someone he judged over an incident that he'd blown all out of proportion, and condemned from what he'd read in the papers.

A sensible man would come right out and ask her why she'd married and divorced twice, why she'd dumped her last fiancé. He assumed it had to do with her being fickle, but maybe it was something else. He couldn't imagine anyone marrying—or staying married to—a man like Chip.

And he *had* read some fairly dismal stories about the indiscretions of her second husband, Leland Lancaster, right up until the time he died. But he'd also read stories about Lauren's escapades, things like naked jaunts on the beach in Rio and flirtations with married men.

As much as he wanted to put her out of his mind, she stayed there, begging him to give her another chance, to get to know her better before he judged her too harshly.

Would it hurt to call her in the morning? Would it be too much trouble to cater her blasted society shindig? Not really, especially when he thought about her softness, the sweet scent of her perfume, and the way she tried her damnedest to make things work. Hell, he wanted to see her again. There was a good chance Miss Palm Beach would crush him like all the other men in her life, but when had he ever turned his back on danger?

A deafening clang forced him to look up from the blur of papers in front of him. Jamie held a soapy copper-bottomed skillet in one hand and an aluminum saucepan in the other, and a mischievous grin brightened her freckled face. "I knew that would get your attention."

"A simple 'Hey, Max,' would have worked just as easily." He put down his pen, closed his notebook, and folded his forearms on the bar, giving Jamie his complete attention. "Okay, I'm all ears."

"Who was that lady you were with today?"

"Lauren Remington."

"She's not a new girlfriend, is she?"

Not at the moment, Max thought. Even though he planned to call her tomorrow, even though he planned to apologize, they had a lot to work out if they were going to have a personal relationship. Hell, she might even hang up on him after today's brutish display.

"There's a possibility I might cater a wedding for her."

Jamie bit her lip and Max knew there was more she wanted to ask, but instead she rinsed the pots and angled them in the drainer on the counter. She rested her elbows on the edge of the sink and scrubbed a spatula. Her eyes slowly drifted up from her chore. "Are you going to see her again no matter what?"

"I don't know."

"Does that mean 'I doubt it' or 'Yeah, I think so'?"

Max laughed. "It's more like 'I don't know,' but I'll keep you posted if the status changes."

"I hope it's 'I doubt it'," Jamie said, slapping the washcloth into the water. At eleven, she considered herself the woman of the house, and she didn't want anyone intruding on her territory.

Of course, there hadn't been many women in Max's life, especially during the last five years. Before his foster father got sick, he'd been in Hollywood and other parts of the country, working and looking for his sister and brother.

After his dad's death, he'd been too busy handling his affairs to *have* affairs. Philippe had left everything he owned—his home, his entire estate—to Max.

He'd also left a catering business that was nearly bankrupt, but Max had turned A Shot of Class into Born To Be Wild, changing the concept from gourmet to luaus, barbecues, and specialty sixties-era parties complete with restored cars, motorcycles, and loud music. He'd built Born To Be Wild to the point where he and his staff could work two and three jobs a day, seven days a week, if he wanted to, and he had in the beginning.

But there were other things he'd wanted to do, like make Philippe's dream of opening a place where kids—underprivileged or underloved—could hang out. Max owed his life, everything he'd become to Philippe, so he'd poured all his energy, all his time into Born To Be Wild until he had the money to open the Hole in the Wall. The Hole was still his pride and joy, but when Jamie and Ryan came into his life two years ago, his entire focus changed. Thankfully his friends had stepped in and took over the day-to-day operation of the Hole.

There hadn't been time for a steady woman in his life. Of course, if he continually treated women the way he'd treated Miss Palm Beach, no one would ever want him.

The kitchen phone rang and Max grabbed it, aiming the remote control at the CD player again to turn down the volume.

"Born To Be Wild," he answered, and for one brief moment hoped that Lauren Remington was on the other end, because he wanted to work out their differences.

"Hello, Max." The deep male voice definitely didn't belong to Lauren—it belonged to the investigator he'd hired to find Charlotte and Zack—and his disappointment surprised him. "How ya doing?"

"Fine. Any news?" Max hated the silence at the other end of the phone. The last time Harry had been this quiet, he'd called to tell Max that after six months of looking, he'd found some information on Max's brother—and the news hadn't been good.

"I might have found Charlotte," Harry said, "but don't get your hopes up."

"You killed any hope I had of finding Zack

when you told me he died in a car fire. I still have hopes of seeing Charlotte again, so whatever you do, don't tell me she's dead, too."

"All I'm trying to tell you is that I found a woman named Charlotte Wilde. She may or may not be your sister."

"Where is she?"

"Phoenix. I'm heading there on Tuesday to check her out."

"Have you talked to her?"

Silence again, until Harry's sigh reverberated against Max's ear. "I talked to the woman she lives with."

He hated the way Harry beat around the bush. "And?"

"She's . . . she's retarded."

"That's impossible. She was perfectly fine the last time I saw her."

"She was four when you saw her last, and from what I've been able to find out, you can't always detect someone's mental capabilities that early. But like I said, she may not be your sister."

Max hadn't seen his baby sister or his younger brother in twenty years, not since their mother had dumped Max on one of her old boyfriends and disappeared with Zack and Charlotte—who she'd eventually abandoned somewhere in California. He wanted to find Charlotte desperately, but he hadn't bargained for this.

"Tell me about her," he said, running a hand through his hair in frustration. "What does she look like? How old is she?"

"She's twenty-four. Black hair. Brown eyes."

The scant description was correct, but that didn't mean much. "What else do you know about her?" Did she still like to dance and sing? he wondered. Was she still pretty?

"I don't know a thing. The woman she lives with was evasive. That's why I'm heading to Phoenix. I can't tell you anything more until I see her and try to talk to her. And like I said, this may or may not be your Charlotte Wilde. It wouldn't be the first time I thought I'd found someone, only to learn that I was way off base."

"I want to find my sister. I want to see her," Max stated. "I don't care what shape she's in. If the woman in Phoenix is my sister, I want to know about it—even if you think I shouldn't be told."

"Don't worry, Max. I'll call you Tuesday night, no matter how bad the news might be."

Max pressed his fingers to his temples after he hung up the phone. He'd spent a lot of years looking for his family and found only his mother, a woman who didn't want to see him, a woman who had started a new life years before and didn't want him to be a part of it. It was just as well, because he had no interest in her, either. All he'd wanted from Loretta Wilde was information about his brother and sister, but she'd blocked them from her mind as easily as she'd shut out Max.

"Are you okay?" Jamie asked, her small, soapy fingers lightly touching his hand.

Nodding, Max slid off the barstool and headed for the sink. He bent down, eye level with his little girl, and touched her face. "Have I ever told you how glad I am to have you and Ryan?"

"A time or two." She bit her lower lip again, and he couldn't miss the worried frown in her eyes. "Will you still want us when you find your sister?"

Max laughed. "I'll always want you."

"But you haven't adopted us."

He stood, lifting Jamie and setting her on the edge of the counter. He put his hands in the warm, soapy dishwasher, taking over the chore she hated. "You have a father," he reminded her.

"He's in jail. I don't even remember him."

"Well, he remembers you, and he doesn't want to give you up."

"Ryan thinks you should talk to our dad. He thinks you could talk him into giving us up."

"What do you think?"

"That you're the only dad I've ever really known."

He dried off his hands and rested a hip on the counter next to her. "Does being adopted mean that much to you?"

Jamie nodded, and slipped her small hand into his much bigger one.

"For what it's worth, it means a lot to me, too." Ryan had come into the kitchen and leaned against the refrigerator. "Sometimes I think you don't want to adopt us."

"It's not that I don't want to, it's just that I hadn't given it much thought."

"Why?" Jamie asked. "Didn't you want Philippe to adopt you?"

He tried to remember if he'd ever had any feelings one way or another about being adopted. Philippe Bernard had been a far better father than Max's real dad had been, and that was enough for Max.

"We never discussed it," Max said. "He was always there for me and I knew he loved me— even though he never said it in so many words. That seemed enough at the time." He smiled at Ryan and Jamie. "You know that I love you, don't you?"

Jamie nodded, but Ryan shrugged and stared at the floor. Displays of emotion weren't that easy for him, not at fourteen. "Yeah . . . I suppose."

Max had been fifteen when Philippe took him in. He'd been a tough kid who hadn't needed or wanted anyone. He saw a lot of himself in Ryan. Jamie, however, was quiet, sensitive, and still a little girl—his little girl.

Two years ago when he'd brought Ryan home, he'd just turned twelve. He was angry at Max, angry at the world, and did little more than sit in a corner and glare. Max had managed to get nine-year-old Jamie a couple of months later, and the very first night she'd crawled into his lap. She'd looked at him with her sweet, baby-blue eyes— eyes filled with tears—and said she hoped he wouldn't get rid of her or Ryan too soon, because she was tired of moving from one foster home to another, tired of being separated from her brother, tired of learning new rules everywhere she went.

Max knew that feeling all too well.

That memory, and his need to comfort her, made him wrap his arm around Jamie and hold her close. Two years ago when Max had asked about the possibility of adoption, he was told that Ryan and Jamie's dad refused to give them up, that he swore he'd get out of prison eventually and take care of his kids.

But their dad had never contacted them. He hadn't made any attempt to cooperate with the system and was denied parole the last time around. Max had come to the conclusion the guy would be in jail for the rest of his life.

But what if he did get out? What if he took Jamie and Ryan away? What if he violated parole again? And what if he got drunk and this time the kids were in the car with him rather than their mother and a couple of friends? What if he had another head-on collision and Jamie and Ryan were his newest victims?

The thought tortured him, made him realize what a special gift he'd been given when Jamie and Ryan came into his life.

He pressed a kiss to Jamie's forehead. "I'll call an adoption attorney tomorrow."

He felt Jamie's arms tighten around him, while Ryan stared at the floor. Slowly Ryan raised his head and Max couldn't miss the moisture welling up in the corners of the boy's eyes. The words "I love you" were on the tip of Ryan's tongue, but they remained unspoken. Sometimes words weren't necessary—he knew that from his own relationship with Philippe.

Max reached out and pulled Ryan against him,

feeling a strong tug at his heart a moment before an uncharacteristic tear slid down his cheek.

Tomorrow he'd take steps to make sure he never lost Jamie and Ryan—to make sure that they never lost him. Because he knew all too well the pain of losing the ones he loved.

 *Six*

$\mathcal{S}$neaking down to the kitchen wasn't a habit of Lauren's, especially at midnight, but she couldn't get the boxes of mini quiche she and Charles had purchased at Costco off her mind. She had no idea if *frozen* mini quiche would taste delicious or if it would taste like cardboard. The same torturous thoughts had also gone through her mind for the past three hours about the pre-sliced chocolate cheesecake, not to mention the platters of shrimp and something called tortilla roll-ups scheduled to be picked up from the deli bright and early Saturday morning. What would Betsy and Bunny Endicott think if they got wind that Lauren had purchased the reception delicacies at a price club?

How would they react when they learned that Lauren had chosen not to have waiters at the fancy affair, that instead the guests would have to walk from table to table if they wanted something to eat or drink?

This was all Max Wilde's fault, of course. How dare he insinuate—no, he hadn't insinuated, he'd blatantly accused her of being a snob. Then he'd walked—no, he'd stormed—away from the most lucrative, glamorous job of his life!

Well, she planned to show him and all of Palm Beach just how good a job she could do without the services of a professional caterer.

"Pride goeth before a fall," Charles had stated in a proper British whisper as he'd pushed the extra-large cart up one Costco aisle and down another. Over and over he'd told her that she should call Max Wilde and beg him to reconsider, but she'd adamantly stated, "No!" Max Wilde was insensitive, insufferable, and he'd deserted her. The nerve of the man!

Flipping on the light, she entered Mrs. Fisk's black and white kitchen. Clean, almost to the point of sterile, it was a place she'd sat in many times chatting with Charles and Mrs. Fisk about the happenings in Palm Beach and Newport, where they often retreated during the hot and humid Florida summers.

It never ceased to amaze Lauren that her butler and cook could tell her what was going on behind closed doors long before she heard exaggerated versions of the stories from her friends. Naturally she listened to all their reports, dispelled rumors when she could, and made it a point never to pass on the information.

Listening to gossip was one thing. Spreading it was quite another. She'd long ago tired of the scandalous tales about her own escapades. Most everyone knew that the tabloids and rumor mill blew everything out of proportion, but all too often something vicious would strike out and hurt someone close—all too often herself.

Of course, people like her—rich society folk— were supposed to be insensitive to backstabbing and name calling. Max Wilde must have thought she was made of steel. Why else would he have treated her the way he did?

She didn't want to think about Max, but it was hard to think of anyone or anything else at midnight, when the house was quiet and she had nothing better to do. Looking at the starkness of her kitchen made her think of his disorderly laundry room and his warm and inviting kitchen, and brought to mind the vivid differences between his life and hers.

She wondered if Max Wilde ever sat around his kitchen discussing the outrageous lives of his friends and neighbors. For some reason she couldn't picture him doing such a thing. Instead, she envisioned him tossing a ball to Ryan while standing at the counter whipping up barbecued ribs, or explaining an algebra equation to Jamie while chopping an onion.

This kitchen had never had that homey feel. There were no pots and pans hanging around, no baskets of tomatoes, bananas, and oranges. Mrs. Fisk kept the cookies tucked away in an air-tight box beneath one of the counters, while Max had a red and black motorcycle cookie jar sitting at one end of the bar. She'd liked this kitchen until she'd sat in Max's.

Max. Why did his name and so many things about him and his life continually pop into her mind? She shouldn't think of him at all, especially when she remembered his hot brown eyes staring at her across the kitchen counter as he laid down the law on what she had to do before he'd work for her.

What an impossible man! One she needed to put completely out of her thoughts, but she couldn't.

He'd been rude to her, teased her, and that had kicked off a chain reaction that had them both zinging verbal jabs at each other. If truth be told, she'd been just as rude picking on his friends when he'd merely tried to help her out—and gone out of his way to do it. She wasn't too sure what a '29 Indian Scout was, but she had the feeling it was a motorcycle, one that he cherished, one that, undoubtedly, was worth a lot of money. And he'd offered it to Bear—all for her.

Maybe she should attempt another apology, but he'd already made it perfectly clear that he wanted nothing more to do with her.

Period.

Tucking an errant strand of hair behind her ear, she opened one of the freezer doors, took out a package of mini quiche, and quickly scanned the instructions, which were written in impossibly small letters on the side of the box.

Opening one cupboard after another, she finally found Mrs. Fisk's baking sheets, then turned on the oven. Three hundred and seventy-five degrees for ten minutes seemed an incredibly long time. With nearly two hundred guests coming on Saturday, with dozens of trays that would need to be filled with tidbits for them to eat, the food would have to cook much quicker. With a flick of her wrist, she twisted the knob to five hundred degrees, carefully placed the quiche on the tray, and popped it into the oven.

She looked at her watch. Twelve-twenty-seven. At precisely twelve-thirty-two she'd check on the quiche.

She paced the floor for the longest time, took one look at her watch, but only fifteen seconds had gone by. Did chefs get bored? she wondered.

Taking one of Mrs. Fisk's cookbooks from the bookshelf, she opened it on the counter and flipped through the pages, looking at all the enticing delicacies. Her stomach growled, and she checked her watch again, anxious to try the quiche.

One minute and thirty seconds had ticked away, leaving her three minutes and thirty seconds. Time enough for a quick phone call.

Grabbing the phone from the wall, she punched in her brother's number. It was only ten-twenty-eight in Wyoming. Surely Jack and Sam would be awake and she could tell Sam about

Betsy's wedding and see if she had some advice. After all, becoming a wedding planner *had* been Sam's idea.

The phone rang three times before Lauren heard the receiver bounce off something hard, before she heard Jack's raspy "Hello."

Oh, dear! Maybe he'd been asleep after all.

"I didn't wake you, did I?" Lauren asked her brother.

She couldn't mistake the grumbling at the other end of the phone. "It's ten-thirty, Lauren. What's wrong?"

"What a silly question to ask. Everything's fine. Absolutely perfect. Is everything absolutely perfect with you?"

"Except for the fact that you woke me out of a sound sleep, except for the fact that Sam's having trouble sleeping and you woke her up from the first good night she's had in weeks, except for—"

"Thank goodness she's awake," Lauren interrupted. Knowing her brother, he could go on for hours saying "except for" and she didn't want to listen to him right now. It was Sam's voice she longed to hear. "Could I speak with her?"

"Hang on a second."

In the background she heard the squeak of the bed, heard Jack's complaining and Sam's delightful laughter as she breathlessly admonished her husband for being such a grouch, all of which brought a smile to Lauren's face. If her brother and sister-in-law didn't choose to live in the godforsaken outback of Wyoming, she'd build a house right next door so she could spend every day in Sam's company.

The same breathless voice that had chewed out Jack said, "Hi, Lauren."

"I am *so* sorry I woke you," Lauren began. "I know it's late, I know you're pregnant, and . . . Oh, dear, I've been so wrapped up in what's going on in my life that I didn't give a moment's thought to the fact that you're carrying around twins, that you must be feeling awful, and—"

"I'm fine," Sam told her, "although your niece and nephew have already begun to fight. Not only that, but one of them continually pushes on my bladder, one has a constant case of the hiccups, and neither one likes to sleep. I can just imagine what life will be like once they enter the world."

Lauren unconsciously put a hand to her belly, wondering if she'd ever know the joy of bringing a new life into the world. It seemed highly doubtful, considering her past and her propensity for making a mess of all her relationships, but she still held out hope that someday she'd have the family she'd always craved.

She tried not to think about her own desires and focused on Sam again, thinking of all the wonderful days she had ahead of her. Of course, there were probably going to be some not so wonderful days, too.

"Mother told me she'd recommended a nanny and that you'd flatly refused to have one."

"Your mother means well, but what do I need

with a nanny? I'm perfectly capable of raising my own children. Jack swears he won't leave my side. Beau's anxious to have a brother and sister. Pastor Mike's already planning a christening, and Crosby's grumbling about having two more mouths to feed. I haven't got the heart to tell Cros that I'll be breast-feeding the babies for at least the first year. As much as he fusses, I think he's secretly looking forward to having children in the house. But enough about us. Tell me about Betsy Endicott's wedding. It's in just a couple of days, isn't it?"

"Saturday," Lauren stated, but suddenly her mind wasn't on Betsy's wedding or her troubles. It was on homes and big happy families. Families like Sam's and her brother's. Children like Max's.

"Is something troubling you?" Sam asked, the concern in her voice bringing Lauren back to reality, tearing her thoughts from a pink-cheeked baby in a bassinet and a husband and wife marveling at the bundle of perfection they'd created. She didn't want to bother Sam with her insecurities about the future, not when Sam had enough to worry about with twins on the way.

"Of course nothing's troubling me," Lauren fibbed. "I just wanted to hear your voice, and tell you about the darling baby clothes I bought the other day. I found a place called Baby Gap that has absolutely adorable things. I imagine I got a bit carried away buying shoes and dresses and would you believe, I even found denim overalls and khakis. I picked up some darling sterling silver spoons at Neiman Marcus, and, well, I could tell you everything, but I want you to be surprised when the packages arrive."

"I'll call you as soon as they come. Now," Sam said flatly, "what's troubling you?"

"Nothing."

"I know you better than you know yourself, Lauren, so spill!"

What could she say? She didn't want to tell Sam about Max, because she'd promised Sam she wouldn't get involved with another man, at least until her business took off. She couldn't tell her about the problems with finding a caterer, because Sam would tell Jack and Jack would send out the Seventh Cavalry to help. She didn't want or need her brother's assistance. She needed to prove to him, just as she needed to prove to herself, that she was perfectly capable of functioning on her own. There was, however, one small thing that had been nagging at her since this afternoon, and she knew Sam would tell her the truth.

"I was accused today of being a . . . snob," Lauren said, her voice nearly a whisper as she uttered the despicable word. "Do you think that's true?"

"Well—"

"Don't lie to me, Sam, and please don't say the polite thing just to protect my feelings. I can handle the truth."

"You're not a snob."

"Thank you," Lauren said, the words rushing out on a gasp of relief. "I couldn't imagine you, of all people, thinking that I had an elitist attitude."

"You didn't let me finish," Sam stated, knocking the wind right out of Lauren.

"Finish? But you said I'm not a snob."

"You're not. You're the loveliest person I've ever met, but sometimes . . ." Lauren hated the sound of her sister-in-law's sigh. "Sometimes you're a little self-centered."

Lauren took a moment to contemplate Sam's words. If they'd come from anyone else, she would have tossed back an immediate rebuttal, but she trusted Sam to tell her the truth. "I didn't realize I was egotistical. I don't mean to be."

"I didn't say egotistical, Lauren. You're not selfish, either. Goodness, I don't know anyone as giving and loving as you. It's just that sometimes you get so carried away with what needs to be done or with what you want to do—like going on a shopping trip or planning a wedding or . . . or calling someone late at night—that you don't take into consideration everyone else's feelings. Sometimes your mind is made up before you listen to what someone else wants or needs."

Lauren laughed lightly. It was either that, or cry. "I don't think I've ever purposely set out to hurt someone, except when I pushed Peter into that lake, and at the time I was secretly praying that there were alligators in the water."

Sam laughed, too. "Peter had that coming, but tell me, why did someone call you a snob?"

Because she was, Lauren realized, remembering the way she'd scrutinized Bear's fingernails, expecting them to be greasy just because he rode a motorcycle. Hadn't she thought Chip was a snob when he'd inspected Max in much the same way she'd checked out Bear?

As for Jazz and Gabe, she didn't know the first thing about either of them, yet she assumed that they'd be lousy waiters. No, she hadn't assumed that at all. She'd assumed that her friends would laugh at them and at her for hiring them. Which made her, without a doubt, a snob.

But she couldn't admit this to Sam. It was far too embarrassing. In light of that fact, she knew she'd have to take steps on her own to lessen her snooty ways.

"Who called me a snob and why isn't all that important," she told Sam. "Besides, it's getting late and I really shouldn't have bothered you."

"You're not bothering me."

Maybe she could get part of it off her chest. "It's a long story, but one of these days when you have a lot of time I'll tell you about Max—"

"Who's Max?"

"Are you sure you want to hear about him now?"

"Positive."

Lauren sat at the kitchen table, crossed her legs, and pulled her aqua silk robe over her knee. "Max is the man who *was* going to cater Betsy's wedding."

"I thought Henri was going to do it."

"He died yesterday. It was just awful. The poor man keeled over from a heart attack and his funeral's Saturday—the same day and time as Betsy's wedding."

"So who's Max?"

"The chef who was going to help out. Unfortunately he wanted to hire a bunch of bikers to wait on people and then he called me a snob because . . . well, just because. So he quit before we even signed a contract, and tonight Charles and I went to Costco because I'm going to cater the entire thing myself."

"You're what?"

"I've decided to cater Betsy's wedding. But please don't tell Jack because he'll worry and then he'll want to help me out and I know I can do this all on my own. After all, how hard could it possibly be to whip up a few little hors d'oeuvres?"

"It's not as simple as it seems," Sam said. "Why don't you let us help?"

"Absolutely not. You've got a date with an obstetrician."

"Not for several months."

"I don't care how much longer you have, you need to rest and Jack needs to be with you, not here trying to help me out. Trust me, Lauren. Everything's under control."

A puff of black smoke suddenly billowed out of the oven.

"Oh, dear!" Lauren shouted, dropping the phone as she ran across the kitchen. "The quiche is on fire!"

The firemen departed at two-twenty-two, taking with them the last of Mrs. Fisk's chocolate-covered pecan cookies. Lauren had hoped to eat a few of them herself before going to bed, but the nice-looking men all decked out in fire-fighting gear had seemed to need them more than she. In fact, their disgruntled attitudes had calmed down immensely after she handed them the entire box.

Why they should have been upset was beyond her. After all, it was their job to respond to fires. Maybe she had told the 911 dispatcher that her kitchen was on fire, when it had been merely a small blaze in the oven, but there was no telling what a flaming tray of quiche could have done to her home.

Fortunately, Charles had put out the inferno with a scoop of baking soda minutes before the fire engine arrived.

Dear, sweet Charles. What would she do without him?

Lauren gathered her soot-splattered robe over her chest with one hand and held the dustpan to the floor with the other, helping Charles sweep up the last of the baking soda and bits and pieces of charred canapés.

When they'd completed their task, Charles stood before her in his short purple silk dressing gown and bare feet and asked, "Is there anything more I can do for you?"

"I don't believe so, but thank you."

"Very well." He walked across the kitchen, stopping when he reached the doorway. Turning slowly, he looked back at Lauren. "I was wondering, Miss Remington?"

"Yes?"

"Do you think Mr. Wilde might reconsider

catering Miss Endicott's wedding if *I* were to ask him?"

"There's no need for you to do that, Charles. I have every intention of doing it myself."

A slow smile touched Charles's mouth. "Very well, Miss Remington."

She didn't like to grovel, especially with a man like Max Wilde, but after tonight, she had no other choice.

 *Seven*

*T*he last thing Max wanted to do was get out of bed at three-thirty-one in the morning, but the incessant knock at the front door forced him to throw off the covers and shoot out of bed before Jamie and Ryan were ripped from their dreams.

He stormed down the hall, stepped on a half-naked Barbie doll sprawling on the living room floor, swept it up before it caused bodily harm to anyone else, and limped the rest of the way to the door.

Getting yanked awake in the middle of the night did not put him in the frame of mind for visitors, especially one knocking nonstop.

Lauren Remington was the last person on earth he'd expected to see when he peered through the security hole, but who else would have the nerve to pay a social call in the middle of the night?

He slid the chain lock off the door, turned the dead bolt, and opened the door a crack. He rubbed his tired eyes. "Do you have any idea what time it is?"

A smile touched her pretty pink lips, and her green eyes sparkled. "It's three-thirty and I apologize profusely for waking you."

He tried not to notice how beautiful she looked standing under the dim porch light, but he wasn't dead, only groggy. He was in complete control of his senses, too, which were yelling, *She may be gorgeous, but what on earth is she doing here in the middle of the night?*

He opened the door a little further, figuring he might as well enjoy the view. "Apology accepted." He attempted to smile in the midst of a yawn. "So, do you mind telling me what you want at this hour of the morning?"

"You."

Obviously he was still asleep because he could swear she'd said she wanted him, even though he looked like hell. He rubbed his left eye, just to make sure he wasn't imagining her. No, Lauren Remington stood on his doorstep looking like heaven. Most women would be in pajamas at three A.M. Some would be naked and in the arms of a lover. But Miss Palm Beach had a green sweater tied about her shoulders, and beneath it she wore a short, silky green dress that showed off her knockout legs. His gaze dipped to her shoes, and he wasn't surprised to see mile-high green spikes.

Her toes were bare, and so were her sleek long legs, and as his eyes drifted up her body he wondered what else she wasn't wearing beneath the dress. Maybe he shouldn't be thinking that way at this time of the morning, but no one had ever accused him of being anything less than a man— no matter what time of day it was.

Slowly his gaze settled on her eyes, pretty green eyes that were giving him the same kind of once-over he'd been giving her.

"Nice pajamas," she said in a tone that was downright sexy.

She had to have rocks in her head if she found his wrinkled white T-shirt and black boxers decorated with flying red hearts *nice*. "I don't wear pajamas." God, he sounded like a petulant fool.

"All right then," she said with that same sweet smile on her lips, "nice shorts."

"Jamie and Ryan gave them to me for Valentine's Day."

"Was Barbie a gift, too?"

"One of many I've given my daughter," he grumbled, and tossed the topless doll across the room, where she made a perfect landing on the couch.

"So," he said, aiming a murderous glare at Lauren, "are you going to tell me why you're here?"

The laughter in her eyes turned to a hesitant smile. "I need you."

If she didn't stop making comments like that, she was going to be in trouble.

"Why?"

Drawing her hand from behind her back, she presented him with a crystal plate bearing a pile of burnt offerings. "Would you like some mini quiche?"

"Is that what that is?"

She nodded. "They're from Costco."

He laughed as he surveyed her culinary handiwork, then folded his arms across his chest and casually leaned against the doorjamb, settling in for what he expected to be a pleasant bit of Laurenesque chatter.

"What happened?"

"I'm not a caterer." She smiled weakly, probably hoping that he'd refute her statement. But he couldn't lie.

"That's obvious."

"You don't have to be so blunt."

"And you didn't have to come knocking on my door at three-thirty."

"But I did, because I have no one else to turn to. Everything's a disaster. I burned the quiche. I nearly burned down my house and I had to call the fire department. I know I'm restating what you already know, but I'm not a cook and I'm very much in need of help. *Your* help. I'm sorry for everything I said today. I was self-centered, judgmental, and before you have a chance to add your favorite choice of words, yes, I suppose I might have come off sounding like a snob. But I'm not. Not really."

She held the plate out to him, and attempting to appear gracious, he took it from her hands.

"I need you, Max," she said softly. "Betsy Endicott's one of my dearest friends. She's in love, Dickie's in love, and I want everything to be perfect for them." She drew in a very deep sigh and let it out slowly. "I need you to help *me*, too. I've failed too many times in my life and . . . and I don't want to fail again." Tears beaded at the corners of her eyes, and her lips trembled. "*Please.*"

Lauren Remington a failure? Hell, she might be a chatterbox, she might not have done well in physics, and more than likely she didn't know one end of a spatula from the other, but she had more spunk than anyone he'd ever met. Her gumption was one of the things he'd admired most about her.

And, hell, he couldn't remember a time when he'd so desperately wanted to kiss a pair of soft, puckery lips, when he'd wanted to wrap an arm around a woman, drag her close, and hold her body hard against him. But not now. Before they launched that kind of relationship, they had some big issues to resolve.

"All right, I'll help you."

"In spite of everything?"

"Yeah, but we've got to straighten out a few things first, like what's going on between the two of us."

"I was thinking exactly the same thing before I burned the quiche. You've been irritated with me for heaven knows what reason and I'm dying to know why. Of course, it's terribly late and I'm sure Jamie and Ryan are asleep, and it would be simply awful to accidentally wake them up if you got upset with me again."

"We're not going to wake Jamie and Ryan because we're not going to talk right now."

"Good. I haven't been to bed yet and you can't believe how tired I am. Maybe you could drop by tomorrow afternoon."

"I'll be there at seven in the morning," he stated, absently sweeping a strand of her soft, wind-blown hair behind her ear. "I'll bring the contract, we can fine-tune the menu—"

"*Seven!* I rarely get up that early."

"And I rarely get up this late." He kept his laughter under control and stepped away from the doorway. "Good night, Lauren."

Her hand shot out, pressing against the door before he could close it. "Couldn't we make it nine instead of seven?"

"*Seven,*" he repeated, refusing to change his mind.

"But—"

"Good night, Lauren."

He closed the door and locked it.

There was silence on the other side, and then he heard the distinct sound of Lauren's heels clicking on the brick walk. He heard her car door open, then close again. Any second now he'd hear the engine, but he was wrong. The click of heels came toward the house, followed by a soft knock.

Again he opened the door a crack.

His leather jacket dangled from Lauren's outstretched hand.

"You left this at my place yesterday."

"Thanks." He took the coat and closed the door.

Once more the knock came. Somehow he got his grin under control before he opened the door.

"What now?" he asked.

"Do you like your coffee black," she asked with a smile, "or do you prefer cream and sugar?"

"I don't drink coffee in the morning. I jog, so we might as well do it together."

Her mouth widened in shock. "But—"

"We can discuss Betsy's wedding in the morning. On the beach. *While* we're jogging."

"But—"

Closing the door on her protest, he bolted it and waited for another knock, for another argument. Instead, he heard Lauren's heels, her car door, and a purring engine.

He went to the front window, parted the drapes a few inches, and watched Lauren's red Mercedes sports car back out of the drive, then zip up the street. Even though she was gone from sight, he could picture her smile, the way she conveyed happiness, guilt, and desperation simply through the tilt of her lips.

Nice lips. Lips he'd wanted to kiss.

What on earth had come over him? The last woman on earth he should want to kiss was Miss Palm Beach. She was a handful. She was out of his league. Worse yet, she'd been married a couple of times. They had nothing in common and— he looked at the remains of charred quiche on the plate he held—she couldn't even cook!

He chuckled as he realized how much Lauren Remington needed him.

And sobered when something deep inside told him that he might need her, too.

 *Eight*

*L*auren looked incredible climbing from the depths of the pink marble pool, with her golden-brown hair slicked back from her face and the morning sunlight glistening off the water that had beaded on her lightly tanned skin. Max's gaze followed the rivulets meandering over her thighs, knees, and calves to form a puddle at her feet, nice feet, which he wouldn't mind massaging late at night as he worked his way up her legs, kneading each extraordinary speck of her body.

When she swept a fluffy white towel from a lounge chair and pressed it to her face, he studied the impressively high cut of her bright yellow swimsuit and imagined the look and feel of the soft, shapely form beneath. Lauren Remington wasn't model material, all bones and hard edges, like some of the women he'd known. No, she came packaged like a goddess, with luscious curves that made him ache.

A mere dance with this woman would never be enough.

He stepped from the shadows of the doorway where, for the past five minutes, he'd contemplated the woman who'd dragged him from bed in the middle of the night, a woman whose image, whose smile, whose tears and confession of being a failure had kept him awake long after.

She saw him finally, their eyes met, and a slow, enchanting smile touched her lips. "Good morning," she said, fastening a sheer piece of brightly flowered fabric about her waist. Her hips swayed provocatively as she sauntered across the patio, a slow-motion picture of perfection.

If she wanted to mesmerize him, she was doing a damn fine job.

If she thought she could sway him from his intentions, however, she was sorely mistaken.

"Ready to go jogging?" he asked.

As if she hadn't heard his question, she sat in one of two white wicker chairs resting beside a glass-topped table, crossed her longer-than-long legs, and smiled. "You slammed the door so quickly last night—"

"This morning," he corrected. "*Early* this morning."

"All right. You slammed the door so *early* this morning that I never had the chance to tell you that I don't like to jog. What I do like to do is swim, which is far more civilized. And when I'm through swimming, I like to have breakfast, beginning with freshly squeezed orange juice." She filled two crystal glasses and held one toward him. "Would you care to join me?"

He'd rather join her in something more *stimulating*, but he nodded slowly and headed for the table. The juice looked good. Lauren looked better—tempting, as a matter of fact. Far too tempting. He had a hell of a lot of nervous energy to burn off, tension that had been piling up since her phone call yesterday morning. She might not want to jog, but he did, and once he set his mind on doing something, he didn't let anything get in his way.

Lauren thought for sure her composure would desert her as Max strolled across the patio, looking at her body as if he wanted to lap the water off every inch of her skin. She couldn't remember any man ever looking at her that way. They normally found her money more enticing than her body.

Tugging her tropical print sarong over her knees to give him fewer places to stare, she took a deep breath and tried to control the rapid beat of her heart. Goodness, she certainly hoped Max Wilde couldn't see the pulse beneath her breasts, even though that's where he kept aiming his eyes!

"I've asked Charles to serve us fruit and muffins," she said, playing the part of the good hostess. It was much too early to entertain, but she'd do anything to keep from jogging on the beach. "It's a lovely morning for talking and . . .

and for straightening out all of those things that caused us so much trouble yesterday. *Or,* if that's too awkward at this time of morning, we could talk about the menu, your fee . . . whatever you'd like."

The slightest grin tilted one side of his mouth. "All right."

There was something very odd in the tone of his voice. It gave her the distinct impression that he didn't want to talk business, or about their continual bickering, that he had more adventurous pursuits in mind. Still, she asked, "What should we discuss first? The wine? What caviar I prefer? The fact that you're a man of too few words, especially early in the morning?"

His silence, the heat in his eyes as he tugged off his T-shirt and bared the most glorious set of pecs she'd ever laid eyes on, put her heart back in uncontrollable motion. Not a good condition for a woman trying *not* to fall under this man's spell.

He tossed his shirt over the back of a chair. His muscles flexed. His mermaid tattoo swished, and a quiver of absolute delight rippled through her insides. "Let's discuss jogging."

That comment brought her emotions skidding under control. "Why don't we talk about current events instead." She took a sip of orange juice and watched his movements over the rim of her glass, while trying her best to turn the subject away from exercise. "Have you seen the paper this morning? It's full of talk about the yacht Dickie's hired for the honeymoon."

"I've told you I don't read the society pages," he said, finally sitting across from her. He took a long drink of orange juice, giving her a chance to study the corded muscles in his neck, the way his Adam's apple rose and fell when he swallowed, his extraordinary chest, and the V-shaped mat of dark hair that spread over his darkly bronzed skin, before disappearing to mysterious territory under his belt.

Oh, dear, she'd never seen such a beautiful man.

"What *do* you read?" she asked, the question inane, but the only one that popped into her mind as he stripped out of his boots and socks.

"The sports pages, mostly." He stood and methodically unlatched his buckle as she watched his slow, seductive movements, and the orange juice she'd been trying to swallow stuck in her throat. "There was an article on jogging this morning." He popped the top button on his jeans. "Studies indicate it's good for your state of mind."

"Is that so?" she choked out, her gaze fixed dead center between his hips as he unlatched the second button and then the third.

"Yeah."

Her eyes flickered from the front of his Levi's to his heated eyes. "My state of mind's perfectly fine," she lied.

"I wish I could say the same." He dropped his jeans and stood before her, his magnificent body decked out in nothing more than a pair of baggy gray running shorts.

Even though her eyes were focused on his

muscular legs, she forced her mind to stay on the conversation. "Something troubling you?" she asked.

"Nothing that a nice long jog won't take care of."

"Jogging leaves me feeling wilted," she responded. "That's why I swim. It's much more refreshing, it's easier on the joints, and I can do it in the privacy of my own backyard."

Obviously he hadn't heard a word she'd said, because he pried the glass of orange juice from her fingers and pulled her out of her chair. "We'd better go before it gets too warm."

"It's already too warm," she stammered, as he tugged her across the patio. "And really, Max, I look dreadful in perspiration."

"I'll be the judge of that." His laughter wrapped around her as he picked up speed. Her feet hit the cool grass and then the sun-soaked sand, and all too soon they were running toward the water.

Oh, dear! She'd wanted to avoid jogging at all costs. She couldn't think of anything more humiliating than having Max see her breasts bounce or her legs and posterior jiggle. But he didn't seem to care, he just pulled her with him into the gentle surf, never once letting go of her hand as she huffed and puffed at his side.

"I hired another waiter," he said, his breathing calm, totally under control, as if they were having a simple business conversation across a table.

"Good. A seasoned professional, I hope."

"One of the kids from the Hole."

She gasped for air, finding the will to stay calm. "And this kid from the Hole? He's experienced?"

"Yeah."

Thank goodness! She didn't want to appear snobbish any longer, but she did so want to have at least one waiter who knew what he was doing. "Has he worked very many Palm Beach parties?"

"Not a one."

Oh, dear! "But you said he has experience."

Max grinned. "He's great at rebuilding engines."

This was not good news. "Please don't tell me you're talking about the kid in greasy overalls? I think Bear called him Jed."

"That's the one."

"But he looks like a hoodlum."

Max laughed, dragging her knee deep into the water. "He looks better when he's cleaned up. And don't worry, he doesn't have a record."

"Has he been in trouble?" she asked, slogging through the surf, each movement of her legs getting increasingly difficult.

"He's got a dad who beats him, and he's got an eye for classic cars. Put the two together and they could easily spell trouble."

She couldn't imagine anyone beating their child, no matter what they'd done. She might not have had the most attentive parents, but they'd never laid a hand on her. Suddenly she wondered why Max was so involved with these children.

"Did you have a dad who beat you?" she asked.

"Yeah, but that's history and not something I talk about." In spite of the anguish that must have been ripping through him, he grinned. "Life's tough. Sometimes you get through it, sometimes you don't. Jed's going to make it, he just needs some nurturing."

He tugged her out of the surf and her water-logged sarong clung to her legs. She gasped for breath and wished Max would stop jogging, but he didn't seem the least bit bothered by the strenuous exercise.

"I'm sorry if I've made rash judgments about your friends," she said, panting again. "I know it's not much of an excuse, but until yesterday, I'd never been around bikers. I've heard some dreadful stories."

"Drinking? Carousing?"

"That and a whole lot more."

"I take it no one in Palm Beach drinks or carouses?"

She gave that question a moment's thought, then laughed. "We just put it in more genteel terms."

"Yeah, I figured that was the case."

His hand felt terribly warm and unbelievably masculine as it tightened around hers. The only thing that didn't feel nice was the ache in her legs and the tightness in her chest when she tried to breathe.

When she thought she couldn't move another yard, Max dropped her hand and slipped in front of her, keeping the same slow, even pace even though he was jogging backward. "Had enough?"

The salt water lapped about her ankles and

calves when she stopped moving. "I had enough twenty minutes ago, thank you," she said, then walked onto the beach and collapsed in the sand, hugging her knees close to her chest. "How's your frame of mind now?"

"Better." He dropped down on the beach beside her. "How about yours?"

"I was perfectly fine before we came out here, even though I'd only had two hours of sleep." She rested her cheek on top her knees and smiled at him. "I hope you don't always conduct business this way."

"Rarely."

"Then why are we here when there's so much to do before Betsy's wedding?"

His eyes trailed up and down her body again, a most uncomfortable—yet delightful—feeling for a woman who knew this exciting and virile man was all wrong for her.

"Because I find you sexier than hell."

Oh, dear! No one had ever found her sexier than anything. "Thank you," she said, "but honestly, Max, what does that have to do with you dragging me down to the beach to jog?"

"I wanted to get you away from that monstrosity you live in."

"You don't like it?"

"Hate it."

"Why?"

"It's too big, too impersonal." He scooped up a handful of sand and let it sift through his fingers and over her toes, the frown on his face making it appear as though he were agonizing over what to say next. "It reminds me that you used to be married to Chip Chasen."

"Why does that bother you so much?"

"Because you deserve better."

His sentiment touched her, but she had her doubts. "Do I?" She lay back in the sand and stared at the clouds floating across the sky. "I've made a mess of every relationship I've ever had."

Max stretched out next to her, lying on his side, his head balanced on his knuckles as he watched the play of emotions on her face. Her vulnerability surprised him. With so much going for her, when she could have the world, she seemed unsure of herself, telling him she'd been unsuccessful at too many things, that she'd failed at one relationship after another.

"You're too hard on yourself," he said.

"Am I? Two marriages? Two divorces? And then, of course, there was that escapade in England with Peter Leighton."

"You mean when you shoved him into a lake?"

"It was a pond covered with lily pads and infested with croaking frogs."

Her quick defense of herself made him smile. "I suppose that means you didn't hit him with a croquet mallet, either."

Her pretty green eyes narrowed as she flashed a frown in his direction. "I thought you didn't read the tabloids or society column."

"It's hard to miss the headlines when you're standing in line at the grocery store."

"Well, if you must know, it wasn't *one* croquet mallet, it was a complete set, and I didn't hit him, he stumbled over the rack in his rush to get out of the pond and away from the frogs. *That's* how Peter broke his arm, but since he's a darling of the polo circuit and since he couldn't play for a while, I was labeled the Wicked Witch of the West."

"So why did you push him in the . . . pond?"

"I didn't like the pre-wedding present he gave me."

"What?" he asked, unable to keep the grin from his face as she pursed her pretty lips. "A set of whips and chains?"

"I'm not into bondage, thank you, but a week's trip to a fat farm was just as crude!"

It would have been easy to tease her, but she'd probably heard enough jokes about Peter's cruel gift. Instead, he found himself studying her body, every curvy inch. "Peter was a fool."

"Thank you, but if truth be told, I'm the fool for picking all the wrong men, something I'm not about to do again."

She was close, so close, and he wanted to kiss her. Instead, he caressed her cheek, letting his thumb graze over her lips. "Are you sure?"

A moment's doubt crossed her face. They were all wrong for each other. He knew it, but couldn't push away the desire he felt; she knew it, too, and didn't have any qualms about pushing away from his touch. "Positive." She sat again, wrapping her arms around her knees. "Besides, I've got my hands full just trying to make a success of my business."

"But you don't need the money?"

"Goodness, no. My grandmother left me a trust that would make your head spin and I've got a financial adviser who's a whiz."

"Then why do you do it?"

"Because it's new and different and I want to earn my way—not just have everything handed to me. I've never had a job before, never had people rely on me, and it feels good. Not only that, but I charge a small fortune for my services, all of which goes into a fund my sister-in-law established for the homeless. My brother's administering the whole thing and doubles every dollar I make."

"Sounds like a nice guy."

"He hasn't always been the benevolent type, but that changed when he met Sam—that's my sister-in-law—and found out she lived in a Volkswagen." Lauren laughed. "You can't imagine my mother's angst over Jack marrying a homeless person, and then when she found out that Sam had suggested I plan weddings, poor Mother was beside herself with embarrassment."

"She doesn't approve?"

"No, but I've tried not to let it bother me. I know I'm good at what I do, and it makes me happy. Of course, having the caterer *die* isn't something I want to go through too often."

"I don't plan on dying."

"I appreciate that." She smiled. "Goodness,

I've gone on and on about myself, as if I'm not the least interested in you, which I am—"

"What interests you?" he asked, taking hold of her arm, pulling her down beside him again.

Oh, dear! They were far too close and she was far too interested in him. She knew full well if she let this go any further she was going to add one more complication to her life. Her friends would never approve of him. Her mother would have a fit. But there was something about him that kept drawing her closer.

"I'd like to know more about your children and why you became a chef." She also wanted to know if his lips tasted as good as they looked, how her breasts would feel crushed against his chest.

He brushed a strand of hair away from her face, and she felt a quiver in the pit of her stomach. "The best thing that ever happened to me was bringing Jamie and Ryan into my life," he said. "I could talk about them for days on end, but I don't want to bore you."

"I wouldn't be bored."

"Wouldn't you?" he asked, dragging his knuckles across her cheek, her chin.

"No. Your life is so different from mine and I want to know more. I look at you and see someone tough, someone unsettled, yet you've got foster kids and a beautiful home. I see a man who looks like a hard-edged renegade, yet you're a chef. You completely baffle me."

"I'm a biker because I like the feel of power between my legs, I'm a foster father because I like kids, I've got a nice home because I want my children to have the things I didn't have, and I'm a chef because my foster dad was a chef."

"You didn't become a chef just because of him, did you?"

He shook his head. "Philippe—my foster dad—was the only man to ever stick by me, even when I got in trouble. He never yelled, never struck out at me, and even though I originally thought cooking was something for sissies, I was determined to be good at it, because I wanted to pay Philippe back for what he'd given me. In the end I realized I enjoyed spending time in the kitchen and creating meals that people remembered. I still enjoy what I do—all of it."

"You're a very lucky man."

"I think so."

She rolled onto her back again and stared at the sky. She was afraid of her emotions but they were hard to ignore, especially when Max Wilde was such a good man.

"What are you thinking about?" he asked, tilting her head toward him with the soft touch of his callused hand.

She couldn't tell him the truth, that she envied his life, that she liked far too much about him. Instead she turned the subject back to business.

"I was just wondering what kind of desserts you're preparing for Saturday?"

"You don't really want to talk business, do you?" he asked, his thumb skimming over her lower lip.

"Not really," she admitted. What she wanted

was to draw his thumb into her mouth, to taste the salt on his skin, and roll into his heated embrace. "But right now I've got to concentrate on Betsy's wedding."

"All right," he said, his thumb lingering at her lips, his fingertips lightly teasing her cheek. "We'll have mango tarts for starters. White and dark chocolate baskets filled with lemon cream and chocolate Grand Marnier."

"Sounds heavenly," she said, succumbing much too easily to the tingle of his fingers grazing down her neck. "And what about the tuxes for your friends? Is that going to be a problem?"

"I don't think so." His palm swirled slowly over her chest. She could feel the tip of one of his fingers tracing the top edge of her bathing suit, the sensation making her tremble inside.

"Bear's got an Armani. Gabe's borrowing one from a friend. The tuxes might not match, but—"

Lauren bolted upright. "What do you mean they might not match?"

He rolled onto his back and folded his arms under his head, laughing as if the situation were funny. "Have you ever tried finding half a dozen matching tuxedos at the last minute?"

"No, but—"

"It doesn't matter if they're not alike, Lauren. No one's going to notice, because no one's going to be paying the least bit of attention to the waiters."

"I'll notice. Bunny Endicott will notice."

He gripped her shoulders and pulled her down on top his chest. She could feel the heat of his eyes, the warmth of his skin as her body stretched over him.

"Bunny Endicott's also going to notice Bear's earrings," he told her, "not to mention Gabe's ponytail and probably one or two of Jazz's tattoos."

"Well, there's not much I can do about those things," she said, pushing away from his chest even though she'd rather lay on top of him indefinitely, "but I *can* do something about the tuxedos."

She scrambled to her feet and half walked, half ran up the beach.

"The wedding's two days away," Max stated, jogging at her side. "You can't get tuxedos now."

"You'd be surprised what I can do in a matter of days."

"I don't think I'd be surprised at all."

She smiled at his compliment, and kept on running. The mismatched tuxedos had been the perfect reason to bolt out of his arms and away from the odd assortment of feelings she had for him—feelings that could much too easily make her forget Betsy's wedding, if it wasn't far too important to remember.

She raced into her garden room when they reached the mansion, grabbed the phone book, and flipped through the pages searching for formal wear. From the corner of her eye she watched Max put on his jeans and his boots, admiring the way his muscles stretched and bunched when he pulled on his T-shirt and tucked it under the waistband of his pants.

For someone who loved her men in Armani, she was rapidly acquiring a taste for Levi's and Jockey, and no one had ever worn those brands better than Max Wilde.

She picked up the phone and punched in the number for Antonio's for Men the moment Max walked into the room.

"May I speak with Mr. Antonio, please," she said into the phone, smiling at Max when he rested his hip against her desk. "This is Lauren Remington, Jack Remington's sister," she said in her sweetest, most sincere voice. "Yes, yes, it has been a long time, but I haven't forgotten you and neither has Jack . . . Yes, he's doing fine, and so is Sam. She's pregnant, you know. With twins . . . She speaks fondly of you, too."

Lauren rolled her eyes, remembering that Mr. Antonio had fired Sam for falling asleep on the job. She despised the man, even though his inconsiderate actions had thrown Jack and Sam together.

"I'm hoping you can do me a favor," she cooed. "A very dear friend of mine, Max Wilde, is in desperate need of a tuxedo for Saturday."

"Not me," Max whispered, and Lauren placed a silencing finger over his lips—lips that felt terribly soft and warm.

"Mr. Wilde and several of his friends will be helping out at a charity event I'm hosting this weekend and, goodness, the tuxes they ordered were lost in shipping. I do realize it's the last minute, but I know you're the most respected men's haberdasher in Palm Beach, and I was hoping you could find it in the goodness of your heart to work a little overtime in order to accommodate their needs.

"That's wonderful, Mr. Antonio. And you did say you'd donate the tuxes, didn't you? After all, it is to a very worthy cause—the homeless—which I'm sure you recall is very near and dear to my sister-in-law's heart.

"Yes, I'll tell Mr. Wilde you'll be happy to help him out, and I'll be sure to pass on your best wishes to Sam and Jack. Thank you, Mr. Antonio."

"You're a con artist," Max said, grinning when she hung up the phone.

"I dislike the man intensely," Lauren announced, jotting the address and phone number for Antonio's on a piece of lacy pink stationery. "Someday when you have the time, I'll tell you how horrid he was to my sister-in-law, how he deserves every misfortune that falls upon his head."

Max laughed. "Those tuxes are going to cost him an arm and a leg. I should pay something."

"Then donate a portion of what I'm paying you to Sam's charity."

"All right."

The fact that he didn't hesitate a moment didn't take her at all by surprise. Max Wilde, in spite of his untamed ways, was a terribly generous man, and she found herself losing a little more of her heart to him because of it.

Opening his briefcase, Max pulled out two sets of contracts. "We never discussed money or anything else."

"I'm sure you're giving me a fair price."

"I've put more in the contract than just the price and the menu. I've also included one condition—our dance on Saturday."

"Why?"

"I want to make sure you don't back out."

"I told you I'd dance with you and I don't go back on my word."

"Good," he said, laying the contracts out on the desktop. He pulled a pen from his briefcase and she thought he was going to line through the clause boldly marked "Dancing," but he scratched through the itemized list of charges instead.

"What are you doing?" Lauren asked.

"I can talk my friends into working for free and you can donate the catering fee."

"But that's a lot of money."

A slow grin touched his mouth. "You're not the only one who's made wise investments. Trust me, Lauren. I'm far from being broke, and the only thing I want from you on Saturday is that dance. That's why I'm not taking that clause out of the contract."

"You're a very difficult man," she said. Difficult . . . but extremely seductive.

He moved close to her, his heated gaze making her body burn.

"I know what I want."

She swallowed hard and forced a smile as she took the pen from his hand. A jolt of electricity zapped through her when their fingers touched, leaving her weak and wanting more. Signing the contract took all her concentration. Her hand shook, her heart pounded, and all she could think of was Max's embrace.

It was a wild thought. A crazy thought, and if he didn't get out of here fast, she might turn on the music and dance with him here and now. But she had far too many things to do for Betsy's wedding, and she really needed to push thoughts of Max Wilde from her mind or she'd accomplish nothing.

She handed the contracts back to Max. "I'll have the money transferred to the charity account today," she said. "Will you need to come by for any reason between now and Saturday?"

He shook his head as he peeled apart the contract, leaving one copy on top the desk for Lauren and stuffing the second copy into his briefcase. "If I need anything, I'll call, but it's going to be chaos around my place for the next couple of days."

She hoped her disappointment didn't show as she headed for the front door to show Max out. The thought of not seeing him for a day and a half left her feeling lonely.

Opening the front door, she almost gasped when she saw her mother walking up the steps.

"Lauren! Darling!"

Lauren's first inclination was to throw her arms around her mother, but in a time-honored tradition, she kept a fair amount of space between them.

Celeste turned her cheek, as she'd always done, and Lauren briefly touched her mother's cool, looking-younger-than-ever skin. "What a surprise to see you," Lauren said, thrilled she was here, wishing she'd come five minutes later, so Max would already be gone. That was a horrible thing to think, but she knew her mother far too well, and dreaded her reaction to Max.

"I hadn't planned on coming, darling, but Chip called yesterday afternoon and told me there was a new man in your life." Celeste's gaze raked over Max. "Naturally I had to meet him."

Celeste's reaction was calm, cool, and calculating, just as Lauren feared.

"Good morning," she said, holding a delicate hand toward Max. "I'm Celeste Ashford. *Lady* Ashford."

Max grasped Celeste's hand, shaking it firmly. Celeste preferred a more discriminating handshake, but she would never show her disapproval. She was graced with beauty, brains, and decorum, although she could dissect a person's appearance and mannerisms in a matter of seconds and rip them to shreds with just one glance. Fortunately she hadn't been too vicious—yet— with Max.

"I'm Max Wilde," he said, then added, "the caterer."

Oh, dear. He could have said anything but that.

Celeste scrutinized his body, offering him a close-lipped smile before turning back to Lauren. Mother obviously didn't approve of Max Wilde, but thankfully she wouldn't voice her opinion here. Opinions were always reserved for behind closed doors.

"Will you be staying awhile?" Lauren asked,

hoping her mother would stay longer than her usual breeze-in, breeze-out trips.

"A little while," she said. "I'm here for Betsy's wedding. She's such a dear girl, and what a catch she's made in Dickie Stribling. Bunny tells me they're in love." Celeste laughed lightly. "Such a shame that *that* rarely lasts."

It wouldn't do much good to argue with her mother, so Lauren let the comment slide. "I was just saying goodbye to Mr. Wilde. Will you excuse us a moment?"

"Of course, darling. I'll ask Charles to serve us tea in the library, and you can join me as soon as Mr. Wilde departs." She smiled indulgently. "I'm sure that won't be long."

"It was nice meeting you," Max said.

"You, too, Mr. Wilde."

Celeste breezed past them, a picture of perfection in a persimmon-colored suit and a jaunty off-white hat with persimmon-colored rosebuds dripping over the brim. The only thing Lauren had in common with her mother was a mile-long pedigree and a love of beautiful clothes. Her visits were few and far between, and Lauren couldn't help but wonder what had precipitated this one.

For the moment, she put thoughts of her mother aside and walked with Max to his motorcycle. He swung his leg over the bike, and caught Lauren's attention when he started the engine. "She doesn't like me."

Lauren laughed. "It's not that, it's just that, well—" Lauren sighed. "All right, she probably doesn't like you, but it's nothing personal. It's just that . . . well . . . it's because you're a caterer."

"And she's a snob."

"I'm afraid it's one of those nasty genes that runs through the female side of my family."

"Then I take it she's not going to like seeing you and me dancing together on Saturday."

"She'll be furious." And Lauren knew she'd never hear the end of it.

"I suppose I should let you out of that part of our contract."

"Would you?" she asked, wanting to dance with Max, but not at Betsy's wedding.

One of his brows rose. "I thought you didn't go back on your word."

"I don't, but you don't know how miserable my mother can make your life and mine."

"I'm not worried about your mother," he said, revving the engine. "I fully intend to dance with you on Saturday." He drew his thumb across her lips, sending a thrill through her entire body. "And when the wedding's over, I'm going to want a lot more than a dance."

Her body continued to quiver as he shot out of the driveway. Max was driving her . . . wild. But she couldn't possibly give him more than just one dance.

Or could she?

Goodness, Max Wilde had an uncanny way of leaving her thoroughly confused.

Running up the steps, she brushed the last remaining traces of sand from her arms and legs, and went straight to the library to face her mother.

Celeste looked up from her paper when Lauren stepped into the room. "What, pray tell, possessed you to hire a caterer like *that*?"

"You know that Henri died," Lauren said, taking a seat across from her mother and pouring herself a cup of tea. "I tried everywhere to find another chef—someone that I knew—but I couldn't, not at the last minute. Fortunately Max came to the rescue."

"Chip tells me that Mr. Wilde specializes in barbecued ribs."

"He does much more than that."

"I'm sure he does. He may have a gorgeous body, Lauren, but he's not in our league. What will Betsy think? What about Bunny, and Dickie's parents, for God's sake? Wasn't it enough of a disgrace for your brother to marry that Samantha Jones without you getting involved with a man with earrings and a tattoo?"

"Jack's lucky to have a wonderful woman like Sam. As for Max, I'm not *involved* with him. He's an excellent chef. *That's* why I hired him."

"I certainly hope so." Celeste turned the page of her newspaper and took a sip of tea.

Lauren lifted her own cup to her mouth and watched her mother. In her mid-fifties, she was beautiful, aided by only a small amount of plastic surgery. Celeste would never admit it, of course, but she worried about growing old. Lauren remembered tagging after her mother whenever she was home—which wasn't often—and seeing her mother looking in a mirror and fretting over the fact that she was getting lines at the corners of her eyes, that her skin wasn't as supple as it once had been.

Lauren had thought her mother was the most beautiful woman on earth, and sometimes had wished that her mother had had a few wrinkles and less suppleness. She'd wanted a mom who'd read her to sleep at night, who'd be a chaperone at one of her cotillions, or who'd take her to the zoo. She'd wanted parents who loved each other, who lived together. But when she knew she couldn't have any of those things, she snatched any spare second and what little attention she could get.

Celeste, unfortunately, gave the biggest percentage of her attention to her husbands. There'd been five of them, and it seemed as if she'd finally found the love of her life. Lord Ashford doted on her and they rarely left each other's side.

So why the sudden visit?

"How's Andrew?" Lauren asked.

"Fine, darling."

Lauren watched her mother's hand shake as she lifted the teacup to her mouth. Something was wrong, but in characteristic fashion, Celeste tried to hide what was upsetting her. Reaching out, Lauren touched her mother's arm. Lauren expected her to flinch, but she didn't. Instead, Celeste's eyes flickered from Lauren's fingers to her eyes, and she smiled softly. "Is something troubling you, Lauren?"

"No, Mother, but I'm worried that something's bothering you. Tell me. Please."

Celeste concentrated on the newspaper, silent for the longest time. Finally, she said, "Andrew spends far too much time working, and that leaves very little time for me." She laughed lightly, as if her worries were of no importance. "I wanted to go to Cannes and he wanted to stay in London. I suggested that we go to Rio for Easter, but he'd rather spend the holiday at our place in the country. He says it would be far easier to work there than in Rio."

Her eyes rose to meet Lauren's. "It's nothing that I haven't been through before, darling, so don't worry about it."

"But I am worried, Mother. Andrew loves you."

Celeste shrugged her dainty shoulders, then turned a page of her paper. "Did you see this?" she asked, her voice ringing with displeasure as she pointed to the photo of a bride and groom. "I can't believe that Erica Brantford would wear such a revealing gown on her wedding day. I hope you've discussed propriety with Betsy."

"Bunny took care of that detail."

"Yes, Bunny's quite good at that."

Lauren added a spoon of sugar to her tea and stirred it, watching her Mother's gaze dart to the sugar bowl, then back to her paper. Surprisingly, she didn't comment on Lauren's sweet tooth.

"Does Andrew know you're here?" Lauren asked.

"I told him I was coming. Whether he heard,

whether he cares, is another subject. But, please, Lauren, I'd rather discuss something else."

Their heart-to-heart talk had been short, but it was the longest, most personal one they'd had in years. "I'm glad you're here, Mother."

Celeste looked up from her paper and smiled. "Did I tell you that I saw Peter in London last week? We met for lunch."

"I hope you had a lovely time."

"How could I not? Peter's a wonderful man. For the life of me, darling, I can't understand why you called off your engagement, or why you pushed him in that lake."

"I didn't love him. He wanted a pencil-thin, picture-perfect wife. I can never be that. And I wanted children, which wasn't in his game plan. That's why I ended our engagement."

"Yes, yes, I understand your reasons, but pushing him in that lake was a little heavy-handed, darling. That broken arm he got in the . . . *mishap* . . . could have ruined his career."

"He could have ruined my life."

"But he still loves you."

"Peter doesn't know the meaning of the word *love*."

She'd told her mother many times that she didn't want or need another rich husband, that all she wanted was someone to love, someone more interested in home and family than in money. Sadly, her mother didn't believe it was possible to have all of those things combined.

Lauren pushed out of her chair and kissed her mother lightly on the cheek. "I've got a busy day today, but why don't I make reservations at Bice for dinner tonight?"

"It's lovely of you to ask, but I've already made plans with Gerald Harcourt."

"Tomorrow, then?"

"Pamela and Jim Carrington invited me to spend the day sailing. But don't worry, darling, I'll be around on Saturday to help with Betsy's wedding. Just to make sure that nothing goes wrong and that neither of us is embarrassed."

Oh, dear! As happy as she was to have her mother's company, she did not want Celeste, Lady Ashford, at Betsy's wedding. If her mother had been embarrassed over Holly's wedding cake sailing into the pool, imagine her mortification when she saw the waiters at Betsy Endicott's wedding—not to mention her daughter dancing with a tattooed, earring-wearing biker.

 *Nine*

Saturday dawned with a bevy of dark gray storm clouds rolling in from the ocean, an ominous sight, something Lauren had prayed wouldn't happen on the day of Betsy Endicott's wedding. But she didn't have time to worry about the weather. Instead, she'd turned her attention and all her time to the flower arrangements Mr. Friedrichs and his crew scattered about the house, the patios, and gardens.

She supervised the chair setup, the table arrangements inside and out, and the construction of the orchestra dais, and tried not to focus on the occasional glimpses she caught of Max and his friends, bringing in food, trays, hundreds of dishes, stacks of linen, plus boxes of crystal and silver.

It was Charles's job to supervise the kitchen. Lauren couldn't handle that task along with everything else. Besides, every time Max flashed across her path she felt an odd flutter in her heart. There was no telling what condition she'd be in if they got too close.

When two o'clock rolled around, the threatening clouds had scurried away, leaving mere puffs of white in the bright blue sky. The light sweet scent of ginger wafted through the mansion, as did the soft tinkling tones of a harp. And under an arbor of white orchids, Betsy and Dickie repeated their vows, words they'd written for each other that were full of passion about their hopes, plans, and dreams for their lifetime together.

Betsy's eyes were misty when she turned around, and Dickie's beamed with happiness when he clutched his new wife's hand and led her up the aisle amid applause and hundreds of fluttering butterflies, released the moment the newlyweds kissed.

Lauren went through the receiving line first, hugging her friends and wishing them all the joy in the world before she hustled outside to make sure everything was impeccable.

The fifteen-piece orchestra was tuned up and the harmonious sounds of violins floated through the air. The ice carving glimmered in the afternoon sun, with beads of water dripping onto the pink and white orchids that encircled it. An odd assortment of tuxedo-wearing waiters stood at attention, trays ready for the guests when they flowed out of the ballroom. Gabe and Jazz seemed perfectly at ease and completely in control of the situation. Ryan fidgeted, Jamie chomped on a wad of gum and blew a pink bubble that popped over her lips, and Jed, well, Lauren had to admit the skinny young mechanic looked rather dashing in his brand-new Armani tux.

Lauren's gaze trailed across the patio, hoping to see Max, but settling on Bear instead. It was hard to miss the giant of a man. Sun glistened on the diamond studs in his ears and almost bounced off his shiny bald pate. He flashed a picture-perfect gleaming white smile, and Lauren felt a growing warmth for Max's friends.

She'd had nightmares about today being a disaster, yet right this moment, everything seemed absolutely perfect.

Finally her eyes settled on Max, looking strong and masculine and devilishly handsome in a white dinner jacket. They hadn't talked since he'd left the house Thursday morning, although she'd made a couple of attempts. Last night she'd picked up the phone to call him. She'd done the same thing the night before, and both times hung up the moment he answered. She had no good reason to call. She didn't want to appear worried about his catering preparations and she didn't want to seem lonely or desperate for his company—although she was.

Goodness, she was falling for Max Wilde, another man who was all wrong for her, and it was happening much too quickly.

He looked up from whatever it was he was doing behind a dessert table and looked directly at her, as if he'd known she was watching. When he smiled, when the tiny lines at the corners of his eyes crinkled, her heart fluttered a little faster.

He strolled toward her, a vision of absolute power, a man in control of everything around him—including her. Except for the earrings and goatee he wore, he could easily pass as a guest, and deep inside, she wished that were the case. No one would question why she was smiling at him, why she was forcing herself to breathe calmly as the distance between them narrowed, and later, no one would wonder why she chose to dance with such a handsome partner. She'd tried convincing herself that the thoughts of her friends and family didn't matter, but she'd always needed their acceptance.

Letting a man like Max Wilde into her world was going to cause all sorts of trouble, but not having him around seemed a far worse prospect.

"Good afternoon," he said, linking an arm through hers and leading her across the lawn, past tables laden with orchids, bird-of-paradise, and frangipani, not to mention silver trays covered with colorfully displayed delicacies.

"I haven't had a chance to sample the food, but it looks delicious," she said, attempting to make small talk about tasty things, which made her long for a kiss.

"It is delicious."

"Are you always so sure of yourself?"

"For the most part."

He plucked a heavenly looking creation from the table. "Try this."

Lauren took a quick peek to make sure no one was looking, and bit into the flaky puff of pastry he held to her mouth. "Mmmm, it's wonderful."

"Caribbean brochette, with the recipe altered slightly to make it special for Betsy's wedding."

"You didn't have to go to so much trouble."

His thumb swept slowly across her lower lip. Their eyes met and—oh, dear—his were far more intense than ever before. "I rarely do the same thing twice," he said slowly. "I want each experience to be a little different, spicier, sweeter, sometimes hotter."

Oh, dear! She struggled to smile. "Henri was a wonderful caterer, but I'm sure I wouldn't have gotten the same quality of service from him."

A grin tilted his lips. "I guarantee you wouldn't."

She didn't have to ask what he was insinuating. Without a doubt, he was talking about something that had nothing whatsoever to do with food preparation and, goodness, she liked the sway of conversation.

He grabbed a glass of champagne from Gabe's passing tray and led her to a secluded spot behind a towering palm. "You look like you could use some of this."

Champagne was dangerous because she got silly if she drank too much. Of course, Max Wilde was dangerous, too, probably a lot more hazardous than the champagne. "Are you playing the devoted servant or my friend?"

"Does it matter?"

"I'd be lying if I said it didn't. I'd also be lying if I told you that I don't want to dance with you, or that I don't care what my mother thinks." She sighed deeply. "You've totally confused my entire life."

"What's so confusing?"

She plucked the champagne from his fingers and took a sip. "My feelings for you."

He backed her against the palm. Bracing one hand against the trunk, he leaned so close to her that she could feel the warmth of his breath against her lips. "You have some?"

"Of course I do, and they make no sense at all. First off, we don't have anything in common, but I enjoy talking to you." He pressed a soft warm kiss to her brow, and her toes tingled. "Second, you're not at all like the men I've always found attractive, yet I find you terribly sexy."

His lips touched the tip of her nose and she felt her legs weakening as his mouth moved to within a fraction of an inch of hers. "Then you'll give me more than the one dance that's in our contract?"

The heat of his eyes mesmerized her. The deepness of his voice and the slow way he spoke rendered her speechless, but she didn't need words to give him an answer. She closed her eyes and leaned toward his lips—

"Excuse me, Miss Remington." Charles's dis-

tinctive throat clearing brought the almost-kiss to
an abrupt halt.

Lauren's eyes popped open and all she saw
was Max's grin. Charles, always terribly proper,
was nowhere to be seen, but she knew he was
close. Peeking around the palm, Lauren smiled at
the gentleman who was a picture of propriety.
"What is it, Charles?"

"I wanted to advise Mr. Wilde that the young
boy who's serving the guests—"

"Ryan?" Max asked. "What's he done?"

"Nothing more than admire the . . . *necklaces* on
several of our female guests."

"Christ!"

Lauren touched Max's arm, wondering why he
was suddenly so agitated. "There's nothing
wrong with Ryan looking at the jewelry."

"It's not the jewelry he's interested in."

"Then what?"

Lauren could see the tightening in Max's jaw.
"He's fourteen and recently discovered the
female anatomy, particularly breasts. It's not the
necklaces he's looking at, it's what's beneath
them."

Charles offered an uncharacteristic chuckle,
but instantly wiped the mirth from his face. "I
would be happy to keep an eye on him for you,
sir."

"That won't be necessary. I'll have a little talk
with him right this minute."

Max stalked off before Lauren could say
another word, which was just as well. She'd

already divulged too much. What was it about Max that made her pour out her heart and soul, not to mention far too many of her secrets? How could he so completely draw her under his spell? The man, not to mention her feelings for him, was totally perplexing.

She took another sip of her champagne as she watched Max disappear into the throng of guests.

"Miss Endicott's wedding is going quite well," Charles said, "and I've heard several guests comment on the delectable canapés. I believe Mr. Wilde was the perfect choice."

"Yes, he's very good at what he does," she admitted, wishing she'd had the opportunity to try out a few more of his skills.

"If there's nothing I can do for you now, I'll see to your guests."

"Before you go, Charles, tell me, have you ever wanted to be something other than a butler?"·

"I don't believe I have. My father was a butler. His father and his father before him served the finest of families. It's what I was born to do. Why do you ask?"

"Oh, I don't know," she said, taking another quick taste of bubbling wine. "I was born to this, too, but sometimes . . . sometimes I wish I could let my hair down and be a little more wild."

"I may have been born a butler," he said, crossing his arms behind him, "I may love my work, but that doesn't mean I dress in formal clothes and serve people on my days off."

"What do you do, Charles? You'd think I'd know after twenty-eight years together."

"I bird watch, occasionally I fish, and I've been known to sit in with one or two jazz bands around town and play piano. I quite enjoy it."

This was a side of Charles she'd never imagined, and now she wondered why he stayed with her when he had so many other interesting pursuits.

"Have you ever thought of playing piano for a living?" she asked.

"I did once or twice when I was younger. In the end, I chose what made me happiest, and that was taking care of you. I still have my love for playing the piano, though, and that gives me the best of both worlds."

She smiled at his heartening sentiment. "Do you think I could have both worlds?"

Charles nodded. "I do believe you could have anything you wanted."

"Thank you," she said, lightly kissing his cheek, an uncommon gesture, for sure, but one that was long overdue.

"You're quite welcome, Miss Remington," Charles said, a slight blush tingeing his cheeks. "Now, I believe I should see to your guests."

Charles was gone in an instant, and not for the first time, Lauren realized how blessed she was to have him in her life.

Slipping away from the palm, Lauren mixed into the crowd, trying to look as if she'd always been there. Her mother was deep in conversation with Chip, the waiters were walking about, serving the guests as if it were something they did every day, and Max was inconspicuously escorting Ryan away from Bunny Endicott, whose hand was clasped across her chest.

Oh, dear. Of all people, why had Ryan picked on Bunny?

Breezing between guests, greeting everyone in her wake, thanking all the ladies who commented on the beauty of her seafoam-green silk crepe Valentino sheath, Lauren finally reached Bunny's side. "Hello, Bunny."

"The strangest thing just happened," Bunny whispered, her face registering complete and utter disbelief. "There was a child here asking all sorts of questions about my necklace. You don't think he could be a front, do you?"

"What do you mean, a front?"

"One of those people who scout out parties, looking for jewelry and other expensive things to steal, before he calls in his accomplices."

Lauren laughed lightly. "I'm positive he's not a front. Your necklace is stunning, and I'm sure he just wanted to check it out."

"Yes, the necklace is stunning," Bunny quipped, "but the child was absolutely obsessed with staring at my chest. And that, of course, made me think he might be doing something else."

"What?"

"This might sound rather vain, and you know I'm not the least narcissistic, but I do believe he might have been checking out my ... breasts." Bunny whispered the word as if it were sacred.

If it was anyone other than Bunny, Lauren wouldn't have been able to smile. But this was Bunny Endicott, who'd not-so-secretly gone under the knife and went from a 32AA to a 34C, and was anxious for everyone to notice. How could Ryan possibly pass up the opportunity to ogle the woman who walked around with her 34Cs thrust forward for everyone to see?

Bunny clasped her hand to her chest again. "Do you think anyone else has been *staring* at my . . . breasts?"

"I should hope not."

Bunny drew her shoulders back a little further, trying to make her 34Cs look like 34Ds. "It's quite embarrassing to think people are looking, so why don't we keep this our little secret?"

"I wouldn't think of telling a soul."

"You are such a dear," Bunny said, then sailed across the patio, more than likely in search of Celeste, Lady Ashford, who loved to share anything the least bit scandalous.

At the far side of the pool Lauren saw Max's daughter picking through the desserts, the same thing Lauren had done when she was a child. She hadn't met Jamie yet, and wondered if she was half as precocious as her brother, although that seemed highly unlikely. Walking toward the little girl, Lauren plucked a glass of champagne from Jazz's tray, and complimented her on doing such a nice job.

"Thank you," Jazz said, a touch of animosity apparent in her soft voice.

When she'd seen Jazz at the Hole all she'd noticed was her platinum hair and wealth of tattoos. Now Lauren saw that Jazz had big blue eyes, a long, graceful neck, and elegant hands.

Lauren took a quick sip of the Dom Perignon, and attempted to make amends with Jazz for all the horrid things she'd thought about her. "I suppose Max told you I had my doubts about you and Gabe working here today."

"He told us," she bit out.

"You must despise me for that."

Jazz shrugged. "I meet all kinds of people in my line of work, and I've been called more names than I can count."

Lauren frowned at her statement. "What kind of work do you do?"

"Stand on street corners and solicit unsuspecting souls."

Oh, dear. Lauren had never met a prostitute before, let alone been served by one. She downed the glass of champagne, put the empty on Jazz's tray, and grabbed another. "Are you happy in that line of work?"

"Can't think of anything I'd rather do." Jazz grinned. "It pays well, the work's stimulating, although it's sometimes exhausting, and sadly I can't handle more than two or three men a night."

"You've taken care of two or three in one night?" Lauren asked, completely aghast.

"My record's six, but I was able to handle three at once."

Lauren felt faint. "Do you ever get frightened?"

"Rarely. I'm trained in martial arts and I carry a gun."

"Isn't that against the law?"

Jazz grinned as she took Lauren's second empty glass of champagne and handed her another. "Not when you're a vice cop."

It took merely half a second for the words *vice cop* to register. "Oh, dear. I do have an annoying way of jumping to conclusions. I can't begin to tell you how sorry I am."

Jazz's blue eyes warmed, and she touched Lauren's shoulder lightly. "I'm afraid I'm the one who should apologize this time. I led you on."

"I suppose I deserved it."

"Then why don't we consider ourselves even," Jazz said, holding out her hand in friendship and Lauren grasped it tightly.

"I've been thinking of teaching the girls at the Hole how to spot come-ons and pick-up lines," Jazz said. "Most of them live in a rough part of town and they're susceptible to far too many jerks. Maybe you'd like to help?"

"Me? I don't know the first thing about teenagers, and I'm afraid the only thing I could teach anyone is how to pour tea and serve watercress sandwiches."

"It wouldn't hurt for the girls to learn some manners. You could start out slowly, volunteer an hour or two a week."

The thought of being with all those kids sounded . . . interesting. But she wasn't a teacher, hadn't been good in school, so how could she possibly help the kids at the Hole? "Could I think about it? I've got a lot of work with my business and—"

"Thinking's quite all right," Jazz told her. "The kids are tough, most of them—including the girls—spout words that would turn your ears scarlet, and sometimes they're a little intimidating. They need encouragement, not to mention role models. But the job's not for everyone."

"Why do you do it?"

"I grew up on the streets. So did Gabe, but neither one of us wanted to settle for the life we knew. We went to school, I became a cop, Gabe a social worker, and we both ended up back on the streets, trying to help others."

"What about Max and Bear?"

"Max was on the streets, too, until Philippe—his foster dad—took him in. Bear was a renegade rich kid. He ran away from home, ended up living off and on with Philippe and Max, and finally realized he didn't want to be broke. He went back home then headed for college and became a dentist."

So that was the reason behind Bear's picture-perfect smile! She should have known.

A few moments later Jazz went back to work and Lauren took another sip of champagne, embarrassed by all the wrong thoughts she'd had about people. Meeting Max and his friends had been an eye-opening experience, gave her insights into a part of the world far removed from her own.

Taking another sip of champagne, and tucking

away thoughts about working at the Hole until later, she headed for the table where Jamie had parked herself. She couldn't help but notice the young girl's bright, sparkling blue eyes, the smattering of freckles bridging her nose, or the abundance of golden-blond curls pulled into a ponytail. She was cute right now, but in a few more years she'd be a knockout and probably a handful for Max.

Setting her glass down not far from Jamie, Lauren studied the array of pastries and tarts. "I'm partial to chocolate," she stated, wanting to draw Jamie into an easy conversation. "What do you like?"

"The chocolate baskets filled with lemon cream."

"Have you tried any?"

"I'm not supposed to touch these. Max said they're for the guests and he'll make some especially for me tomorrow or the next day."

"My mother didn't allow sweets in the house when I was growing up," Lauren said nonchalantly, "and I wasn't supposed to touch them when I went to parties."

"Really?"

"Really." Tilting her head toward Jamie, she grinned. "But I didn't let that stop me."

"What did you do?"

"I'll show you." Lauren swept her finger through the lemon cream filling and quickly shoved it into her mouth, licking away the deliciously sticky concoction.

Jamie giggled. "Max would murder me if he caught me doing that."

"So would my mother, I'm afraid, so why don't we do it the right way."

Lauren took a dessert plate from the table, scooped up two chocolate baskets, and set them in the center of the delicate china plate. She took two forks and napkins and sat on a cushioned wrought-iron bench near the end of the table. "Oh, dear!" she exclaimed. "I've taken much more than I can eat." She smiled at Jamie. "Would you mind helping me?"

"You're sure?"

"Quite."

Jamie sat next to her on the bench, took the fork Lauren offered her, and dug into the dessert. Lauren followed her lead, finding the creamy concoction even tastier than it looked.

"I'm Lauren Remington," she said, taking a second bite.

"I know," Jamie said, licking lemon cream off her lips. "I keep track of all the women Max dates, even the ones he's just thinking about dating."

"Are there a lot of them?"

"Hundreds."

Hmm. Lauren easily recognized the young girl's jealousy. She remembered having a similar conversation with one of the many blond bimbos her father had dated when she was young. Reece Remington, an All-American retired rancher with whom she'd spent a few weeks out of every summer, still dated blond bimbos, usually two at a time. Max, however, didn't seem like the blond bimbo type. That could, however, just be wishful thinking on her part.

Lauren helped herself to another bite of lemon cream. "Which one of Max's girlfriends is your favorite?"

"I don't know," Jamie answered. "Probably the stripper."

Lauren coughed, nearly choking on the filling that had stuck in her throat. "*A stripper?*"

"Yeah. Max says he likes her moves."

Oh, dear!

Jamie pushed up from the bench. "Well, I'd better get back to the kitchen. If Max sees me out here having fun when I should be working, he'll have my head."

The little girl skipped off, leaving Lauren all alone with her lemon cream, thoughts of a nearly naked buxom woman suggestively hugging a pole, and the sound of footsteps that came to a stop behind her.

"I've been looking for you."

Lauren spun around, a dizzying feeling hitting her when she did. She closed her eyes a moment, wishing she hadn't had so much champagne, then opened them slowly, focusing on the man standing over her. "Gerald?"

"I'm glad you haven't forgotten me completely."

"Of course I haven't forgotten you." That would have been an impossibility. Her mother had brought up the name Gerald Harcourt in nearly every conversation they'd had in the past few days.

Rising slowly, Lauren wobbled and was grateful when Gerald offered a helping hand. "Thank you."

"You're welcome."

Gerald Harcourt was one of the most distinguished-looking gentlemen she'd ever met, and she'd met quite a few. Tall and slender, he wore Armani like a champ. The black and white tux looked rather nice against the richness of his tan, one he'd probably gotten lying in a thong on the sun-drenched Fiji island he'd purchased. The last time she'd seen Gerald, his hair had been dark brown; now it was mostly silver. One thing about him definitely hadn't changed. His hands were warm and far too skilled, and she couldn't forget that he liked women. A lot of women.

"Would you care to dance?" he asked. "It's been a long time."

She looked about her, finding it difficult to believe that she hadn't noticed other people dancing, that she hadn't heard the orchestra, that she hadn't observed Max standing near the kitchen door. Watching her. Glaring at Gerald.

"I really should take care of my guests," she said, trying to pull away, but Gerald held on to her hand and playfully spun her against his chest.

"Nonsense," he whispered against her ear. "Everything's well under control."

Again she looked toward the kitchen, but Max

had disappeared, and her heart sank in disappointment. She'd wanted to dance with him, but she had guests to entertain, and he had guests to serve.

"You look troubled," Gerald said. "The best way to deal with that is dancing." He led her far too easily to a place near the pool where at least a dozen couples swayed to the music. Sliding his hand behind her back, he pulled her closer than she wanted to be held. It was only one dance, she told herself, and he *was* her guest.

"You're very beautiful," Gerald said, as he swept her about in a dizzying circle. "I've thought of you often over the years."

"How could you possibly find time to think of me? Mother tells me you've been terribly busy."

"It doesn't take all that much time to purchase a summer house on Martha's Vineyard or an island in Fiji, it merely takes money. Both places are quite lonely, though."

"Then why did you buy them?" she said, not really interested, but trying to be a good hostess.

"I'd hoped to share them with my wife."

Or one of his many girlfriends, Lauren imagined, but she was far too polite to make that comment. "I'm sorry things didn't work out between you and Jessica."

"Sometimes marriages work, sometimes they don't. She was a beautiful woman and I enjoyed her company. Unfortunately, she had a deathly fear of flying and didn't like accompanying me on my trips around the world."

"You could have stayed home."

"I did in the beginning. I gave her everything I could—my time, homes, beautiful jewelry. But I missed traveling, seeing my friends in other countries. Long separations led to other troubles I needn't bother you with. Surely you understand?"

"All too well."

His mouth moved close to her ear. His breath was warm. Too warm. "We're very much alike. You realize that, don't you?"

"Champagne?"

Lauren jerked away at the sound of Max's voice. "I'd love some." She took a glass from his tray, relieved that he'd rescued her. She smiled, but met nothing but Max's blank stare.

"And you, sir?" Max asked, holding the tray toward Gerald.

Gerald's lip almost curled as he stared at Max. It was just a flash of animosity that turned quickly to a polished smile. He took a glass and in his most gentlemanly voice said, "Thank you."

"You're quite welcome, sir."

Max turned to Lauren, his expression still cool and detached. "Is there anything else I can get you?"

What on earth had she done to annoy him this time?

"I believe our contract called for a dance."

His eyes narrowed into a frown, not exactly the look she'd expected. "Yeah, it did," he said. "But don't worry, I'm not going to hold you to it."

"But—"

"If you'll excuse me, I've got work to do."

Max stalked away, disappearing into the crowd and leaving her annoyed with his actions and hurt by his indifference, because little more than an hour ago they were nearly in each other's arms.

"What was that all about?" Gerald asked.

"Nothing," she answered, trying to ignore the ache in her heart, but it seemed to blot out everything around her.

"Do you make a habit of dancing with the caterers?"

She wanted to tell him no. Wanted to pretend that she felt nothing for Max, but she couldn't hide her deepening emotions. "He's a friend. A dear friend."

There. She'd said it, and the world hadn't crashed in on her.

"Your mother told me you'd developed an odd attraction toward a caterer. Is he the one?"

"I told you, he's a friend."

"And decidedly jealous, I daresay."

Could Max really be jealous? She'd done nothing more than dance with Gerald Harcourt, a bore who meant nothing to her. Goodness, she'd have to straighten Max out the next time she saw him.

But she didn't see him again. Max Wilde had made himself completely invisible, while Gerald Harcourt stayed glued to her side, flashing his million-dollar smile so many times she wanted to scream. Instead, she drank champagne, flitted from one acquaintance to another, entertaining her guests while trying to figure out a way to get rid of Gerald, other than knocking him unconscious.

But Gerald wouldn't be put off. He urged her to stand with the other single women when Betsy tossed her bouquet, and pulled her back to his side when she missed. They ate cake together, drank more champagne, and tossed fragrant white plumeria at the bride and groom when they ran off for their round-the-world honeymoon.

She had no idea how much time had gone by, but the warmth of the air, the smoothness of Gerald's voice, and too many glasses of champagne lulled her, made her rest her head against his shoulder. She wanted to close her eyes. Wanted to sleep.

And then she could dream of dancing with Max, since it appeared that was as close as she'd ever get to reality.

Gerald's cologne was strong and sweet, so different from Max's, which had been light and musky and natural. Gerald's hand was small, soft against her back, where Max's was large and strong, with calluses on his palms. Gerald's hair was perfect, while Max's was wild. She lifted her head and looked into pale blue eyes that weren't the least bit intense, showed no sign of danger, only sophistication and the ultimate in breeding, and she wished that she were looking into Max's fiery brown eyes.

She didn't want to be with Gerald any longer. It was getting late, people were starting to drift away. "It's time that I say goodbye to some of the guests," she told him, pulling far away.

"I could do that with you."

She shook her head. "You've been wonderful all afternoon, but there are a few people I'd like to see on my own."

He didn't argue. "Perhaps tonight—"

"I have plans."

"Then I'll call tomorrow."

She smiled gently, not wanting to tell him that she wasn't interested. Unfortunately, she'd done little to prove that point in the past few hours.

The orchestra continued to play, a few couples swayed on the veranda, and Lauren searched for the only man she wanted to dance with.

"Have you seen Max?" she asked Bear, who stood behind the bar, looking devilishly handsome in his tux.

"There was a problem at the Fabianos' party. He asked me to take charge here."

A sinking feeling hit her heart. "He's gone?"

"Not more than a minute or so." He turned a glass upright on the bar. "Would you like a drink? I make a hell of a martini."

"Some other time, thank you." She skirted quickly past friends and acquaintances, past her mother, who tried to catch her attention, toward the driveway that led to the side of the house. She prayed she could catch him.

A black van with a sleek motorcycle and Born To Be Wild painted in screaming reds, yellows, and greens on the side was backing out of the drive, and she raced after it. "Stop, Max. Please."

The van continued to move backward, slowly

maneuvering around a Rolls and a Bentley. "Max!" she cried out again. He didn't stop until the vehicle reached the street. She was breathless when she got to the rolled-down driver's window.

Max had stripped off his tie. His jacket was gone and the top button was loosened on his shirt. He looked wonderful, and she wished she could climb into the van and run away with him.

"I hoped I could catch you."

"Why?"

She couldn't miss the annoyance in his voice. "Because we need to talk."

"I don't have time."

"I know. Bear told me there was an emergency at the Fabianos', that you had to rush off, but—" She smiled weakly. "But maybe we can talk later. Maybe you can come back tonight and we can have our dance."

He laughed far too cynically. "You traded in our dance for a dozen dances with Gerald Harcourt."

"I would have given you a dozen dances if you'd been anywhere around, if you hadn't turned me down when I asked."

"You were busy."

"I was entertaining my guests."

"*One* guest!"

She put her hands on the door and leaned close. "You're jealous!"

"Damn right!"

"But why? Gerald's a bore!"

"Chip's a bore, too, but you married him. Then there were Leland, and Peter, and God knows how many others. Hell, Lauren, you dispense with husbands and lovers easier than I get rid of motorcycles and cars."

"You don't know enough about my marriages or the rest of my life to go throwing the past in my face."

"I don't have to throw it in your face. It's with you all the time. Your ex-husband is always around. You live in the house he bought you."

"It's just a house, Max. A big, empty, lonely mansion that has no sentimental value to me at all. It's where I live, it's where I entertain, nothing more. As for Chip, I don't love him anymore. My life might not be anything like yours. You might not like the way I entertain my guests. You might not like my friends or the way I've lived my life. But this *is* my life and I'm not going to give it up—no matter how much I want you."

He stared at her, and a deafening silence and all their differences, not to mention her past, formed a wall between them.

She dropped her hands from the side of the van and took a deep breath to regain her composure. He was cruel, and jealous, and totally wrong for her, and she refused to let him see just how much he'd hurt her.

"Thank you for everything you did to make Betsy's wedding such a success," she said, and didn't wait for another vindictive response.

Instead, she turned and walked back toward the house, far away from the first man to make her truly happy, and far away from the first man to leave her feeling completely lost.

Ten

$\mathcal{L}$auren strolled through the conservatory, tending her orchids, sticking her finger into each pot to see if the soil was damp and watering the plants that were far too dry. The gardening she did in this room was therapy for most everything that ailed her, but tonight it was only barely taking care of a headache induced by too much champagne and an injured heart. She sighed as she pinched off a wilted bloom from a lemon-yellow lady's slipper, wishing she could pinch away the agony she felt at losing Max just as easily.

Unfortunately, life didn't work that way. That was something she knew all too well.

She looked up at the sound of her mother talking to Charles in the next room, ignoring their words as she carefully dusted the mottled leaves with a soft cotton cloth. When Charles walked up the grand staircase, her mother came into the garden room, looking refreshed after a two-hour nap and a massage from Lauren's masseuse.

"The wedding was lovely, darling," Celeste said, taking a seat in one of the white wicker chairs and crossing her legs neatly. She smoothed the skirt of her amethyst shantung suit and casually leaned back, watching Lauren at work. "The flowers were beautiful, the music gorgeous, and Betsy's dress was fabulous."

Lauren wiped her hands on a towel and slid closed the tropical-painted panel that hid her potting supplies. "Betsy told me she'd never been happier," she said, taking a seat across from her mother.

A blasé smile touched Celeste's mouth. "Dickie and Betsy have so much going for them. For their sake, I hope the marriage will last."

"I'd put odds on them."

"I heard that Chip was doing that very thing during the reception."

Lauren frowned as she picked up her cup of lukewarm tea, letting her mind drift back to the wedding celebration she'd shared with Chip. "He took bets during our reception, too."

"Surely that's just a rumor that was circulating at the time."

"I'm afraid not. He gave us six months, not a day longer. He would have made a lot of money if anyone had taken him up on it, but no one thought our marriage would even last *that* long."

"I'm truly sorry, darling. I didn't know."

"It's history," Lauren said, taking a sip of her tea. "Believe it or not, Chip and I have laughed about it a time or two. He's even apologized."

Celeste smiled uncomfortably and picked up a copy of *Town & Country*. She flipped absently through a few pages, obviously as uncomfortable with the conversation as Lauren. Talk between mother and daughter should come easy, Lauren thought, but it always seemed as if she and Celeste were only casual acquaintances.

"You also received many compliments on the food," Celeste said, her eyes never leaving the magazine.

"Max Wilde was completely responsible." For everything—even for a painfully splintered heart. "I'll drop him a note and tell him how delighted the guests were."

Celeste glanced up, quickly studied Lauren's face, then looked back down at her magazine, as if she'd heard the note of unhappiness in her daughter's voice, but didn't know how to respond.

"Did you try the pastries?" Lauren asked, forcing her mind to more pleasant thoughts of the day.

"You know I don't eat sweets, darling."

"I know, but the lemon cream was delicious." Remembrances of the tangy flavor and the sweet scents of lemon, sugar, and chocolate came back to her, as did the conversation she'd shared with a jealous little girl. She leaned back in her chair, closed her eyes, and pictured herself taking Jamie into the shops on Worth Avenue, ducking into an ice cream parlor and indulging in a hot fudge sundae, or discussing things little girls could only talk to a mother about. Her eyes popped open again when she realized those were things that would never be—as if there'd ever been a chance for them in the first place.

She had to put Max and Jamie completely out of her mind because that brief interlude in her life was over.

Celeste poured more tea into her cup, frowning as if an unpleasant thought had just come to her. "I hate to bring this up right now, darling, considering how well Betsy's wedding went, but in spite of the compliments on the food, I did hear several people complaining about the waiters, particularly the young boy and girl. I can't believe in this day and age a man would be so unenlightened as to hire children."

"They're Max's children and they don't wait on people as a rule. His other waiters were busy and—"

"There's no need to make excuses for him. I overheard the conversation between you and Mr. Wilde."

Lauren frowned. "You didn't follow me to his van, did you?"

"Of course not. I was walking Holly Rutherford to her car and we both heard your argument. Face it, darling. Max Wilde is not the man for you, nor is he the type of person who should be catering our parties." Her mother leaned forward and uncharacteristically placed a gentle hand on Lauren's knee. "I hope you're not too upset by this incident."

Lauren smiled softly, hoping to fight off her threatening tears. "I suppose it's difficult for you to understand, but I liked him, much more than I ever expected."

"It's not difficult to understand. I once felt that way about your father, who was terribly handsome in a rugged way." A slight smile touched her lips. "It was a long time ago, of course. Did I ever tell you how we met?"

Lauren shook her head, wanting to know a part of her mother's past that she'd never shared before.

Celeste leaned back casually, her gaze fixed on one of the potted orchids. "Bunny Endicott—she was Bunny Barrett then—dragged me to a rodeo on a lark. The place was awful. Too much dirt being kicked up, and I detested the smell of the cows, but I couldn't take my eyes off one of the bronc riders. Reece Remington was big, strong, terribly brash, and extremely wealthy. I was eighteen, he was twenty-three, and he could have swept me off my feet even if he'd been poor."

"So why didn't your marriage work?"

"He hated Newport and Palm Beach, and I could never adjust to Wyoming. You've been there. You now how desolate it can be." She took a sip of tea, holding the cup close to her lips. "I gave him six good years and two beautiful children, but the love we had wasn't enough to keep us together, not when we wanted such different things in life. That's why I've encouraged you to choose men with the same breeding and social standing as you."

"But they've never made me happy, never made me feel good."

"Gerald can do that for you."

"I'm not interested in Gerald Harcourt."

Celeste smiled as she put down her cup. "Don't brush his attentions off too lightly, Lauren. You love to travel, and so does he. You love the tropics, and he's just purchased that island in Fiji. I've heard the home he's building is magnificent, and if you don't wait too long, you could have a say in the decorating scheme, although you could always have the rooms changed later."

"I have a big house, Mother. I could travel to Fiji any time, I could go anywhere I want, but I love Palm Beach, even in the summer when everyone's gone and the weather's at its worst. Somehow or other I've become a homebody, and all I want are family and friends around me." She smiled at her mother. "I want more moments like this."

"Maybe you want too much."

"I just want what I've never had."

Celeste fidgeted with her wedding ring, obviously searching for some kind of response, but she was saved from answering when Charles walked into the room. "Pardon me, my lady, but the car's ready."

"I'll be out in just a moment, Charles."

"Very well," he said, and much too formally left the room, a posture he'd always maintained in Celeste's presence.

"I hadn't expected you to leave so soon," Lauren said, putting down her cup of tea when Celeste rose from the chair and tucked her handbag under her arm. "We've hardly had any time together."

"But, darling, Bunny wants me to fly down to Rio with her for a few days, and Charles is taking us to the airport. After that, I may go back to England. As much fun as I'm having, I do miss Andrew. Of course, you know what they say about absence making the heart grow fonder." A cunning smile touched Celeste's lips. "Maybe I'll come back here after Rio and give Andrew a little more time to miss me."

"Please go home after Rio," Lauren said, knowing her words sounded abrupt, but she hated to see her mother testing Andrew's devotion.

Celeste laughed lightly. "I thought you wanted me here."

"I do. I'll miss you when you're gone, but I think it's more important for you to be with Andrew."

Celeste squeezed her daughter's hands when they reached the car. "Will you really miss me, darling?"

"I've always missed you when you've gone away."

Celeste slowly, somewhat uncomfortably, wrapped Lauren in a tender embrace. "I love you," she whispered.

Lauren couldn't remember ever hearing her mother say "I love you"—not to her. She tried to respond, but her own words stuck in her throat as Celeste pulled away.

"I'll call you from Rio," Celeste said, sliding gracefully into the backseat of the Bentley. "Please, darling, don't fret over losing that man. You'll find another."

Lauren waved as the car drove away. It seemed as if she was always saying goodbye to the people she cared about. But it wasn't her mother's leaving her that bothered her most, not now, not after she'd said, "I love you." Celeste would always come back, in a few days, a few weeks, a few months. This time when her mother disappeared, Lauren wished with all her heart that Max were the one coming back.

The house was far too quiet, Lauren thought as she crept down the stairs at ten. Charles had gone to a friend's, Mrs. Fisk would be in Tahiti for a few more days, and the crew that had been hired to clean up had long since departed. No one would ever guess that a wedding and reception had been held there only a few hours before.

The mansion seemed big and lonely. Lauren almost wished she'd gone to Rio with her mother. She'd even considered flying to Aspen, or heading to Milan or Paris, where she could immerse herself in shopping and socializing, but none of those ideas interested her anymore.

Crying had seemed like a good idea after her mother had gone. For nearly half an hour she'd cried over losing Max, cried because he'd hurt her feelings, cried because she'd let a man trample all over her emotions. Unfortunately she didn't feel the least bit better when the crying jag was over. Instead, she had another headache and puffy eyes, and she was in no mood to garden this time of night.

Instead, she headed into the kitchen, dragged the Hershey's syrup from the back of the refrigerator where Mrs. Fisk usually hid it, squeezed a healthy portion into a glass, and added a tiny bit of milk. Chocolate could cure anything!

Curling up in her big wicker chair in the conservatory, she opened the latest issue of *Vogue* and thumbed through the pages while sipping chocolate milk. Maybe she'd feel better if she made a few more changes in her life. Perhaps she should throw caution to the wind and dump her pastel suits and dresses for something bold. She'd loved Jean Paul Gaultier's collection last year, especially his tropical selection. Maybe she should buy a new wardrobe and head to Tahiti. But the thought of lying around on the beach all day sounded too ho-hum. She'd done that far too often in her life.

She folded over the edge of one of the pages, marking a sequin and fringe number, something she imagined a woman like Jazz would wear to work. Was that the kind of look Max enjoyed? she wondered. Maybe he'd like tight black leather or something see-through. She could change her entire look, become a daring vamp, and really give Max a reason to be jealous.

Wouldn't that make the tongues of Palm Beach wag! Of course, enough gossip would be flying around town tomorrow, because Holly Rutherford had heard her argument with Max, and Holly wasn't above telling tales.

Well, let the tongues wag. She was tired of being the polite, do-what's-expected socialite Lauren Remington. She wanted to be the rash and carefree Lauren Remington who didn't cry for half an hour after she'd been dumped by a man.

Tossing the magazine onto the table, she headed for the stairs and raced up to her bedroom, where she could be anything she wanted to be, because no one would ever know. Nearly two years ago she'd bought something totally outrageous, an outfit Peter had despised. "It's too flamboyant," he'd told her. "Too tight for your figure." So she'd shoved it aside and forgot all about it—until now.

She stood before the bank of closets, trying to remember where she'd hidden the snakeskin bomber jacket and matching silk pants. Not in the wardrobe with her evening wear, not in the one where she kept her shoes. More than likely it was with the athletic gear she seldom needed.

Pushing open the sliding door, she stepped into the closet, sorting through ski jackets, jogging suits, and the ridiculous riding-to-the-hounds outfits Chip had insisted she buy right after their marriage. There, between a fringed buckskin jacket her brother had sent her a few years ago for Christmas and the tie-dyed beach cover-up she'd worn at sixteen hoping to get some attention from her mother, was the shimmering snakeskin.

She pulled it from the closet and laid it out on her bed. It was perfect for knocking on a biker's front door, which she wouldn't do ever again, or for breaking out of her traditional, monotonous fashions.

She turned on her CD player, and Phil Collins came into the room, his voice brightening her world as she searched for a sexy black bra and just the right thong. If she was going to make a change, she planned to go all the way. Fortunately she had a few lingerie drawers filled with all the naughty items she'd had the guts to buy but never to wear.

Suddenly she remembered a pair of black patent Manolo Blahnik stilettos that were completely and utterly wicked!

She stripped down to nothing, then slid into the thong, knowing immediately why she'd never worn a pair before. Several times she tugged at the straps and the tiny strip of silk in the front, deciding a thong might take some getting used to. Of course, there was no time like the present to give it a try.

The bra was totally sinful, sheer black lace that barely covered a pair of breasts that Peter had once suggested she have reduced. She laughed out loud, enjoying the sound of her own voice ringing through the room. Peter had been jealous in a way Max could never be jealous—she was pretty darn positive of that! Poor Peter, he'd hated the fact that she was more than amply endowed on top, while he'd been decidedly lacking down below.

Enough thinking about Peter, or men in general. This was her night, her moment to have fun.

She stepped into the soft faux-snakeskin pants, loving the feel of the silk against her legs. Tightening the drawstring, she slipped into the matching bomber jacket, zipping it up so just the tiniest bit of black lace bra showed beneath.

Her hair came next. A little gel, a little spray, and suddenly it was slicked back from her face. She pushed several platinum bangles onto her wrists, some dangly diamonds into her ears, applied darker eye makeup, heavier blush, and scarlet lipstick, then stepped into her heels and stood in front of the full-length mirror.

She liked what she saw. Wicked. Erotic.

Maybe not quite wicked and erotic enough!

She slid the zipper down a few inches on the jacket, letting more of the bra—not to mention her breasts—show.

"That's perfect."

Her head snapped around. Max leaned against the doorjamb, an incredible vision in faded jeans, a T-shirt, and a leather jacket. In spite of his drop-dead-gorgeous looks and the fact that her heart was racing, she didn't feel the least bit cordial.

"What are you doing here?"

"I forgot my briefcase."

Her gaze took a quick tour of the room. "It's not up here."

"I'm well aware of what's up here and what's not."

That was a seductive come-on line if she'd ever heard one, and she'd heard more than enough in her life—none of which sounded as appealing as his. Still, he'd made her cry, made her eyes get all puffy, and given her a headache. She wasn't about to be civil . . . yet.

"Do you mind telling me how you got into my house?"

"I knocked. I even rang the doorbell, but no one answered."

"That doesn't explain how you got inside. Did you crawl through a window or something?"

"I opened the kitchen door and let myself in. You should lock the doors when you're home alone."

"Yes, I should. You never know what kind of loathsome character might walk right in."

He grinned, walked across the room, and sat down in a pink and white striped chair. The contrast between the chair's ruffles and Max's attire was shocking. She'd always loved that chair and where it was placed in the room. Suddenly she wanted to replace it with black leather.

He extended his legs, crossing his ankles, looking far too relaxed, as if he'd been invited to stay. His hot brown eyes raked over her body—every inch of her—and then a slow, deeply satisfied smile touched his lips. "This new look suits you."

"Thank you." She owed him that much courtesy, considering his compliment. Then she hit him with a scowl. "How long were you standing in my doorway?"

"Not long enough."

"How much did you see?"

"Not enough."

His answers weren't the least bit helpful. She wanted his assurance that he hadn't seen her fiddling with the thong to find a comfortable position for the straps, that he hadn't seen her bending over and shaking her breasts until they fit perfectly into the skimpy black bra.

She wanted him to tell her what he was doing in her room when hours before he'd seemed to detest her. Since she knew he wouldn't come right out and tell her on his own, she simply glared at him and said, "Would you mind telling me why you came up here, when you know perfectly well your briefcase has never traveled past the first floor?"

"It wasn't just the briefcase I came for."

"No?"

"I came because you owe me a dance."

"I tried to dance with you at Betsy's wedding reception, but you walked away from me. Do you expect me to forget that? Am I supposed to forget the argument we had earlier? Pretend it never happened?"

"That's the idea."

"I don't forget that easily."

"I don't, either. But this time's different," he said, his voice low, sincere, making her believe he might have a soft place for her in his cold, hard heart. He sat up, no longer relaxed. "This time I care too much to let what happened keep us apart."

"It's not the argument we had that's the problem, and you know it," Lauren said, bound and determined to air out their grievances. "I've been married twice. I almost got married a third time." She took a deep breath, wishing her life had been different. "That's my past, Max. It's not something I'm proud of, but it's something I can't change."

He got up from the chair and came toward her, cupping her arms, his eyes hot as he stared into hers. "Divorce goes against everything I believe in, and I'd be a liar if I said your past doesn't scare the hell out of me. But right now, the thought of not having you in my future scares the hell out of me, too."

"Please don't say anything more," she said, stunned at the feelings going through her, a mixture of wanting him and not wanting him. "You've already given me puffy eyes twice today, and I don't want to go through that again."

"Okay, I promise, not another word," he said, dragging her hard against his chest. She didn't know who was breathing harder, him or her, but she forgot all about breathing the moment his mouth captured hers.

Opening up to him was the simplest thing she'd ever done. Feeling his tongue against her lips, gliding lightly over her teeth, then melding with her own tongue made her dizzy with desire and need. And she'd never desired or needed a man as much as Max. He was nothing like the men she'd ever known, nothing like the men she'd ever wanted.

She hadn't really known what her heart desired. Until now.

Warm hands slipped beneath her jacket and pressed against the small of her back, drawing her closer, as the rapturous beat of the music around them turned soft and mellow.

Their bodies began to move together, slow and easy, perfectly in sync. The room spun around her, and she was lost in his passion, in the taste and feel of his kiss, in the tingle of his fingers trailing down the curve of her spine.

She'd never been held so close while dancing, never had a man hold her hips so tightly against him that she could feel every hard contour, every slow, seductive movement.

And she'd never experienced such lustful cravings. Never wanted to be with a man so badly. She wanted to touch him, wanted to trail her fingers over every speck of his magnificent physique. She wanted to make love to him—and that frightened her.

Don't rush into something, she told herself, even while she was falling under the spell of his kiss. *And whatever you do, don't let him rush you.*

All too suddenly she felt his fingers on the zipper of her jacket, could hear the nylon teeth sliding down, down, down.

She pushed away, drawing in a deep breath as she walked to one of the tall bedroom windows and looked out at the moonlit ocean.

Strong hands rested on her shoulders and drew her back against his chest. "What's wrong?" he whispered into her ear.

"This is going too fast for me."

He nibbled her earlobe. "I thought the pace was perfect."

Against her better judgment, against all that

was sane, she tilted her head slightly so he could have easier access to her sensitive skin. "I would have thought it was too slow for you," she said, sighing as his lips teased her jaw, the corner of her mouth.

"All right," he said, turning her around and backing her against the window. He braced a hand on either side of her head, and leaned close. "I want to make love to you. Right here. Right now."

She wanted exactly the same thing, but this was all too soon. "I can't."

"Why?" he asked, trailing kisses down her throat, kisses that made her want so much more. "You like this, don't you?"

"Of course I do," she panted. "You don't know how much of me wants to rush into something with you, but I've rushed too many times before. I've had too many disastrous relationships, and this one has all the earmarkings of another."

"Relationships don't come with a guarantee." He stared into her eyes, as if he wanted to read her mind. "I can't swear to you that you won't get hurt, any more than you can promise me the same thing."

"Please understand, Max. I need more time. We need to know each other better before we'll know if it's right, before we can even think about guarantees or promises."

His gaze trailed to her lips, to her breasts, his knuckles taking the same path, skimming over her skin until he grasped the catch on the jacket's zipper. She ceased to breathe. Her fingers trembled at her sides and her mouth quivered, part apprehension, part need, wondering if he planned to take what he wanted, hoping he wouldn't just walk away.

Slowly he drew the zipper up till the lacy black bra disappeared from view. Then he wove his fingers through hers and tugged her toward the door.

"What are you doing?"

"Taking you out on the town."

Goodness, she'd never known a man whose moods changed so drastically and so rapidly. "Isn't this all rather sudden?"

"I like spur-of-the-moment things."

"But I'm not dressed to go anywhere."

He spun her around and looked her up and down. Flames nearly leaped from his eyes as he peeled the zipper back down an inch. "You'll blend in perfectly where I'm going to take you."

"Please don't tell me we're going to go visit Jazz on one of her favorite street corners."

"Nope, somewhere even better."

"Couldn't you at least give me a hint?" she asked, her stilettos slipping and sliding on the marble floor as she tried to keep up with his rapid pace.

In spite of his hurry, she couldn't miss the grin tilting his lips when he swung his leg over his motorcycle. "You really want to know?" he asked. She snuggled up behind him, latched onto his waist, and nodded.

"My *real* hangout."

He gunned the engine and blazed out of the driveway.

All sorts of sordid visions flashed through Lauren's mind, and she couldn't help but wonder what kind of mess she'd gotten herself into this time.

 *Eleven*

*T*attoo Annie's Saloon sat on a lonely stretch of road on the outskirts of West Palm Beach, where the roar of several dozen motorcycle engines and the hoots and hollers of leather-clad bikers wouldn't bring out the cops late on a Saturday night. Hell, Tattoo Annie's wasn't the kind of place that would bring Max out, either. His usual hangout was the pool in his backyard or sitting in front of the television losing one video game after another to his kids.

But he wanted to see Lauren with her hair down. Tattoo Annie's was the perfect place for that.

Bear had told him he'd be here tonight, showing the Scout off to a bunch of guys he went to the Sturgis Rally with every year, so he knew there'd be at least one familiar face in the crowd. Bear hadn't exaggerated by using the term *showing off*, either. The big guy and Max's prized '29 Indian were the center of attention inside Tattoo Annie's. The classic bike, with Bear sitting like a king on the leather seat Max had hand-rubbed again and again to make it soft, sat in the middle of the peanut shell–covered dance floor with at least two dozen gawkers listening to him tell how he came to be in possession of the thing. His story was a bald-faced lie about winning it and a whole lot more in a game of strip poker with a chick from Miami.

"That's not the truth," Lauren said, outraged by the tale.

"Bear likes to embellish his stories. Sort of like a fisherman talking about the size of his prize trout," Max said, pulling her away from that crowd, which only flowed into another. With an arm grasped tightly about her waist, he headed for the bar, trying to talk over the clamor. "No one ever believes the tale, but they listen to every detail, making sure they get the facts straight so they can one-up the guy the next time around."

"I see. Sort of like if I told you I'd spent a week sunning on the sand in Monte Carlo, you'd follow up by saying that you spent a week by the palace pool, and that the prince of Monaco served you his special lemonade?"

"That was last year." Max grinned and drew her even closer. "I'm thinking of inviting the prince to stay with me this time around."

Lauren smiled, the red and yellow neon lights

twinkling in her already sparkling eyes. "I'm sure you'd be terribly bored. The prince is a lovely man, so are his children, but, honestly Max, Monte Carlo and the palace can't compare with Tattoo Annie's."

"You really like it, huh?"

"It's . . . different. Do you come here often?"

"Once or twice a year, maybe less."

"But I thought you said this is your hangout."

"If I'd taken you to the place I normally hang out, we'd be saddled with two kids for the rest of the evening."

"You're not telling me you're a homebody, are you?"

"If you'd asked me that a few years ago I would have laughed. Now, I figure it's not such a bad thing to be."

He ordered a couple of draft beers when they were able to push their way through to the bar, then led her to a just emptying booth.

Taking a swallow of beer, he watched Lauren over the top of the frosty mug, thinking he'd never seen anyone so pretty. The room was warm with the press of people and pulsing neon lights, and he was taken completely by surprise when she touched her icy mug to her chest. That didn't seem like something Miss Palm Beach would do, but neither did going to a biker bar.

What other surprises lay in store? he wondered. Every moment with Lauren he seemed to find out something new, something that made him care for her and want her even more.

She took a sip of beer and licked a speck of

foam from her upper lip after setting the mug back on the table. "It's been a long time since I've had a beer," she said, "it's been even longer since I've been in a place like this."

"I thought this would have been a first for you."

"It's a second. I was in finishing school the first time."

"Not part of the curriculum, was it?"

"Goodness no. Betsy Endicott and I sneaked away from school one night and ended up in this terribly sleazy place. Poor Betsy. She was worried sick because we were under age, and she spent the longest time trying to drag me away, but I was having far too much fun. I didn't know, of course, that I was drinking strawberry daiquiris instead of fruit punch, and I surely didn't know that drinking three of those things in less than an hour would make me horribly uninhibited."

Max folded his forearms on the table and watched the animation in her face. "What did you do?"

"A partial striptease, I'm afraid."

"Would you do that for me if I ordered you a strawberry daiquiri?"

"I'm not seventeen any longer and definitely not as gullible as I was back then."

"Then how can I entice you to strip for me?"

"Order me another beer, keep on smiling at me the way you've been doing, and who knows what will happen."

Max fetched another round from the bar, more

than glad to oblige, grabbed a bowl of peanuts, and sat down for more Laurenesque chatter.

"Want to tell me why you did only a partial strip?" he asked, watching her again press the icy mug to her chest. His eyes were drawn to her breasts, to the silkiness of her skin, the tantalizing black lace of her bra, and he wanted to strip her himself. But, hell, she wanted to go slow, and he was bound and determined to give her anything she wanted, operating in the hope that someday she'd give him everything he wanted in return.

"It's warm in here," she said, "just like it was that night."

"Want to go outside?"

"No, I like the music. The beer's delicious. The company's the best I've had in a long time." She took another long sip, watching him over the top of her mug. "I was having a good time that night, too, dancing with anyone and everyone, and before I knew it, I was up on a table, unbuttoning my blouse because it was far too hot, and doing some kind of dance that I definitely didn't learn in Mrs. Stravinski's ballroom dance class. The men were watching me, lights were flashing, and my head started spinning. Before I got to the last button, I threw up." She giggled. "Goodness, you would have thought I was firing an Uzi around the place the way everyone was screaming."

Max couldn't stop his laughter. "You didn't throw up on people, did you?"

"There were a lot of gawkers egging me on in that striptease and, I'm sorry, but I was only seventeen, they'd gotten me drunk, and they deserved everything I hit them with." She took a long sip of cold beer and rested her arms on the table, leaning close, her pretty face only inches from his. "I can still hear the men yelling at me, and if poor Betsy hadn't dragged me out right then and there, I'm sure I would have been lynched. I don't remember how she got me back to school and I don't remember going to bed, but I do remember my rude awakening."

"What happened?" he asked, as she picked a peanut from the bowl, cracked the shell, and popped one of the nuts into her mouth.

"The headmistress flashed the front page of the local newspaper in my face and started to shout things about me ruining the school's reputation. My poor mother was beside herself when the tabloids ran their own version of the story, saying they couldn't print the X-rated photographs. My father, who I ended up staying with for a few weeks after I was kicked out of school, made me shovel horse manure as punishment." She popped the other nut between her teeth and slowly licked her lips, a gesture that kept Max's eyes riveted on her mouth. "I haven't been in a sleazy bar or had another daiquiri since."

"Did you ever go back to finishing school?"

"A different one, I'm afraid. I wanted to run away from that one, too." She took another sip of beer and leaned forward. "May I make a suggestion?"

"Shoot."

"Don't ever send Jamie to finishing school or

Ryan to a military academy. They're terribly boring and, really, Max, children need their parents raising them, not the butler, even if he is one of the loveliest people on earth, not a nanny, and not total strangers."

Max shelled another peanut and held the nuts against her lips, definitely liking the feel of her mouth closing over his fingers and licking off the salt. He wondered if she had any idea what she was doing to him, wondered how he was going to keep his sanity when she was the most innocently erotic woman he'd ever encountered.

For days he'd wanted Lauren, in his arms, in his bed, but tonight he realized he might want even more from her.

"Do you want children?" The way the question slipped casually from his mouth surprised him. It seemed to surprise Lauren, too.

She lifted the beer and drank slowly, watching him. If she was trying to figure out why he'd asked the question, she probably wouldn't find the answer in his eyes, because he wasn't too sure himself.

"I've always wanted children," she said softly. "Lots of them. But I don't have the foggiest idea how to take care of a child, and how could I possibly be a good parent when I haven't had the best role models?"

"Instinct, I imagine. My dad disappeared when I was eight and my mom dumped me on one of her many boyfriends when I was ten. I didn't have good role models either, until Philippe took me in."

"But you're a good dad."

He shrugged. "I wing it every day. Sometimes I make mistakes, sometimes I do things right. I haven't found a book yet that answers all the questions, so I do the best I can."

Sliding out of the booth, he took her beer from her hands, because she'd already had too many, and pulled her out to the dance floor and into his arms. "You'll be a good mother when the time comes," he whispered against her ear, and let the subject drift away as Steppenwolf took them on a Magic Carpet Ride.

Her skin was warm and damp, and God, he liked the feel of her cheek against his as they moved to the beat, their hips, their thighs, her soft breasts and his chest melding together and swaying with the pounding tune. Her fingers twisted in his hair, and his found their way under her leather jacket to the curve of her waist, the swell of her hips.

"Don't ever dance naked for anyone but me," he said, caught up in their sensual dance, thoughts of her long-ago escapade recurring in his mind.

"I don't think I'll be dancing naked for anyone."

"Why?"

"My thighs jiggle and so do my breasts."

"I know." His tongue and lips briefly explored the sensitive hollow beneath her ear, and he thought about exploring other parts on her anatomy, especially the parts that jiggled. "I kept an eye on your body the other day on the beach."

"Oh, dear."

"I liked watching you. I like everything about you. Your honesty, your drive, the way you make the things you do look so easy."

"Throwing parties is something I've done all my life, that's why my planning looks easy."

He pushed her far enough away that he could look into her eyes. "Why do you always downplay everything you do? Why are you so unsure of yourself?"

"Because I've failed at all the things that really matter."

"Such as?"

"I've told you that before and you've thrown it in my face. I'm a lousy wife."

"But you had lousy husbands. Have you ever wondered how good you'd be at something if you had someone encouraging you, making you feel good about yourself and the things you've done?"

She just looked at him, tears welling in her eyes. Hell, hadn't anyone ever told her what a wonder she was?

He would have told her himself, right then and there, but Bear slapped him on the back and whipped Lauren right out of his arms.

"You've monopolized this little lady for far too long. It's my turn now."

The room buzzed with Credence Clearwater Revival, more Steppenwolf, and an endless stream of favorite biker music and Lauren switched partners more times than Max could count. She laughed, shook her delicious hips, and every so often Max cut in, slowing down her pace, loving the feel of her against him, tasting the beer and peanuts on her tongue and the salty perspiration on her neck. She was hot and erotic and she'd had too much to drink, but he was sure it had been years since she'd let her hair down, so he let her go.

That proved to be a big mistake.

"Have you seen Lauren?" Max asked Bear, when he'd lost track of her in the crowd.

"Ten, fifteen minutes ago, I guess. Why?"

Max plowed his fingers through his hair. "I can't find her."

"Did she go home with someone else?"

"She wouldn't do that."

Bear raised an eyebrow. "You're sure?"

He had to think about that question for a moment. Earlier today he thought the woman thrived on men and would latch on to anyone who paid attention to her. But rage and jealousy had been doing his thinking earlier. He was somewhat levelheaded tonight. "I'm positive."

"Did you check the john?"

"No, but I will. Keep an eye out for her, will you?"

"Yeah."

Max headed for the hallway and the dim red exit sign. He looked in the men's head, just in case she'd accidentally stumbled in there and passed out. Fortunately, all he saw were men. God, he shouldn't have let her have those few extra beers.

He knocked on the women's rest room door, and when no one answered he checked inside. Empty.

Where had she gone?

Pushing through the exit, he went out back, hoping she wasn't in the alley with some other biker, praying she hadn't left with someone else, frightened that someone might have led her out when she wasn't thinking straight.

He blasted back inside, making his way through the crowd, asking everyone he knew and even people he didn't know if they'd seen the tall, voluptuous woman in the snakeskin jacket. Heads shook everywhere, until he got close to Tattoo Annie's artistic parlor. A guy waiting in line to add another illustration to the collage on his arms thumbed Max toward the door. "I think she's inside."

"Ah, Christ!"

Max tried the doorknob.

"I'm busy," came the woman's voice from within. "Get in line and I'll be with you later."

"I don't want a tattoo," Max shouted. "I want to know who's in there with you?"

"I think she said her name's Lauren. I'd ask her, but she passed out halfway through."

Damn! "Open the door and let me in, okay?"

"Can't. Not till I'm done."

"But she's drunk and I don't think she really wants a tattoo."

"Honey," Tattoo Annie hollered back, "she knew what she was doing when she asked for this thing, and she plunked down good money to pay for it. Now if you don't mind, I'm busy."

Max let out a deadly sigh and slammed himself up against the wall to wait. The next fifteen minutes seemed to be the longest wait of his life.

Finally the door opened and Tattoo Annie, a woman with every visible inch of skin covered in embedded dye, stepped out of the room and glared. "Are you the one waiting for the woman?"

"Yeah."

"Well, she's dead to the world. I've got customers waiting, so you're gonna have to haul her out of here." Tattoo Annie slapped a piece of paper in his hand. "There's instructions on there for cleaning my artwork. My phone number's there, too . . . just in case."

"Thanks," Max said, and stalked into the room, where he couldn't miss Lauren lying flat out on a cushioned table, facedown, eyes closed, mouth open wide and snoring.

Bending over, Max managed to heft Lauren onto his shoulder, grabbed her purse, and headed into the bar.

"Well, this is a pretty sight," Bear quipped.

"Breathe a word of it to anyone and you're dead meat."

"I wouldn't think of it. So, how are you gonna get her home?"

Max shoved his keys in Bear's hand. "I'm calling her butler and I need you to follow behind on my bike. I'll bring you back here after I've got her tucked in bed."

Bear put his hand on Max's unencumbered shoulder. "Is she worth all this?" he asked.

Max had been fairly unsure of a lot of things in his life, but he had no doubt at all about the answer he gave Bear. "Yeah, she's worth all of this and a hell of a lot more."

Lauren had the awful feeling that she'd fallen asleep in a construction zone somewhere and that a big burly guy had mistakenly thought her head was old asphalt that needed to be pecked away with a jackhammer.

The pain and the excruciatingly loud noise subsided a moment, then started up all over again.

"Excuse me, Miss Remington."

Cracking open one heavy eyelid, Lauren saw Charles's blurry figure walk toward the bed. "I haven't died, have I?" she asked, clasping her palms to her aching skull.

"Not yet, but your mother is on the telephone. This is the fourth time she's called today and I couldn't put her off again."

"Fourth time? Where was I the other three?"

"In various degrees of agony caused by the consumption of too much alcohol."

"Oh, dear."

"Would you care to take your mother's call now, or do you have an excuse I could use to explain your absence? I do believe I'm fresh out of explanations."

Lauren ran her fingers through oily hair and had the feeling she looked even worse than she felt. But somehow she rolled toward the phone. "I'll talk to her."

"Very well, miss."

"Before you go, Charles, do you by any chance know a hangover remedy?"

"I believe I might be able to concoct something. I'll bring it up shortly."

"Thank you," she muttered as he walked out the door. Taking a deep breath, she lifted the phone. "Hello, Mother."

"Lauren, darling, I'm so glad you're finally home. The most dreadful thing has happened."

"What is it, Mother?" Lauren asked, forcing herself to listen carefully when she heard the nervousness in her mother's voice. "Are you in Rio? Has there been an accident?"

"Yes, Bunny and I are in Rio and no, there hasn't been an accident. However, Bunny and I were preparing to go out this evening and she opened her jewelry case to find out that her emerald necklace is missing."

Lauren sighed with relief. "Calm down, Mother. I'm sure Bunny just forgot to pack it. You know how forgetful she can be at times."

"I thought the same thing, darling, but she showed it to me before Betsy's wedding. She couldn't make up her mind which necklace to wear, and we sorted through several before she found the right one. You didn't see it lying on the floor in the bedroom where Bunny changed, did you?"

"No, Mother, and I'm sure Charles would have let me know if he'd found it."

"It's worth a small fortune and can't be replaced."

"Is Bunny sure she didn't leave it at home?"

"She hasn't touched the jewelry case since the wedding. We left for Rio so quickly that she brought everything with her, rather than returning it to her safe deposit box."

Lauren could almost hear the flutter of her mother's heart, the nervousness she felt over Bunny losing her jewelry.

"I'll go to Bunny's home if you'd like," Lauren offered, then wondered how she could possibly get there in the shape she was in. Still, she said, "I'd be happy to look around."

"She's already called her maid, talked to her butler and her cook, not to mention the chauffeur to see if it might have been misplaced in the car. Having you look would be useless, darling. Bunny and I are positive it's been stolen."

Lauren laughed lightly, the sound vibrating heavily between her ears. "That's always a possibility," she said, trying to soften her voice, "but if it was stolen, it could have happened anyplace. On the plane, in Rio, at her home."

Her mother was silent a moment. "I hate to bring this up, darling, because I know that you like that man who catered Betsy's wedding, but he had some very disreputable people working for him. One in particular."

"And which one would that have been, Mother?" Lauren asked, angry that her mother would even think such a thing about Max and his friends.

"Well, Bunny told me there was a young man at the wedding who was admiring jewelry. She was under the impression he was talking about her breasts, of all things, but now she's sure he was looking for things to steal."

Lauren hadn't wanted to hear this. Not now. Not ever. "That was Ryan, Mother."

"You know him, then?"

"He's Max's son, and I know the entire story behind him looking at Bunny's jewelry."

"Then why don't you tell me."

"His hormones are in overdrive." She could hear her mother's gasp; young men's hormones were something ladies didn't talk about! "I know you're going to find this reprehensible, but Ryan was looking at Bunny's *breasts*, not her *jewelry*, and Max had a long talk with him about not doing it in the future."

"I certainly hope so. But if the boy didn't take Bunny's necklace, I'm sure one of those other people could have."

"You're wrong about Max and his staff, and I'm sure you and Bunny are wrong about it disappearing during Betsy's wedding."

"Those people had access to every room in your home, for several hours, I might add. You're giving them too much credit."

"Max's friends aren't thieves," Lauren stated adamantly. "Jazz is a cop. Bear's a dentist and Gabe's a social worker."

"That doesn't mean they can't have the inclination to steal."

"The same could be said for a hundred percent of the people who were at Betsy's wedding."

Lauren heard her mother's frustrated sigh. "That man's got you beguiled, Lauren. Wake up and realize that he lives on the wrong side of the tracks—"

"He lives in a beautiful home."

"Don't tell me you've been there!"

"Of course I have. I like his friends, I like his children, and Max is warm and genuine and—"

"And he knows exactly what kind of power he has over you. Don't be a fool, Lauren."

"I'm not, Mother. I know perfectly well what I'm doing."

"He'll take you for everything you've got."

"And what would that be, Mother? A mansion that's cold and empty because I have no one to share it with? Jewelry, money, and fancy cars, none of which crawl into bed with me at night?"

"You're being ridiculous."

"I'm being honest!"

"There's no reasoning with you when you're this way, so just listen for one moment to what I have to say."

Lauren didn't want to listen, but she'd never had the courage to hang up on her mother. She didn't have the courage now.

"The man's no good, Lauren. You let him into your life and he's not only going to walk away with everything you own—those things you don't feel are all that important at the present time—but he's also going to walk away with your heart. Take my advice, Lauren, don't ever let a man steal that, because when it happens, when you find out he's the wrong one for you, you'll end up a very cold, very lonely and bitter woman."

Hearing the dial tone didn't come as much of a surprise. Too many conversations with her mother over the years had ended with Celeste hanging up when Lauren attempted to disagree with her.

Moving slowly, she put down the receiver, slid her legs over the side of the mattress, and sat up. She was in her panties and bra and nothing more, and for the life of her she couldn't remember how she'd gotten into bed. As for how she'd gotten home from Tattoo Annie's Saloon, well, that was a complete mystery, too.

Putting a hand on the bedpost, she steadied herself as she stood. The room spun around her. The inside of her mouth felt like cotton. And her mother's nonsense swam through her mind.

Max was not a thief. Max's friends weren't criminals. She'd never believe that ever in a million years. As for Max being out for her money, she didn't believe that, either.

Losing her heart to him was another matter completely. He was good and kind and he hung out in biker bars with all the wrong kind of people. He was honest and loyal, but that didn't matter to her friends and family. If something went wrong, they'd look at someone like Max first.

He'd never be accepted in her world and, God, did she really want to go back to his, considering the way she felt right now?

Somehow she trudged toward the bathroom, stripped out of her underwear, and stared at herself in the mirror. Dark shadow and heavy mascara had smeared under her eyes. Her goopy hair shot out at various angles from her head. She didn't know the woman staring back at her. That Lauren Remington was a complete stranger, a woman who had tried to be something she wasn't, just to please a man. That thought annoyed her more than her mother's words, more than getting drunk, more than anything.

She put her hands to her face and started to cry. For once in her life, she wanted to be loved for who she was. She didn't want to change to get a man or to keep a man.

She heard Charles's knock at her door. "Just a moment," she called out to him, her words pounding against her head. Grabbing a brush, she tried to put her hair in some kind of order, splashed cold water on her face, and took her robe from the back of the door.

What she saw in the full-length mirror stunned her. She moved closer, turned her backside toward the door, and stared at some kind of fish tattooed on her cheek. Oh, dear, it wasn't a fish. It was a merman, with bulging pecs and biceps, shoulder-length black hair, and hoops in his ears.

What had she done? she asked herself, as tears flowed again from her eyes. More importantly, what was she going to do now?

* * *

Max wound his way through the tight confines of J. C. Penney's lingerie department, wishing there were some way he could hide from prying eyes. What people thought of him rarely mattered, but he'd never gone shopping for bras before, and doing it with an eleven-year-old girl made the task a thousand times more uncomfortable.

For both of them.

How could Jamie have gone from flat as a pancake one day to needing a training bra the next? Why couldn't she be happy with the perfectly acceptable plain white cotton stretchy things the clerk kept suggesting she try?

"They're ugly, Max!" she said a little too loudly.

"You're not going to be wearing them out in public," he stated as low as he possibly could, while still trying to get his point across.

Jamie had her fists planted firmly on her nonexistent hips. "I have to change clothes in PE and all the girls will look at me."

"And I'm sure they're all wearing training bras, too."

"Nikki Constantine's mother took her to Victoria's Secret to buy her first bra and it pushes her up to make her look bigger."

"Well I'm not Nikki Constantine's mother, I'm your father."

"You are not!"

"Well, I will be real soon, but that's neither here

nor there. I don't want you to look bigger. Not now, not ever!"

Big tears welled up in Jamie's eyes and poured down her cheeks.

"Christ!"

The saleslady gasped, and Max came close to throwing his arms up in the air in frustration. Instead, he looked at the training bra the woman held in her hands and said, "We'll take a dozen of those."

"You really don't need that many, sir."

"Then give me however many you think we'll need so we can get out of here."

"Perhaps you'd like to come back when you're in a better frame of mind."

His eyes narrowed as he stared at her. "There's nothing wrong with my frame of mind, I just don't like shopping for bras!"

"Ryan thought you should take me to Victoria's Secret," Jamie blubbered. "He said they had women's bras there, and you'd probably like them better."

Hell! He didn't even like women at the moment, one in particular, the one who'd disappeared from Palm Beach without a goodbye, an I-hate-you, or a drop-dead. Damn her!

He'd called again and again to talk to Lauren that first day, and Charles continually told him she was unavailable. She was hung over, they both knew that, and Max figured she was asleep the first couple of times he'd called. But Miss Palm Beach couldn't possibly have slept for twenty-four hours. She must have gotten his messages—but she hadn't bothered to call, she'd just up and run away. Damn her!

He plunked down cash for the bras, grabbed the bag that Jamie refused to hold, latched on to his little girl's hand, and marched out of J. C. Penney's thinking that Jamie was growing up far too fast, thinking, too, that he'd made a big mistake losing his heart to Lauren Remington. She was a scheming, conniving, spoiled brat, who had a knack for chewing men up and spitting them out. He'd known that days ago, and he'd walked right into her trap.

But damn if he didn't still want her!

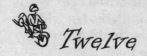 *Twelve*

*W*ednesday morning came with its usual fanfare. Jamie refused to go to school because she'd been teased unmercifully about her new bras on Monday and Tuesday. Ryan hadn't done his homework the night before and refused to go because he was certain his teacher would give him an F.

"You knew a week ago that that assignment was due today," Max grumbled, while hacking up a bunch of carrots to go in Jamie's and Ryan's lunches.

Ryan dribbled his basketball, glaring at Max as if school and homework were no big deal. "I forgot."

"You've got an assignment calendar on the wall

in your room. There's one on the refrigerator and one in your notebook. 'I forgot' doesn't cut it."

Ryan dribbled the ball beneath his leg without missing a beat. "You don't have to get all over my case just because you're pissed—"

Max shot Ryan a look the kid knew full well meant, *Watch your language.*

Ryan, as usual, rolled his eyes. "Okay, you don't have to get all over my case just because you're *ticked* off at that Lauren Remington woman."

"I'm not ticked off."

"Well, that's what Bear told me."

Max hacked the carrots one more time and took a deep breath as he threw the shreds into two plastic bags. Yeah, he had been mad. His exhaustion hadn't helped. In the last couple of days he'd talked to the adoption lawyer, he'd gathered up old report cards to prove how much the kids had progressed since they'd come to live with him, he'd catered a car dealer's luncheon and an engagement dinner.

Except for his insane foray to Tattoo Annie's, he'd worked nonstop for days. He'd had trouble sleeping. Jamie refused to speak to him, Lauren still hadn't called, which hurt his pride and, God forbid, his heart, and the investigator hadn't phoned. He'd hired a chef to substitute for him at the engagement party last night because he hadn't wanted to leave the house and possibly miss Harry's call. But he'd gotten no word about his sister. Even the messages he'd left on Harry's voice mail had gone unanswered.

It seemed the only one interested in talking to him these days was Ryan, and their conversation was going nowhere.

He shoved his hands through his hair. As tired as he was, as hurt and angry as he felt, he didn't have to take his frustrations out on the kids.

He poured fresh-squeezed orange juice into a glass and shoved it across the counter to Ryan, who managed to gulp down half of it while dribbling the basketball.

"So," Max said, leaning against one of the refrigerators, "what's the *real* reason you didn't get the assignment done?"

"I for—" Max's eyes narrowed when Ryan started to once again feed him the lousy "I forgot" excuse. "Okay, I hate history, my teacher's boring, and I'd rather play basketball."

"Do you have a game plan?" Max asked.

"What do you mean?"

"What are you going to do? Drop out of school?"

Ryan finally put the ball on the counter and poured himself some more juice. "I've thought about it."

"What's that going to get you?"

Ryan shrugged. "Freedom to do what I want."

"Freedom to live on the street when you're older is more like it. Freedom to be poor, to work at some fast-food joint." Max took a swallow of Ryan's juice and poured some more, keeping his eyes trained on Ryan's face. "You might be better off staying in school."

"Why?"

"Because you're good at basketball. Stick around school, get good grades, and you might get a scholarship. Who knows, you could end up good enough to play professional."

Ryan laughed. "In my dreams."

Max shoved sandwiches, carrots, and cookies into two brown paper bags. "I've seen dreams come true," Max said, "but I've also seen people working darn hard to make that happen. There aren't too many fairy godmothers waving magic wands around these days."

Ryan picked up one of the banana pecan muffins Max had made that morning and took a bite out of the side, watching Max, apparently contemplating his words. Max merely leaned on the counter, watched and waited for Ryan's response.

"It's too late to do anything about the F on my history paper that's due today," Ryan said. "You got any suggestions?"

"See if you can work something out with the teacher," Max told him.

"Maybe you could call him for me?"

Max shook his head. "You didn't do the assignment. You have to take care of the problem."

"What am I supposed to tell him?"

"I don't know. Maybe you could ask to do some extra homework."

"I can't do that! It'll mess with my basketball time."

"It's up to you," Max said, then turned his back on Ryan and went to the refrigerator for milk.

He supposed he should have chewed Ryan out

for not turning in the assignment. Maybe he should have taken away his basketball, grounded him for a few weeks, but it seemed some kind of positive reinforcement would work better. It wasn't exactly the kind of tough love he'd heard people preach about, but it was the only kind of love he planned to give his kids.

The phone rang and he grabbed for it, hoping it was Lauren, hoping it was Harry. "Hello."

"It's Harry." Relief flooded through him. So did disappointment that it wasn't Miss Palm Beach. "Sorry I couldn't get back to you last night."

Max didn't care about apologies, he just wanted to hear the news. "Did you find my sister?"

"I found a woman named Charlotte Wilde, just like I told you the other day. She's the right age, dark hair, brown eyes."

All too soon Harry was silent.

"What else did you find out?" Max asked, positive by now it wasn't good.

"Not a thing. The woman she's living with isn't anxious to lose her and Charlotte doesn't remember her past."

Max hadn't wanted to hear that. Maybe he'd gotten his hopes up too high that this Charlotte Wilde was his real sister, that she wasn't as mentally challenged as he'd been led to believe, that she suddenly remembered she had a brother and was anxious to see him again.

"Do you think she's the right one?"

"I don't know."

"What's your gut instinct?" Max asked.

"I don't form gut instincts," Harry answered. "I go on fact, nothing more. If you want to be sure, you'll have to come here yourself."

Max let out a frustrated breath. He had to cater a birthday party tonight. He'd neglected Jamie and Ryan too much lately. The laundry was piling up.

He needed to call Lauren—again.

But he needed to learn the truth about the woman in Phoenix.

He looked at his watch. "Let me see if I can get a flight out this morning, or this afternoon at the latest. I've got to get a sitter for the kids, make a few phone calls."

"My flight home's not till late tomorrow," Harry said. "You've got my cell phone number. Just let me know when you're getting in and I'll let the woman here know you're coming."

Max hung up the phone and braced his hands on the counter top. He stared out the kitchen window, seeing nothing but the memories of his little sister.

Ryan leaned on the counter beside him. "Where you going?" he asked.

"Phoenix, if I can get a flight."

"You could take me and Jamie with you."

In spite of the turmoil roiling through him right now, he managed to grin at Ryan. "Why, so you can have an extra day to work on that history assignment?"

"It seemed like a good idea."

"I don't think so."

Max grabbed for a box of cereal, not caring what he pulled out of the cabinet, and set it on the counter. "I've got to get your sister out of her room, I've got some phone calls to make, and—"

"Do you think this one might be your sister?" Ryan asked, taking cereal bowls down from a shelf.

"I don't know. I hope so."

Ryan poured Cheerios into one of the bowls. "I hated it when Jamie and I got sent to different foster homes." He looked up briefly as he poured the milk. "I didn't think I'd ever see her again."

Ryan's gaze darted quickly back to his bowl and he shoveled a spoonful of cereal into his mouth. He never talked about his mother's death or his father's imprisonment, and rarely mentioned the fact that he and Jamie had been separated for nearly three years. Max didn't bring it up, either. He knew all too well what separation was like, knew the good and bad aspects of the foster system. He was thankful Philippe had taken him in; thankful that he himself had taken in Jamie and Ryan.

He hadn't given much thought to becoming a foster father until Ryan showed up at the Hole. He was an angry twelve-year-old who wanted to run away from everyone and everything. He was tough, far too often he had a smart mouth, and he was this close to getting in trouble with the law.

They were two of a kind. It had taken Philippe a few years to straighten Max out, and Max figured it would take at least that amount of time to work on Ryan. They'd had some major battles in the beginning, but once Max learned that Ryan had a little sister, once he'd found Jamie and brought her into their home, the troubles had eased. They still had their problems, but he refused to give up.

"You want me to get Jamie off to school for you?" Ryan asked, looking up from his cereal. "She's a pain in the butt most of the time, but you've got stuff to do."

Max looked at Ryan, wishing he could tell the boy how much that offer meant. But Ryan considered himself too old for verbal or physical displays of affection, so Max just said, "Thanks."

"You want us to go to the Hole after school?"

"No, come home today. I'll see if Jazz can watch you tonight."

"I'm old enough to take care of Jamie."

"I know, but humor me just this once, okay."

Ryan shoveled another spoonful of cereal into his mouth. "Okay."

Max fluffed Ryan's hair, another display of affection the boy hated, and headed for his office. He had a million things to do and far too much on his mind, the last of which should have been Lauren Remington.

But right this moment, he wanted to be near her, wanted to feel her arms holding him tight. He was worried about seeing the woman in Phoenix. Afraid she wouldn't be his sister; afraid she would. He'd never shared his troubles with a soul, never known anyone he'd wanted to share them with.

Until Lauren.

* * *

Lauren drummed her fingers on the red crocodile Gucci handbag she'd picked up at Bergdorf Goodman yesterday, and watched the traffic whizzing past the car as Charles drove along Ocean Boulevard. She was anxious to get home. More anxious, in fact, than she'd been to get away from Palm Beach and what had seemed like a miserable existence a few days before.

The impromptu trip to New York for a shopping spree on Fifth Avenue hadn't solved any of her problems, hadn't erased any of her worries, and definitely hadn't taken her mind off Max.

He was all she'd thought of. That and the fact that she wished she'd called him instead of running away, wished she'd fallen into his arms and poured her heart and soul out to him. He was the first man she'd ever confided in. Oh, she'd cried on more than a few shoulders, but usually over superficial things. She'd never told anyone how much her past bothered her. Never told anyone how frightened she was of being hurt again. She'd never wanted to share those things with anyone.

Until Max.

Now, however, it was highly possible that he wouldn't want to speak to her again. After all the things Charles had told her about what he'd done—carrying her out of Tattoo Annie's and tucking her in bed—she should have called and at least said thanks. She should have called to tell him where she was going, but she'd just run away, needing time to sort out all the things going through her mind.

Hiding in New York had been her way of protecting herself, her way of not saying yes to Max when she needed to say, "Someday." It was her way of making sure she didn't let him take over her life.

But she couldn't run away from Max or her fears forever. He was too firmly embedded in her mind and heart, and it looked like he was there to stay.

The phone was ringing when she walked into the house, and she picked up the extension in the foyer. "Hello."

There was silence on the other end of the line and she almost hung up, but then she heard Max's voice. "So, you finally decided to come home, or have you been there all the time, refusing to take or return my calls?"

She deserved his anger because he was good and kind and wonderful, and she'd been horrid.

"I was in New York." A lump formed in her throat when she heard nothing but silence at the other end of the line. "I'm sorry, Max. I owe you an apology for so many things, it's hard to know where to begin."

"Why not start by telling me why you left? I was under the impression things were going pretty good between us. I thought we'd get together Sunday night, or Monday night, or even last night, but hell, no, you went to New York!"

"Things *were* going well. I don't remember any time with any man ever being so special."

"So why'd you run away?"

She sat down in a chair and stared at the cold marble floor. "I was scared."

"Of what?"

She couldn't tell him that she was afraid of a lot of things, like becoming someone different and losing friends who might not approve of her relationship with Max.

All of those things were too complicated to talk about now, especially over the phone. So she told him the one thing that he could probably understand. "I'm scared of falling in love with you. I may have made some mistakes in my other relationships, but I was hurt every time one of them fell apart. If I give myself to you and things don't work out, I don't think I'll recover as easily as I have in the past."

"So," Max said, sighing in frustration. "What are you going to do? Tell me that you don't want to see me again, because you don't want to fall in love?"

"No," Lauren admitted. "I came back to tell you that I *do* want to see you again, whether we fall in love or not, whether you break my heart or not, because you're worth taking a chance." She wiped away an escaping tear, wishing he'd say something—afraid of his silence. "What about you, Max?" she asked. "Am I worth taking a chance on, too?"

"I told you last Saturday night that I wanted you. That hasn't changed."

A flutter of relief raced through her. "Then maybe we should start over again. Tonight, if you can get away. We could go to dinner, go dancing, or just sit on the beach and talk."

"I can't tonight. I've got a flight to Phoenix in an hour and I'm not sure when I'll be home."

With some other man she might have considered the words a brush-off, but she heard the troubled tone in Max's voice.

"Is everything all right?"

"Yeah." He was silent a moment, and then he sighed. "No, everything isn't all right. I'm having troubles finding someone to take care of Jamie and Ryan while I'm gone."

Surely he wasn't going to ask her? "What about Bear? Or Jazz or Gabe?"

"Jazz has to work tonight and Gabe and Bear are out of town."

"Couldn't somebody at the Hole watch them?"

He was silent again. A deafening silence. And then he hit her. "I was thinking you could do it."

"Me?"

"Yeah, you," he chuckled.

"But I don't know the first thing about kids."

"They're eleven and fourteen. They don't need their diapers changed and they can eat pizza for dinner. I just need someone to stay with them to make sure they don't get into any trouble."

From the little she'd seen of Ryan, he could be the poster boy for "Trouble," and Jamie wasn't the least bit crazy about Lauren tampering with Max's affections. But there was something special about Max's kids. She saw a little bit of herself in Jamie and a whole lot of Max in Ryan.

How could she possibly turn Max down when

he needed her help, especially after he'd come to her rescue more than once.

"All right," she said, apprehensive—but excited—at the prospect of being a makeshift mom for a day or two. "Just give me a few minutes to gather up a few things, and I'll be right over."

"I owe you for this," Max said, his voice filled with the warmth that Lauren had never known in other men.

"You don't owe me a thing," Lauren said. "But if you insist on paying me back, I wouldn't mind another dance."

"I'd like to give you more than that."

Lauren leaned back in the chair and smiled, thinking of all the delicious things Max could give her. "There's really only one thing I want," she told him.

"And what's that?"

"You. Just you."

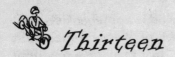 *Thirteen*

*T*he staring contest ended within half an hour. It started shortly after Ryan made it perfectly clear to Lauren that he didn't want or need a baby-sitter. That was followed by Jamie's declaration that she took care of Max and she didn't want or need a rich woman moving in. So all three of them sized each other up for twenty-seven minutes and twelve seconds. Lauren knew the exact time, because she'd continually looked at her watch, wondering how long it would be before Max returned.

Finally Ryan turned on his Nintendo game—with the sound excessively loud, of course—and Jamie took the vacuum cleaner from a closet and began cleaning floors. Apparently they thought the noise would drive Lauren out.

They were wrong.

Lauren smoothed out a wrinkle in her orchid print sundress as she lounged on the black leather sofa in Max's family room. Crossing her legs, she flipped through an issue of *Elle*, raising her eyes only when she sensed Ryan or Jamie was watching her—looking for just the right moment to strike.

"Max has lots of girlfriends," Jamie said, pushing the vacuum cleaner back and forth, dangerously close to Lauren's toes.

They'd had a similar conversation at Betsy's wedding reception, but Lauren humored her. "Is that so?"

"Yeah. At least three or four a week 'cause he gets tired of the same old thing all the time."

"My dad was exactly the same way. After he divorced my mother, I think he dated every eligible woman in the state of Wyoming." Jamie's eyes widened in shock, as Lauren continued. "I didn't get to spend much time with my father—*or* my mother—but when I did, I wanted them totally to myself."

Jamie nodded, obviously having the same sentiments.

Lauren didn't bother telling Jamie that after Reece Remington exhausted the women in Wyoming, he'd handed the ranch over to her brother Jack and moved to New Mexico because he needed fresh pickings.

"My dad likes blonds," Lauren said over the noise of the vacuum. "What about Max? Does he have a preference?"

Jamie pushed the vacuum cleaner within a quarter of an inch of Lauren's lavender spikes, but Lauren didn't flinch a muscle. Jamie was not going to get the upper hand. With the vacuum roaring next to Lauren's legs, Jamie stared over the handle at Lauren's hair. "Max likes blonds, too," she announced. "He thinks redheads are okay, but he doesn't like brown hair."

Lauren drew a lock of her own hair forward and stared at it. Crossing her eyes gave her a headache, but Jamie would probably appreciate the fact that Lauren looked ridiculous. "I've always considered this dark honey-blond," she said. "Brown's *so* drab."

Jamie switched off the vacuum and plopped down on the couch. "My mom had honey-blond hair. I don't remember her much, but I think her hair was a lot lighter than yours."

"Honey-blond comes in all shades, light, dark, in between." Lauren leaned close to Jamie and whispered. "Most of mine comes from a bottle."

A small smile touched Jamie's lips. "I told Max I wanted to dye mine black so I'd look more like him, but he said no."

"Your hair's much too pretty to dye." Lauren threaded her fingers through the curly, pale blond ponytail. "I like your hairstyle, too, and your bangs are absolutely perfect. You must have a wonderful hairdresser."

Jamie giggled. "Max cuts it for me."

"*Max cuts it?*"

"Yeah. He's got an extra pair of really sharp

kitchen scissors and every once in a while, he just whacks it off."

"You mean to tell me you've never been to a salon?"

Jamie shook her head.

How was this possible in this day and age? Lauren wondered. "Have you ever wanted to go?"

Jamie's shoulders rose and fell. "I never gave it much thought, and Max isn't into frills."

"Well, we're going to change all that."

Jamie frowned. "How?"

"I'm going to make an appointment for you with Frederico."

"Who's that?"

"The man who does my hair. And"—she lifted Jamie's hands and stared at her blunt, chewed-off fingernails—"we'll get your nails done, too."

"Really?"

"Of course, but first things first."

Lauren dropped her magazine on the glass and chrome coffee table and pushed up from the couch. "Ryan!"

He tilted his head toward her, shooting her a withering glare. "What?"

"It's homework time," Lauren announced, remembering that Max had left specific instructions that homework had to be done right after school. She'd let that rule slide for nearly an hour, which was definitely long enough. "You can play Nintendo later."

"I'm in the middle of a game," Ryan argued.

"Which, I'm sure, you can get back to some other time."

"But I've got a high score."

Not knowing what else to do, Lauren emulated one of her boarding school teachers and tapped the toe of her shoe on the carpeting.

Ryan offered her a long-winded sigh, then flipped off the TV and Nintendo. "I'll do my homework in my room," he said, and started to storm off.

"Wait a minute, Ryan."

He turned around and glared. "What now?"

"I just wanted to tell you that I didn't like school either."

"So."

"*So*, I got lousy grades because I didn't do my homework. Then my mother married this old guy—his name was George Rhodes, not that that matters to you—but George was a whiz at math and history and when my mother and George were in town, which wasn't often, he'd help me with my homework."

Ryan rolled his eyes. "Is there supposed to be a moral to this story?"

Lauren smiled, touched by Ryan's lack of charm and social skills. "Only that I didn't mind doing my homework so much when someone was around to help me."

"Max is around."

"Do you let him help you?"

"I don't need help."

"No, I suppose you wouldn't."

He frowned, his look suspicious, as if he was

certain Lauren had something up her sleeve. "Can I go to my room now?"

"If you want, but it's going to be terribly boring for me the next couple of hours while you and Jamie are doing your schoolwork. I was thinking you might let me help—just so I'll have something to do."

"All I have is history. I don't think you want to help with that."

"I have to write an essay," Jamie chimed in. "It can be on any subject. You can help me."

"Well," she said, smiling at Jamie and then at Ryan, "as I said, George was a whiz in history. Ask me a question, any question, and I'm sure I can answer it. As for essays, they're only as good as the subject you pick, and I know an awful lot of interesting subjects. So, grab your books, we'll get the homework done, and then we'll pay a visit to Frederico and get Jamie's hair done."

"Wait a minute," Ryan blurted out. "I'm not going to do homework just so I can spend the rest of the night sitting in some old beauty shop."

"Frederico's isn't old, and I have no intention of taking you there," Lauren shot right back. "Your hair's perfectly fine. There is, however, a sports store next door."

"What do you know about sports?"

"Absolutely nothing, although I'm a terrific spectator and I know how to yell with the crowd. However, I've made numerous purchases from this store for my nephew Beau, who's just a few years older than you, and I'm acquainted with the owner. He used to play pro basketball, and if you can be civil for an hour, I'm sure he would give you some tips."

Ryan's eyes narrowed suspiciously. "And all I have to do is my homework?"

"I'd take you whether you did it or not," Lauren said flat out. "But you know what? Max has got an awful lot on his mind right now, and I think it would be nice for him to come home and find that you'd done your homework and chores without me even suggesting it. What do you think?"

This time his eyes narrowed to mere slits. "You mean you're not going to tell him that I gave you a hard time?"

Lauren smiled. "Have you given me a hard time?"

His eyes rolled once again. "Okay, but you'd better be really good at history, because I'm lousy," Ryan said, heading off to the kitchen.

Lauren wasn't about to tell him she was pretty lousy at history, too. They'd just have to fumble through it together.

Jamie had already pulled out a notebook and was working away at the coffee table. "Okay, Jamie," Lauren said, "how can I help you?"

"I'm pretty good at essays, but there is something else you can help me with."

"What's that?"

"Come here." Jamie tugged Lauren toward her bedroom, her small hand warm against Lauren's palm, and a lovely feeling hugged her heart.

Her good feelings nearly collapsed when she

saw the horrid decorating scheme in Jamie's room. The walls were plastered with posters of motorcycles and cars, when Lauren had fully expected to see frills.

"This is *your* room?" Lauren asked.

"I keep telling Max that I want posters of the Backstreet Boys and 'N Sync," Jamie said, "but he seems to think I'm not quite ready to like boys."

"Are you?"

Jamie wrinkled her nose. "They're okay. I figure I'll like them more in another six months or so, but my girlfriends all like boys, and it's kind of embarrassing when they come in here and see all these posters."

"Do you want me to talk to Max about it?"

"No," Jamie said, "he's not ready for me to make the leap from motorcycles to boys, so I'll wait awhile."

"So what is it you wanted to show me?"

"This," Jamie said, her voice full of defeat when she pulled a white J. C. Penney's bag from a drawer, opened it slowly, and drew out a plain white brassiere. "I needed a bra," she said, her pretty blue eyes frowning as she dangled the horrendous piece of stretchy cotton on her finger. "Max and I went shopping on Sunday, and *this* is what he said I should get."

"Oh, dear."

"I told him we should go to Victoria's Secret."

Lauren sat on the edge of the bed. "You're not quite ready for Victoria's Secret," she said, "but there's a wonderful lingerie shop on Worth Avenue that carries the most divine bras and panties. I shop there all the time and I bet we could find something perfect in your size. A little lace. A little silk. I think you'd look lovely in pink or green."

"I like lavender," Jamie said softly.

"Then that's what we'll get. Right after the homework's done."

Jamie sat beside her on the bed. "You know what, Lauren?"

"What?"

"Max doesn't really date a lot of women."

"Not even a stripper?"

"Heck no!"

That was a relief.

"And," Jamie added, "I think he likes brown hair, even if it is dyed."

Lauren smiled. She'd never been flattered quite so nicely. On top of that, she'd come to the conclusion that her instincts weren't half bad, and she might even make a pretty good mother after all.

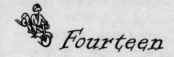 *Fourteen*

*M*ax rolled down the window to let the warm spring air blow about him as he followed Harry's directions to the house where Charlotte lived, just a twenty-minute drive from the Phoenix airport. Saguaro cactus and sand streaked by as he headed along the highway at seventy-five. He'd stopped in Phoenix ten years before, when he'd made his first trip to Hollywood to look for his brother and sister. He wondered if Charlotte had lived there then, if he might have seen her on that trip, and not even recognized her.

He passed a run-down trailer park with a sign hanging lopsided over the entrance reading SHADY GROVE, reminding him of a trailer he'd lived in with his mom, dad, brother, and sister, a one-bedroom single-wide parked in the vacant lot behind the Boardwalk Tavern, where his mom waited tables.

Max rarely allowed his mind to wander back to his childhood, to a father who drifted from one minimum-wage job to another until he drifted completely from sight.

Larry Wilde had a heavy hand and a fast-action belt, and he'd used both whenever and wherever the mood struck, his target most often Max. His mom, Loretta, never raised her hand against her husband, never raised her voice. She just put up with the man.

It went without saying that Larry hadn't been much of a dad, and Max couldn't remember wanting to know what had happened to him. He'd gone away, and good riddance had been Max's only thought.

When his mother left, Max had a different attitude. He'd just turned ten, and he was hurt, angry, and not about to stay with Rich Hunt, the man who owned the Boardwalk Tavern, just one boyfriend out of many Loretta had used. Before Rich shoved Max off on the foster system, Max had run away three times. Then he'd run away from five or six foster homes before he ended up with Philippe.

Loretta Wilde had promised to send for him once she got settled in Hollywood, but Max couldn't remember her being all that good at keeping promises, or caring all that much about what happened to him. Whether or not she ever tried to find him, Max didn't know. But he doubted it. The only kids she'd seemed to have had some feelings for were Charlotte and Zack, because she'd taken them with her when she headed for California.

Zack was seven, Charlotte only four when he saw them last. Zack had had pudgy cheeks, curly black hair and wanted to be a cop. Charlotte's eyes had been big and brown, and she'd loved to sing and dance.

They'd eaten a lot of Kraft Macaroni & Cheese when they were little. A lot of canned pork and beans. In the afternoons they'd watch soap operas with their mom, and one night a week they were allowed to stay up late and watch the *Dukes of Hazzard*. Max had few memories left of those days, because he'd blocked everything but his brother and sister out of his mind.

Zack was dead now, killed in a car accident six months before Max tracked down the cemetery where he'd been buried. The only thing he'd been able to find out about his brother was that he'd been a cop, that he didn't have a family, his friends said he was a good man, and he shouldn't have died . . . but he had.

Max had placed flowers on the grave, cursed his mother for separating them, and became even more resolved to find Charlotte. With all his heart, he hoped the woman he was about to see was really his sister.

Max found the house on the outskirts of town. It was a sprawling place with white stucco walls and a red-tiled roof. The yard was sand instead of grass, landscaped with yucca, saguaro, and cholla cactus. Desert flowers bloomed yellow and red in the sunshine. It was a much nicer place than the trailer he and Charlotte had shared as kids.

Pulling into the drive, Max couldn't miss Harry, a barrel-chested man in a blue polo shirt and khakis leaning against a white Ford Explorer. Harry Crow said he'd meet Max there at two P.M., and he was as good as his word.

Max walked toward the man with the gray crewcut. "Afternoon," he said, shaking Harry's hand.

"Good to see you, Max."

Max's gaze drifted toward the house. He could see a woman's silhouette behind the white lace curtains. "Is that Charlotte?" he asked.

"No. Mrs. Ryan, her guardian."

Max watched the curtains flutter behind the window, and then the woman's silhouette disappeared. "She is expecting me, isn't she?"

"Yeah, and she's not too receptive to the idea of you coming. At first I thought this was a care home, that she got money for looking after Charlotte, but I was wrong. This is a real home, clean, neat, and she and Mr. Ryan treat Charlotte like a daughter. You'll see when you go inside."

That was the best news Max had heard about Charlotte so far. He didn't know Charlotte's mental capabilities, but he'd been afraid of finding his sister living in squalor, unbathed, unloved, and left to fend for herself. The first foster home he'd run away from was like that, where the people who had taken him in did it for money only. He knew that the system tried to provide the best environment for children—and even adults who needed to be in assisted living—but sometimes the system failed.

He was glad Charlotte Wilde—whether she was his sister or not—had ended up in a home where she was loved.

He looked at the house again, took off his sunglasses, and tucked them in his shirt pocket.

"You want me to go in with you?" Harry asked.

Max shook his head. He had twenty years worth of emotions bottled up inside. He didn't care if Harry saw him cry. That wasn't why he wanted to go in alone. He just wanted a few private moments, time to look at this Charlotte Wilde, to remember the little girl he'd laughed with, played with . . . then lost. He wanted time to adjust to finding her again, or to deal with his heartache if this was another wild-goose chase.

He grabbed a bouquet of spring flowers from the front seat of his rental car and walked toward the house. The screen door opened before he could knock.

"I'm Mrs. Ryan," the woman extending her hand said. She was average height, slender, and her short hair seemed to have turned solid gray far too early, considering the youthfulness of her face.

"I'm Max Wilde," he said. "I'm sure Harry told you why I'm here."

Her gaze traveled to Harry, then back again to

Max. "I can appreciate you wanting to find your sister, but I'm sure Charlotte's not the woman you're looking for."

"Why do you say that? I was under the impression you didn't know much about her background."

Mrs. Ryan studied him for a long time, summing him up, Max imagined. "I don't want to lose her," she admitted, a touch of sadness in her eyes, making Max wonder if what he was doing was right, but he'd come this far. He couldn't back down now.

"I didn't want to lose my sister, either," Max told her, "but I didn't have any say in the matter."

"I understand that, but—" She looked away, but Max couldn't miss the moisture in her eyes. She sighed heavily. "I'm sorry, but this has taken me by surprise. After all these years, I never expected someone to show up claiming they're related to Charlotte."

"She might not be my sister, Mrs. Ryan, but I'll never know if you don't let me see her."

She stared at him a moment, then stepped aside and gestured for him to enter. "Charlotte's been with my husband and me for eight years now," she said, closing the door behind Max. "There are times when she makes me want to tear my hair out. Times when I wonder what possessed me to take on this responsibility. But when Charlotte smiles, when she puts her arms around me and says, 'I love you,' I realize I wouldn't give her up for the world."

She walked across the cozy living room decorated in shades of blue with lace and ruffles everywhere, and stood at the entrance to the hallway. "Charlotte was—we guess—about fifteen when she came here. She's beautiful, Mr. Wilde. She's sweet . . . and even though she's a grown woman, her mental age is only around five or six."

"Was she in a foster home?" Max asked, needing to know more about her history. "Is that how she came to live with you?"

Mrs. Ryan shook her head. "Some hikers found her in the desert. She'd been beaten and . . . molested." She put her fingers to her mouth, but Max could still see her trembling lips. "My husband's a sheriff's deputy and he was the one who brought her in. She didn't have any ID on her, she didn't fit any missing person's reports, and she couldn't give them any information at all. She just stared at the wall. It took a long time for her to remember her name—but she's never mentioned her past. We don't know if she doesn't remember, or if she chooses not to talk about what she does remember."

"She doesn't talk about her family? Old friends?"

"Nothing from before she came here. Seeing you—if you are her brother—could be the best thing for her. Then, again, you could frighten her, send her back into that not-talking stage."

"I've spent twenty years wanting to see my sister," Max stated. "I don't want to hurt you, and the last thing I want is to hurt the woman you've been caring for. But I need to see her. I need to know if she is—or isn't—my sister."

Mrs. Ryan stared at him again, at the flowers clutched in his hands. She took a deep breath and walked down the hall.

She put her hand on the doorknob, and looked at Max. "She knows you're coming. I've told her you're a friend of my husband's and that you wanted to meet her."

"Is she used to strangers?"

Mrs. Ryan nodded, a small smile touching her face. "She has a job two days a week, working for a recycler. It's supervised, she gets to spend time with friends—people she can relate to—and she gets a little spending money. She likes to buy stuffed animals. You'll see."

Mrs. Ryan opened the door, and the first thing that caught Max's eye was a canopy bed at the far side of the room. The sheets, pillows, and canopy were decorated with Winnie-the-Pooh. Stuffed animals littered the floor and every imaginable surface. There were two big windows, and the sun streamed through one, casting light on a young woman sitting cross-legged on the floor, with an oversized picture book open in her lap.

"Charlotte," Mrs. Ryan said, her voice sweet, kind. "This is the man I told you about. Max Wilde."

Charlotte *was* beautiful, just as he'd been told. Her hair was long and black, and she wore it in a braid that hung over one shoulder. Her eyes were big and brown and she had a beautiful smile. If only she would stand, Max thought. His mother had been tall. If this Charlotte was, too, that would be another characteristic that might prove she was the sister he sought.

"You have the same last name as me," Charlotte said. She spoke slowly, as if she had to concentrate on how to string a sentence together, but he liked the childish delight in her voice and the sparkle in her eyes.

Twenty years had gone by without seeing his sister, and now he didn't know what to say, so he merely walked across the room and handed her the flowers.

"Thank you," she said politely. "I like flowers. These are carnations." She pointed to the fluffy yellow chrysanthemums, and Max ignored her mistake. Hell, not everyone knew the difference between the two flowers.

"What are you reading?" he asked, sitting cross-legged on the floor in front of her.

"*Beauty and the Beast*," she said, dragging her finger from word to word as she spoke. "Mama reads it to me a lot. I'm not a good reader. Mostly I just look at the pictures."

"Would you like me to read it to you?"

She looked to Mrs. Ryan for approval, and when the older woman nodded, Charlotte handed him the book.

He heard Mrs. Ryan's shoes on the floor and watched her out of the corner of his eye. Sitting on the edge of the bed, she picked up one of the stuffed animals and held it tightly in her lap. Max wanted time alone, but he couldn't help but admire Mrs. Ryan for not leaving Charlotte with a "stranger."

He opened the book to the first page, remembering back to the days long ago, when he'd read to his sister and brother most every night. It didn't matter to Charlotte and Zack what Max read, as long as the three of them were together.

And then they'd been pulled apart.

Max flipped to the second page where the story began. "Once upon a time . . ." he read, his gaze fluttering up occasionally to look at Charlotte, wishing there was some way he could know for sure if she were his sister. Her hair was the right color, so were her eyes. He couldn't remember any birthmarks, couldn't remember any scars. Twenty years had wiped out a lot of memories, and now it seemed that the only way he'd ever know for sure was through blood or DNA testing. He hadn't wanted to resort to that, but it seemed there was no other choice. He needed to know the truth.

Charlotte moved closer to him as he read, repeating his words, pointing out Belle, Mrs. Potts, and Chip, the same way his own Charlotte had pointed out characters when he'd read one of her favorite stories.

Across the room he saw Mrs. Ryan lift her glasses to wipe her eyes with a tissue, and Max was afraid he couldn't take Charlotte away from this woman, even if he did find proof she was his sister.

He finished the story and closed the book.

"Read another one," Charlotte said.

"One's enough," Mrs. Ryan told her. "Mr. Wilde has a plane to catch."

He didn't, of course, because he hadn't known when he'd be leaving or whether he'd need one seat or two on the return trip. He knew the answer now. He'd be heading home on his own.

Cradling Charlotte's cheek in his palm, he felt a heaviness in his heart. She was sweet and lovely, but *this* was her home now. He could never take her away from here. "It was nice meeting you," he said softly. She smiled back, opened another book, and stared at the pictures.

Mrs. Ryan led him from the room, closing the door behind him. "Is she your sister?" she asked, a touch of worry lining her brow.

"I don't know. I don't have any pictures. No fingerprints. I'd like to have some blood work done."

Mrs. Ryan shook her head and tears fell from her eyes. "No. I've let you see her. I've let you talk to her—but that's enough!"

"I need to know for sure, Mrs. Ryan, and that's the only way I'm going to find out."

"Then you'll have to get a court order."

Max plowed his fingers through his hair. Mrs. Ryan didn't want to give up her daughter and he couldn't give up trying to find out if he'd finally found his sister. "I know you love her, but—"

"I'm not going to let you take her away. I don't care if she's your sister or not."

"I don't want to take her away. I did at first, but it's obvious she belongs here. I just need to know the truth."

The door opened, and Charlotte stepped close to Mrs. Ryan. "What's wrong, Mama?"

Mrs. Ryan smiled. "Nothing at all," she said, smoothing a hand across Charlotte's cheek. "We were just talking a little too loudly, I'm afraid. Why don't you go back in your room and play while I say goodbye to Mr. Wilde."

"Could I go outside and water the flowers?"

"Of course."

Charlotte looked at Max with big brown eyes. " 'Bye, Mr. Wilde," she said, waving as she made her way down the hall, letting Max see for the first time that she walked with a limp, that one leg was decidedly shorter than the other.

He stared at her, remembering the way his own Charlotte had loved to dance, that her legs had been perfect.

"I rarely notice Charlotte's limp," Mrs. Ryan said, when Charlotte was out of sight. "I should have mentioned it before, but it isn't something I think about. The doctors told us she was born that way. It isn't something that happened when she was abused. I know you think I might be lying, to cover up her identity. But you can contact our doctor for verification if you wish."

"I believe you, Mrs. Ryan."

She touched Max's arm gently. "Did your sister ever have trouble walking?"

Max shook his head. "No," he said, fighting back the well of disappointment behind his eyes.

"Then I'm sorry," Mrs. Ryan said. "I don't want to lose Charlotte, that's why I was against you coming here, why I didn't want you doing blood tests. But part of me was hoping she was your sister, just so you could tell me what she was like as a little girl."

"I'm sure she's always been wonderful," Max said, then headed for the front door. He had to get out of this house, back in the car. He needed to be alone with his thoughts.

He shook Mrs. Ryan's hand when he reached the front door. "I'm sorry I bothered you. I hope I didn't cause any problems for Charlotte."

"She'll be fine," Mrs. Ryan said, and a tear slipped from her eye. "I hope you find your sister."

"Thanks."

Max opened the door and let himself out, waving to Mrs. Ryan when he reached the car.

The door closed behind her, and he took a deep breath before looking directly at Harry.

"Any luck?" Harry asked.

"No," Max said, and shook Harry's hand. "I guess that means you're still in my employ."

"Not exactly the words I wanted to hear, but I'll be back at work tomorrow, hot on the trail. I'll find your sister, Max. Trust me."

"I'm holding you to that. She's out there somewhere, and I don't plan to ever give up looking."

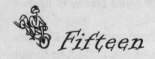

Fifteen

*T*he flight out of Phoenix was late and Max almost missed his connection in Dallas. He'd run through the terminal, was the last passenger to board the plane, and had to squeeze into the middle seat, between an elderly woman wearing too much perfume and an overweight, sweaty businessman who continually mumbled about his bad day as he slugged down one drink after another.

Max had tried to sleep, but the plane tossed and turned through storm clouds. His own mind was just as turbulent, as thoughts of Mrs. Ryan, the Charlotte Wilde he'd seen today, and his own sister thundered through his mind. Exhaustion told him he should give up his search, that he'd never find the real Charlotte, that he was wasting time, money, and energy. His heart said just the opposite.

He pulled into his driveway at two A.M. The lights were off in the house and all was quiet. If this were any other night, if he'd had someone other than Lauren watching the kids, he'd send the sitter home and head for bed. But tonight he needed to talk. Tonight he needed to hold someone—and Lauren was the woman he wanted in his arms.

He wondered if Jamie and Ryan had tortured her, if they'd made her afternoon and evening absolute hell with their playful bickering, their refusal to do chores and homework. They could be a handful. Of course, Lauren could be a handful, too, and he had the feeling the kids had met their match.

Walking into the laundry room was a shock. The socks and towels that had been scattered on the floor that morning were nowhere in sight, and the month's worth of smelly gym clothes Ryan had emptied out of his locker at school had been laundered and folded, and sat on top the washer next to a purple tote bag. He could smell the sweetness of Lauren's perfume on the bag, and ran his fingers over it lightly as he headed for the kitchen.

The dirty dishes he'd expected to see stacked a mile high on the counter didn't exist. A vase full of plumeria sat in the middle of the table, the strong fragrance wafting through the kitchen, which usually smelled of spices, fruits, and barbecued meat. The change wasn't bad. In fact, he could get used to having flowers in the house on occasion.

The key he'd left for Lauren in a potted fern that hung on the patio lay on the table beside a list of emergency contacts and phone numbers, plus homework and bedtime instructions. A bold red checkmark followed each one of the assignments and chores, and scribbled at the bottom he read:

Dear Max,

Thank you so much for asking me to watch Jamie and Ryan. This was the second best time of my life. The first was Saturday evening with you.

Lauren

He chuckled to himself, folded the note, and stuck it into the inside pocket of his jacket, just in case she ever needed a reminder that kids could be fun, or that Lauren had spent the best night of her life with him.

He dropped his leather jacket over a kitchen chair, realizing that he was just as big an offender as the kids when it came to messing up the place. He pulled off his boots and socks and crept into the living room, not wanting to wake Lauren if she was asleep on the couch.

The coffee and end tables should have been cluttered with bags of chips and half-full cans of soda. MTV should have been blaring on an unwatched TV. But the room was spotless except for schoolbooks, neatly closed.

Lauren must have bribed them. He couldn't think of any other reason the house would be clean, unless Lauren had done the work herself. That thought made him laugh. Miss Palm Beach might not be all that domestic, but the little things she did brought joy to his life. What more did a man need?

Heading down the hallway, he eased open Ryan's door and stepped inside, maneuvering around basketballs, gym clothes, tennis shoes, and jeans. The clean house stopped at the red and white DO NOT ENTER sign posted on the outside of Ryan's bedroom door. Ryan liked the "feel" of his mess and didn't want anyone touching his stuff. Max didn't come unglued about the state of the room. If Ryan wanted to live in a pigsty, that was his choice. He'd outgrow it sooner or later.

Over the past two years Ryan had amassed a roomful of sports memorabilia, not to mention walls covered with Michael Jordan, Larry Bird, and Kareem Abdul-Jabbar posters. On the table next to his bed was the lockbox where he kept his collection of basketball cards, including the ones signed by Magic Johnson, Charles Barkley, and his all-time favorite, Wilt Chamberlain.

Max had no doubt Ryan could end up with a basketball scholarship. He'd encourage the boy in every way he could, but he wouldn't make decisions for him. Ryan knew right from wrong, he knew what he had to do to get ahead, but the choices were his own to make. If he stumbled and fell, well, he'd just have to pick himself up and move on. That's what Max had been taught, and it had served him well.

That didn't mean, however, that he didn't have a soft side.

Looking at Ryan sprawled on top of his bed, the covers in a heap on the floor, his arms curled around a basketball, made Max realize just how much he loved him. He leaned over the bed and pressed a kiss to Ryan's forehead, something he wasn't allowed to do when the boy was awake. Philippe had kissed him that way, too, always late at night when he thought Max was asleep. Max hadn't liked outward displays of affection anymore than Ryan did. But he'd liked it when Philippe had come into his room, pulled the covers up to his chest, and gently cupped his hand around Max's shoulder. Max had never opened his eyes, never let Philippe know that he was awake. He just enjoyed knowing he was loved.

Making his way back through the hovel, he closed Ryan's door and went to Jamie's room. That's where he found Lauren, sitting in a chair beside Jamie's bed with an open book in her lap, her eyes closed, her head tilted to one side as she slept. It didn't matter how many times he saw her—or how she looked when he saw her—he always found her beautiful. This morning, though, sitting by his daughter, she was prettier than ever.

He wanted to wake her, wanted to hold her, but he let her sleep, and went to Jamie instead. He sat on the edge of the bed and brushed a lock of hair from his little girl's brow. Pulling the sheet up to her shoulders, he kissed her forehead. She stirred, her eyes fluttering open then closed again as she tucked her hands beneath her cheek, and settled back into sleep.

He stood slowly, noticing in the moonlight that the far corner of Jamie's room was piled high with white, black, pink, and gold shopping bags with the names of exclusive Palm Beach shops emblazoned on their sides. The bribe! He should have known.

"We had fun." He turned at the sound of Lauren's whisper. Her eyes were open, watching him, and he held out his hand to her. The minute their fingers touched, he realized how much he needed her, how much he loved her warmth, the comfort that he found having her near. They'd known each other just a few days, but it seemed a lifetime.

"You look tired," she said, gently touching his cheek when they stepped into the hallway and he quietly closed Jamie's door.

"It's been a long day."

"I could tell that from the phone message you left." She reached out and smoothed a strand of hair from his brow. "I'm sorry you didn't find your sister."

"This isn't the first time I've gone on a wild goose chase."

Her fingers lingered at his cheek then slowly curled around his neck. "Why don't I fix you a drink?"

"That's not what I need." He lowered his mouth to hers, finding something far more potent than liquor to enjoy. His kiss was soft at first, but the feel of her breasts against his chest and the beat of her heart matching the rapid thump of his own made him want so much more.

He pressed her against the wall, his hands cupping her face, holding her mouth close as his tongue swept inside, danced with hers, and tasted her sweetness. His breath was ragged, his body hard with need. God, he wanted her. He needed her to wipe out the frustration and regret of the day, but reality surfaced.

His kiss slowed, gentled. "I want you more than I've ever wanted anyone," he whispered, "but not in the hallway, not with Jamie and Ryan close by."

She slipped her fingers through his and tugged him down the hallway. When they reached the laundry room, she grabbed the tote bag and her shoes from the top of the washer. "It's been a long day, Max. You need to sleep and I should head for home."

"If I went to bed right now all I'd do is toss and turn. I need to talk about today, about you and me, about where we're going from here."

Her gaze shot to her purple bag. "I brought a swimsuit." Her hands slipped up his arms and did wonders on the hard, tense muscles in his shoulders. "It's warm out and the pool's inviting. We could talk. You could relax."

Relax? Hell, he hadn't forgotten how seductive she'd looked walking out of her swimming pool, hadn't forgotten her alluring curves, the way his body had hardened at the sight of her. "Getting into the water with you could be dangerous."

"All I plan to do is swim."

"I might have other ideas in mind."

Her soft lips tilted into a smile. "I'll take my chances."

Had he gone plumb loco? he wondered, when she headed to the bathroom to change. How could he get into the swimming pool with Lauren and not do something rash? He didn't want her in a swimsuit, no matter how sexy she looked. He wanted her naked, and he wanted to spend hours exploring all her luscious curves, every nook and cranny.

But not in his backyard pool. Not when Jamie or Ryan could wake up and stumble outside to find them. Somehow or other he was going to have to keep his lust under control, but that was easier said than done around Miss Palm Beach.

He went to his room, stripped out of his clothes, and pulled on a baggy pair of swim trunks. Stepping in front of the mirror, he took a look at himself, wondering what a woman like Lauren Remington could possibly see in him—especially now. He had a day's growth of heavy black stubble on his cheeks and dark circles ringed his eyes. Not an impressive sight.

A few quick swipes with a razor took care of the stubble. There wasn't much he could do about the exhaustion that was evident on his face, but he took a toothbrush to his teeth and felt somewhat human again.

He also felt like a schoolboy on his very first date.

Lauren, however, was far from being a schoolgirl.

Grabbing a couple of towels from the linen closet, he headed outside into the warm night air. Lauren was already there, standing breast deep and looking drop-dead gorgeous with the moonlit water lapping about her body. He dropped the towels on a patio chair and dove into the pool.

The underwater lights shimmered on her legs, which fluttered back and forth, keeping her afloat. He circled her body, stroking her hips, the outsides of her thighs, as he swam, and watched, and felt his need for her rise to an all-time high.

Putting his hands on her hips, he pulled himself to the surface. Their eyes met. Danger and desire were only a heartbeat away. He moved in for a kiss, but she shoved away from him, laughing as she swam to the steps at the shallow end.

"Frightened?" He focused on her pretty green eyes, while stroking through the water toward her.

She shook her head. "Not of you."

"What are you afraid of then?" he asked, standing over her, water dripping from his hair to her upturned face.

"My reactions to you. I need to go slow, but I want to move fast, and those two emotions are doing battle with each other."

"Just do what feels right to you."

She put her hand on his stomach, swirling her

fingers through the hair on his chest. "Touching you feels right." He gritted his teeth as she kissed his navel, and fire shot through his loins.

Bracing his hands on her knees, he spread her legs gently. He wanted to slide his fingers under her bathing suit and feel the heat inside her. It would have been so easy, but that wasn't his intention now. He lowered himself into the water, sat between her thighs, and they squeezed around him.

Like a woman born to pamper a man, she kneaded the muscles along his spine with her fingers, working her way up to his shoulders, his neck. "Relax," she whispered.

His head fell forward as her fingers worked their magic.

"Tell me about your sister," she said, drawing his head back to rest beneath her chin as she gently massaged his temples. "What's her name?"

"Charlotte."

"Do you think she might have changed her name? That she might have been adopted? That might be why you're having trouble finding her."

"I've thought a million things since I started searching, the only thing I won't allow myself to think is that she might be dead." He closed his eyes, drew one of her hands to his mouth, and pressed a slow, lingering kiss to her palm. "Sometimes, like today, it seems useless to keep looking."

"Why?"

"I've been searching since I was twenty. I spent

a couple of years riding from town to town trying to come up with leads, but I couldn't find a thing, except my mother, and she was a dead end." He pulled Lauren's arms around him, hugging them close to his chest, soaking in her comfort. He told Lauren about being deserted at ten, about his mother driving off with his brother and sister and promising to send for him, about finding out that Zack was dead.

"When I found my mother she was living in Brentwood, in a place that was a far cry from the trailer where I'd been raised. She had a rich husband, she had the life she'd always dreamed of, and she didn't want memories or the reality of her past messing up what she had."

"But she must have been happy to see you."

Max laughed. "I showed up on her doorstep and you would have thought I was a complete stranger. She told me to go away, but I walked right into her house, for all the good that did. She didn't want to talk to me, claimed she didn't know who I was talking about when I mentioned Charlotte and Zack, and said she'd never had a son named Max. Then she picked up the phone to call the police. That's when I left, and I didn't bother going back again."

"I'm sorry, Max."

"It's history. I don't think about her. I try not to think about Zack because I can't bring him back, but I can't get Charlotte off my mind."

"You'll find her," Lauren whispered, and kissed his shoulder before he pushed away from her and easily switched places, drawing her luscious hips between his thighs, her sleek back against his chest.

"It's my turn to ease some of your tension," he said, sliding his hands over her arms, her shoulders, gently kneading the tightness at the base of her neck. He could easily run his fingers under her bathing suit and drive her mad with passion, then satisfy his own burning need, but holding her, touching her, talking to her tonight was what she needed. And that made him feel good inside.

He kissed the top of her head, resting his chin in the softness of her hair. "Tell me about your day."

She swirled her fingers over his thigh, her touch driving him mad, making him want to forget all about talking. But when she started to recount the day's events, he was caught up in the happiness of her voice.

"I think I might make a good mother after all," she said. "I didn't have to threaten or raise my voice, and once Jamie and Ryan realized that I couldn't be intimidated, we got along fine."

"I suppose the shopping trip did wonders, too?"

She tilted her head upward, and he could see the smile in her eyes. "Shopping is one of the highlights of life."

"I saw a new basketball in Ryan's room. Did he get that before or after he did his history assignments?"

"After, of course. I thought we'd never get his

homework done. Goodness, Max, he hates history more than I do."

"And what about Jamie?" he asked, trailing his fingers along the top edge of her suit, fighting the urge to circle them over the hardened nipples he could see through the stretchy lavender fabric. "What did you buy her?"

"Girl stuff. Some adorable shirts, a pair of sandals, some panties and bras."

His fingers stilled. "Did she talk you into that?"

"Of course not. It was all my idea."

"But she has clothes, she has sandals, and she *has* bras!"

Lauren twisted around, hitting him with a frown. "You call those dreadful things you bought her bras?"

"She's eleven years old, for God's sake! What more does she need?"

"Something frilly and feminine, which is exactly what I purchased."

"Not at Victoria's Secret, I hope?"

"Of course not. We went to the boutique where I buy most all of my lingerie. I actually found a few things that weren't too expensive."

His entire body tensed. "And what exactly is your definition of not too expensive?"

"A hundred dollars or so."

"For how many? Half a dozen?"

"Don't be silly. That was for one bra and a matching pair of panties, and I couldn't believe our luck that they had the same thing in seven different colors."

"So you bought all seven?"

She smiled sweetly. "A set for each day of the week."

Max plowed his fingers through his hair. "You know, Lauren, I do okay with my catering business. I've got a house that's paid for and I've made some smart investments that help me live comfortably, but if I have to buy hundred-dollar bras every time I turn around, I'll be broke in a year."

"What I purchased today was a gift. Purely a girl thing, because honestly, Max, Jamie needed someone like me to take her shopping for bras. Of course, she'll grow out of them soon—"

"I don't want to hear about it."

"It's a fact of life."

"I'm only interested in one pair of breasts," he barked, staring at the objects he'd become quite fond of in recent days. "*Your* breasts are the *only* breasts I want to talk about, the *only* breasts I want to think about, and the *only* breasts I want to touch."

Lauren smiled. "Oh, Max, you say the sweetest things."

"Don't get too used to it." He grinned. "It takes a lot of energy for me to say something that creative."

"I don't think it takes any energy at all." She moved closer and lightly kissed his lips. "You just get disgruntled and all sorts of things flow from this wonderful mouth of yours."

"Getting disgruntled comes easily when you're around."

"I know," she said, pushing away from him

and climbing from the pool. "That's why I'm leaving," she said, combing her fingers through her hair and smoothing it away from her face. "If I stick around much longer you're going to be all tense again, and you won't be able to sleep."

"I'm tense right now, and the last thing I want to do is sleep." He followed her across the patio and wrapped one of the towels about her.

"I know what you want to do," she said, lifting his hands to her mouth and kissing his knuckles. "I want the same thing."

"Then don't leave. I'll turn out the lights, we'll get back in the pool."

"There's a time and place for everything," she said, the voice of reason when all his sensibilities had left him. "This isn't it."

"Tomorrow night, then. I'll get someone to watch the kids."

She stilled his words with another kiss. "Mrs. Fisk, my cook, came home this afternoon. My mother's gone and my house is virtually empty. Why don't you come for dinner at eight? Maybe you can tell me again that my breasts are the only ones you want to touch."

He kissed her lightly. "I'll show you instead."

She smiled, and all too soon pulled away from him, grabbed her tote bag, and headed for her car. His arms felt empty; he wanted her back. But tomorrow night she wouldn't leave. Tomorrow night he'd have all that he wanted.

Lauren rolled down the car window after she started the engine. "I'll have Charles bring up the best bottle of wine from the cellar, and I'll tell Mrs. Fisk not to bother with dessert."

"Good," Max said. "We'll have each other instead."

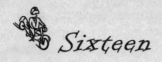 *Sixteen*

*L*auren spent half the morning zipping in and out of Ralph Lauren, Chanel, and Cartier, looking for the perfect clothing and accessories for a romantic evening. She had the oddest feeling that Max didn't give a fig for what she wore, in fact, he'd probably prefer her in nothing at all, but she did want to look her best when he peeled away every speck of her attire.

When noon rolled around, she strolled into Frederico's for the works. Pasta and shrimp was brought in for her while Frederico did her hair. She sipped Perrier as Lola manicured her nails and Linda gave her a facial. She opted for Chablis when Shirley applied the wax to her legs and other portions of her anatomy. As often as she'd gone through this routine, it still made her tense, and the wine soothed her anxiety.

"Holly Rutherford was in here early this morning," Shirley chirped, then happily ripped off a strip of cooled wax. "That woman can definitely talk up a storm. Naturally I heard all about the disaster with her wedding cake for the umpteenth time."

"Is she still blaming it on me?" Lauren asked through nearly clenched teeth.

"Well, of course she is, but we all know you weren't responsible." Shirley leaned close to Lauren's ear. "Mrs. Rutherford's very chintzy when it comes to tipping, unlike you. On top of that, she's informed every one of us that we're to call her *Mrs.* Rutherford and not Holly any longer, considering that she's a married woman now." Shirley shook her head. "That woman's attitude is just too high and mighty to suit me or anyone else around here, so she doesn't get special privileges. And when it comes to who we like and who we don't like, as well as who we believe and who we don't believe, she's at the bottom of the scale and you, sweetie, are right up there at the top."

"That means a lot to me, Shirley."

"We like the fact that you're not a gossip, either. Holly Rutherford, on the other hand, goes nonstop from the moment she walks in here till the moment she leaves. I don't know anyone in Palm Beach who's escaped that woman's tongue. And now she's hitting on people in West Palm Beach. Can you believe that?"

Shirley spread wax high on Lauren's inner thigh and kept right on talking. "This morning she gave me the complete low-down on her stolen jewelry."

Lauren's ears perked up at the mention of another jewelry theft. "Did she say what was taken?"

"Naturally, and of course we didn't escape hearing *any* of the details. A fifty-four-carat aquamarine and diamond pendant. Mrs. Rutherford was very explicit about the size of the aquamarine, wanting us to know that's she filthy rich, as if her high and mighty attitude didn't give us a clue."

"Did she say when it was stolen? Where?"

"She believes it happened last Saturday, probably at Betsy Endicott's wedding." A gasp escaped from Shirley's lips. "Goodness gracious sakes alive! Betsy's wedding was at your place. You didn't have anything stolen, did you?"

"Of course not." Lauren wasn't about to tell Shirley about Bunny Endicott's necklace or the fact that Bunny was sure it had disappeared during the wedding. She definitely wouldn't mention Bunny's suspicions about Max's friends.

"I bet Holly misplaced her necklace," Lauren stated. "You know how forgetful people can be at times."

"Mrs. Rutherford said she *might* have misplaced it, because she can't remember if she wore the missing necklace or another diamond and aquamarine pendant to the wedding. *But* she did tell the police that it may have disappeared at

Betsy Endicott's wedding because, *apparently*, Bunny Endicott *swears* a piece of her jewelry disappeared that day, too."

Oh, dear! "Have the police done anything about it?" Lauren asked, as Shirley finished the last speck of Lauren's inner thighs.

"Mrs. Rutherford called them buffoons, said they weren't terribly concerned about her fifty-four-carat aquamarine and diamond pendant. Apparently they told her to report it to her insurance company."

"That's it? No investigation?"

"Well, she did say that there'd been some rather odd people catering Betsy Endicott's wedding. That's what I was saying, about her going on and on about *those* people from West Palm Beach. Obviously she didn't realize that *I* live in West Palm Beach. Then again, maybe she didn't care that she offended me. Anyway, she said she told the police that any one of *those* people could have been responsible."

Oh, dear!

"She also said, if I'm not mistaken, that the police went to your house and talked to your butler."

"*They did?*"

"I believe that's what she said, but why wouldn't you know anything about that if it was true?"

That was a question Lauren was dying to get an answer to as well.

* * *

Lauren found Charles sitting at the kitchen table with Mrs. Fisk, listening to one of the cook's tales about her escapades on the beach in Tahiti. "He was absolutely gorgeous, Charles. Simply stunning, and he made the most delicious mai tai. Rose—you remember her, my friend from Miami? Well, Rose thinks the bartender must have been gay, but I don't care. I could have sat at that bar on the beach and stared at him all day long."

Lauren cleared her throat. "Excuse me for interrupting."

"Oh, don't worry at all about that, Miss Remington," Mrs. Fisk chortled, waving a freshly baked cookie in the air in front of her. "I was just telling Charles about the bartender I met in Tahiti. Why, if I was twenty-five again instead of sixty-three, I would have scooped that young man up in a moment—gay or not."

"I'm glad you had such a lovely time."

"It was wonderful, thank you." Mrs. Fisk took a bite of cookie. "By the way, I've decided on the entrée for tonight. A new dish that a friend of mine has raved about—asparagus cannelloni with chanterelles. And Charles brought a lovely '96 Chateau St. Jean Chardonnay up from the cellar."

"I'm sure the dinner will be perfect, as always," Lauren said, although dinner was the last thing on her mind at the moment. She was far more concerned about the accusations being aimed at Max and his friends.

She turned her eyes on her butler. "Could I see you a moment, Charles?"

"Of course."

He followed her to the conservatory, where Lauren paced from one end to the other, several times, before Charles asked, "Is something troubling you, Miss Remington?"

She stopped, folded her hands behind her lemon chiffon halter dress, and hit him with a frown. "Were the police here recently?"

Charles's gaze darted toward the pink marble floor. "Why, yes, I do believe they were here while you were in New York."

"Mind if I ask why?"

"They had a few questions about the possible theft of some jewelry during Betsy Endicott's wedding."

"I see." She paced again, hating the fact that Charles was so secretive. "And were you able to help them?"

"I was able to tell them nothing," he said flatly, as if he'd been annoyed that the police had even come around. "I told them I did not see anything out of the ordinary during the wedding or reception. I told them that I did not see any suspicious-looking characters, nor did I see anyone wandering around the house as if they were looking for something to steal."

"Did they ask you about anyone specific?"

His white brows knit together. "They asked about Mr. Wilde and I told them that neither you nor I had any reason whatsoever to suspect Mr.

Wilde of being anything but a gracious and admirable chef. When they asked about his assistants, I also put in a good word for them. And then I advised them that one of the assistants was a vice cop."

Lauren smiled as relief flooded through her. "Thank you, Charles."

"You're quite welcome. I might also mention that I informed the officers that there were nearly two hundred guests here during Miss Endicott's wedding to Mr. Stribling, and that I would gladly give them a list of names, addresses, and phone numbers, because any one of those guests—rich or not—could have absconded with the jewels. I also mentioned that Mrs. Endicott and Mrs. Rutherford had made a point of showing their baubles off to everyone in attendance."

"You might have gone a little far with that last statement," Lauren said, even though she'd watched Holly showing off her latest acquisitions and Bunny had definitely displayed her *baubles*.

"Be that as it may," Charles added in his defense, "I felt their actions needed to be addressed."

"May I ask you one other question, Charles?"

"By all means."

"Why didn't you tell me about any of this?"

"I felt I could dispel all rumors and I didn't see the need to worry you."

"I appreciate that, but in the future, would you let me know so I don't hear these tales from the woman waxing my legs."

He folded his hands behind his back. "Very well."

"One other thing," Lauren said, walking across the room and staring Charles right in the eye.

"Yes?"

She slipped her arms around his neck, pressing her cheek against his. "I just wanted you to know that I love you, that I always have, and always will."

Lauren felt a little of the stiffness drain from Charles, felt one of his hands pat her gently on the back. "The feeling is mutual," he said, clearing his throat as he pulled from her embrace. "If you'll excuse me, I'll call Mr. Friedrichs and have him deliver a special centerpiece for tonight's dinner. Is there anything else you'd like?"

It was Lauren's turn to gaze down at the marble floor. She cleared her throat. "If it's not any trouble, could you put a bottle of Dom Perignon in my room during dinner tonight."

A hint of pink touched Charles's cheeks. "I believe I could do that. Might I also suggest dark chocolate Godivas. I picked up a box for myself just this morning and they haven't been touched. They might go quite well with champagne."

Lauren smiled, thinking they might go quite well with Max Wilde, too. She'd always enjoyed chocolate topping on her desserts. "You do think of everything, don't you, Charles?"

"I do my best."

"And I'm extremely grateful."

"I'll remind you of that when Christmas rolls

around," he said with a grin, then strolled out of the room without giving Lauren a second look.

With thoughts of stolen jewelry pushed from her mind, Lauren pulled her address book from her desk and scanned the names, looking for friends who'd recently announced their engagement.

She'd had fun planning Holly Rutherford's wedding and it had been a huge success except for the accident with the cake. And even though Henri had died and Betsy's wedding had almost fallen apart, Max had come to the rescue and the affair had turned out perfect.

Now that life was looking bright, it was time to drum up a little more business.

Paige Carlyle, the daughter of one of her mother's oldest and dearest friends, was first on her list.

"How are you?" Lauren asked, once the preliminary salutations were out of the way.

"I couldn't be more wonderful," Paige exclaimed. "Jeffrey and I just purchased a home in Newport. We're having it completely refurbished. Lillian Spradling, the decorator who did my parents' home in the Vineyard, is selecting all the furniture and art."

"It sounds lovely," Lauren said.

"It's going to be. Of course, it's nearly a year-long project, but Lillian's promised we'll be able to move into it right after our wedding and honeymoon next spring."

"You've set a date then?"

"February twelfth. Less than a year away."

"Goodness, the year will fly by with so much to do, selecting a place for the wedding and reception, finding the right dress, the perfect invitations. It amazes me sometimes how many details there are."

"I know what you're leading up to," Paige said, the disdainful tone of her voice taking Lauren by surprise. "I know you mean well, Lauren, but I need a professional planning my wedding. Too many things tend to go wrong when you're in charge."

"If you're referring to that silly cake incident?"

"Of course I'm referring to that. It was an utter disaster, and then there was the caterer you hired for Betsy's wedding."

"The food was delicious."

"Yes, that's true, but there's much more involved with catering than good food."

As if Paige Carlyle had any idea what was involved with anything!

"Betsy's a dear," Paige went on, "and I know she'd never say anything, but I'm sure she was absolutely mortified when she caught a glimpse of the waiters and found out that their normal routine is serving barbecues and luaus."

"I appreciate your opinion," Lauren said graciously, biting back her hurt. "If you'd like, I could recommend another planner."

"We already have several in mind and I'll be interviewing them soon."

"Well, I know you're busy and I don't want to take any more of your time," Lauren said. "If there's anything I can do to help—"

"Yes, I'll keep your offer in mind," Paige said. "I have to run now. Goodbye."

Lauren listened to the dial tone then glared at the phone. "I hope your cake falls in the pool, too!" she snapped.

She paced across the room, waiting for her anger to subside, then went back to the phone and punched in another phone number. She was not going to let an imperialistic snoot like Paige Carlyle get her down.

Blaine Whitfield, an old friend from Lauren's finishing school days, was much more congenial, but she hit her with a similar line. "Sorry, Lauren. Your weddings don't quite live up to our social status."

Kitty Burke was in tears when she answered the phone, having broken her engagement early that morning when she found her husband-to-be in the arms of another man.

And Suzie Frost, who'd once dated Chip and Leland and had had grand hopes of marrying one of them, was bitingly honest. "Your friends are laughing at you behind your back. Be careful, Lauren, or someday you'll look at your social calendar and find it's empty."

The names in the address book suddenly became one big blur as tears filled Lauren's eyes. As hard as she'd tried to plan the perfect wedding, as much as she'd wanted to succeed in business, she'd failed . . . again.

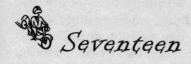# *Seventeen*

*M*ax was Lauren's salvation.

Only Max could take her mind off her troubles, and he did it with so little effort. A simple smile, the twitch of his mustache, and, of course, there was always his touch, which never failed to make her quiver inside.

The subject of her latest failure would not come up tonight. Tomorrow she might share her fears, but this evening she wanted to share something completely different—the passion that they felt for each other.

Taking one last look at herself in the hallway mirror, she assessed the sinfulness of her red silk dress. It plunged low in the front and even though the hem stopped well below her calves, the left side was slit nearly to her hip. She wore nothing under it but a skimpy red silk bra and even skimpier silk thong, and her only accessories were a pair of dangly ruby and diamond earrings, which set off her slicked-back hairdo, and her red-beaded Manolo Blahnik heels.

She needed nothing more to complete her new look—except Max.

She was halfway down the circular stairs when she saw him, a stunning sight in his black leather jacket, a white button-down shirt, black slacks, and a killer smile.

Later tonight, that smile would be the only thing she'd allow him to wear! And goodness, all her troubles would definitely fly out the door.

"Good evening," she said, taking the hand he held out to her and letting him pull her into his arms, the place she'd longed to be since she'd left him at three A.M.

"You're beautiful," he whispered against her ear, kissing her lightly and sending shivers of absolute delight through her entire body. She could stand here for hours enjoying the touch of his lips against her skin, but she planned to spend hours in his arms after dinner. Right now, she wanted to enjoy his laughter, their small talk. She wanted to share a fine bottle of wine and a good meal, and when she was relaxed, she'd take hold of his hand and lead him to her room, where champagne and Godivas awaited them.

She slipped just far enough away from him to hold on to what was left of her senses, and asked, "Would you like a drink before dinner?"

Apparently he didn't want her holding on to her senses because he pulled her right back into his arms. "I was thinking we might start with dessert, and skip dinner altogether."

His fingers roamed over the silky fabric, teased the curve of her spine and splayed over her bottom, tugging her against his hips, leaving no doubt at all where he wanted to start this evening.

"Dessert sounds lovely," she moaned against the soft, thrilling kisses he pressed to her lips. "But Mrs. Fisk has made something wonderful for dinner tonight, and it wouldn't be fair not to enjoy it."

"We could enjoy it in bed. You feed me. I'll feed you."

She tilted her head, hoping he'd kiss the soft spot beneath her ear that longed for his touch. "I don't think we'd get that far."

"We could try." He nibbled her earlobe, the sensations drumming up all sorts of devilish thoughts about Max nibbling away at her anatomy . . . after Mrs. Fisk's romantic dinner, if she could just hold on.

"It's tempting. *You're* tempting, but—"

"Lauren, darling!"

Lauren jerked out of Max's arms, spinning around to see a moment of scorn and then a superficial smile on her mother's face.

She took a deep breath, hoping her face and chest weren't red, hoping she wouldn't die from complete mortification right here and now. "What are you doing here, Mother?"

"Keeping you from doing something you shouldn't," Celeste offered, laughing lightly.

She walked toward Max in her bold, sophisticated manner and shook his hand. "How lovely to see you again, Mr. Wilde."

How Max managed to smile so politely was beyond Lauren's imagination. Never in her life had she wanted so desperately for her mother to disappear, and when Gerald Harcourt strolled into the room looking far too cultured in his tux, Lauren wished they'd both go *poof!* Unfortunately she didn't think she was on good terms with the fairy godmother lately.

"May I introduce you to Gerald Harcourt," Celeste said, glaring at Max, smiling at Gerald.

"I believe we've already met," Gerald said, but still he held out his hand to Max, and Lauren couldn't miss the animosity in their shake, not when both men's knuckles turned white. Obviously Max's jealousy hadn't completely subsided, and it appeared Gerald was still under the impression that she was interested.

"I thought you were going back to London," Lauren said to her mother.

"Andrew had some pressing business to take care of—naturally. I thought about staying in Rio for a few more days, but Gerald called and suggested we—the *three* of us," she said pointedly, treating Max as if he weren't in the room, "go sailing."

Celeste linked her arm through Gerald's. "Gerald sailed in the America's Cup last year." She turned her artificial smile on Max. "Do you sail, Mr. Wilde?"

"I ride motorcycles."

"Oh, yes, how could I forget?"

"He restores motorcycles, too," Lauren said. "As well as classic cars."

"I have a penchant for the classics," Gerald added, leading Celeste to the living room, not taking any notice if Lauren and Max had followed. Of course, they had, because Max seemed determined to keep an eye on the man he despised.

"My collection includes Pierce-Arrow, Isotta-Fraschini, Duesenberg," Gerald continued. "In fact, I've recently purchased a '32 Walker-LeGrande SJ, a magnificent vehicle." He stood behind the bar and aimed his superior gaze at Max. "What about you?"

"A '68 Corvette convertible," Max said, leaning casually against the grand piano.

"I see."

Gerald didn't see a thing, Lauren thought. He was stuffy, arrogant, and sure that anyone and everyone would fall all over him and his wealth. Well, that wasn't quite the case where she was concerned.

"Gerald and I were thinking of going to Bice for dinner," her mother said. "Perhaps you'd like to join us."

"Max and I are having dinner here," Lauren stated, trying hard to stay composed, to keep a smile on her face. "Mrs. Fisk is back from Tahiti and she's preparing something new."

"I'm sorry, Mr. Wilde," Celeste said, "I thought you were here on business. Picking up a check or something you might have left behind when you catered Betsy Endicott's wedding."

"I'm here strictly for Lauren," he stated, sliding his arm possessively around her waist, his fingers clutching her side as he tugged her against him.

"How lovely." Celeste turned to Gerald. "You know, darling, I've been traveling so much lately, it might be nice to have dinner at home tonight. You wouldn't mind, would you?"

Gerald had already made himself at home and was pouring Chivas Regal into a glass. "Not at all."

"I'm afraid—" Lauren's protest was cut off by Max's fingers digging into her side.

"I'm glad you're going to join us," Max said, far too cordially. "I've been looking forward to getting to know both of you."

So much for her evening alone with Max!

"If you'll excuse me a moment," Lauren said, hoping no one could hear the gnash of her teeth, "I'll ask Mrs. Fisk and Charles to plan on four for dinner."

"Thank you, darling." Celeste turned to Max and, assuming the job of hostess, said, "Gerald makes a wonderful martini. Would you care for one?"

"I prefer beer."

"Yes, of course. I should have known."

Lauren walked out on the conversation, the

click of her heels on the marble floor drowning out the forced congeniality going on behind her. Shoving through the kitchen doors, she collapsed in one of the chairs. "This evening isn't going to go too well," she said to Charles and Mrs. Fisk.

"Why is that?" Charles asked, casually wiping a crystal goblet with a white linen towel.

"My mother has returned, along with Gerald Harcourt."

"Oh, dear."

Lauren couldn't help but laugh. "I think you've been around me far too much, Charles. You're beginning to sound like me."

"I could never be around you too much, Miss Remington." He set the glass on the counter and took another from Mrs. Fisk, who was swirling them in soapy water. "Is there something I could do to alleviate this situation?"

"Short of hog-tying Gerald and my mother and throwing them in the wine cellar, I can't think of a thing."

"I believe I might be able to find some rope in the garage."

Lauren grinned. "You really would do that for me, wouldn't you?"

"Quite possibly."

"And I'd help," Mrs. Fisk added. "How dare they interrupt a romantic evening, not to mention make me have to prepare additional food!"

"In all fairness, they didn't know they were interrupting anything."

"If you ask me," Mrs. Fisk went on, "you're

much too forgiving with Lady Ashford. I know she's your mother and all, but really, Miss Remington, it's high time you stood up to her."

"I quite agree," Charles stated. "There was a time when she was a lovely young woman, not unlike yourself, I daresay. She was in love with your father but she let convention, social status, and an imperialistic mother come between them. When that happened, the part of her that I loved so well disappeared." Charles put a hand on Lauren's shoulder. "I pray the same thing does not happen to you."

Lauren rested her hand over Charles's fingers. "It seems my social status has taken quite a beating lately. As for convention, does this dress look like something my Palm Beach sisters would wear?"

"Heavens, no, and more's the pity," Mrs. Fisk chortled.

Lauren smiled as she stood, thankful to have such generous friends in her employ. "Thanks for bolstering my courage. I believe I'll head back out and make sure Mother and Gerald haven't done anything evil to Max."

"I'm quite certain Mr. Wilde can take care of himself," Charles said. "Quite certain, indeed."

When Lauren walked back into the living room, it didn't take but a moment to realize that Charles was, as always, correct.

Max leaned against the piano, relaxed in spite of the venom that was spit at him with every word coming from Lady Ashford's mouth. The woman disliked him, plain and simple, and he was doing his best to bite his tongue.

As for Gerald Harcourt, the guy was a pompous ass, smiling, joking, and laughing at everything that was said. At least Lauren's mother was open and honest with her hatred—and he'd always admired honesty.

Max took a long, cold swallow of Budweiser from the bottle Gerald had found in the refrigerator behind the bar, and watched Lauren return from the kitchen. She was stunning in that scarlet dress that showed off an awful lot of her soft, warm skin. He'd wanted to see even more tonight, but it looked like Gerald Harcourt had come between him and his plans—once again.

"So, Gerald," Max said, latching on to Lauren and pulling her against his side. "What do you do for a living?"

"Nothing quite as intriguing as being a chef, I'm sure. I spend my days dabbling in investments, buying property, traveling."

"He's just purchased an island in Fiji," Celeste added. "Have you been to Fiji, Mr. Wilde?"

Max took another drink of beer. "I went to Catalina Island once. I was working as a stuntman in an action-adventure film."

"Is that how you broke your nose?" Lauren asked, drawing a slender finger over the bridge, which raised a cold look of disdain from Celeste.

"I broke it the first time when I was eight. A car accident," he said, remembering the long-forgotten incident where his drunken father had run their old Impala into a parked car. Zack was in the front passenger seat, buckled in. Max and Charlotte had flown forward on impact and hit the windshield. He frowned, remembering that Charlotte's head was cut, that she probably had a scar. He tucked the thought away and took a swallow of beer.

"The second time I broke it was in Catalina."

"Please tell us more, Mr. Wilde," Celeste suggested. Was she interested? Max wondered, or just being polite?

"I was in a chase scene. Two boats racing across the water. The one I was in was rigged to blow up *after* I jumped overboard, but the timing was off. I ended up with a broken leg, a busted arm, a fractured nose, and a concussion that put me in the hospital for nearly two weeks." Max looked directly at Gerald. "That doesn't happen in Fiji, does it?"

"I live a quiet life on the island."

"My first husband, Lauren's father, was a rodeo star," Celeste said, turning her attention—*again*—to Max, which surprised the hell out of him. "Reece, that was my husband, was hurt quite often, too. I remember a time—"

"Why did you give up being a stuntman?" Gerald asked, interrupting Celeste. Max couldn't miss the annoyance in her eyes.

"My foster father was ill, he needed someone to run his catering business, and I wasn't making any money in Hollywood." Max turned to Celeste. "Stunt work's a lot like rodeoing—some make good money at it, some don't."

"Do you make much money now?" Celeste asked. Max saw a small touch of warmth in her eyes, and thought they might be able to like each other—someday.

"I'm comfortable," he answered, figuring she didn't want too many details.

"And you have two children?"

Max nodded. "Jamie and Ryan."

"Foster children, I believe Lauren said." Celeste smiled, and took a dainty sip of the martini Gerald had made for her. "And they work for you, too, I understand. Is that why you brought them into your home?"

So much for the two of them getting along, Max decided.

"That was a one-time thing," Lauren said, coming to his rescue. Max might have tossed back some cynical comment, but he heard the butler clearing his throat.

"Dinner is served."

"Thank you, Charles," Celeste said, tucking her arm through Gerald's. "We can continue this lovely conversation over wine and one of Mrs. Fisk's delectable meals."

Gerald led Celeste toward the dining room, but Max didn't move from the piano. "What would happen if we didn't follow them?" Max asked Lauren, pulling her hard against his chest.

"My mother would send out the hounds, and they can be terribly vicious."

"I'm not afraid of dogs any more than I'm afraid of your mother. If it was someone else who'd interrupted us, I wouldn't let them stand in our way. But I don't want to cause you any trouble."

"Thank you," she said, whispering the words against his lips. "I'll make it up to you."

He smiled. "I'm counting on it."

They strolled arm in arm into the dining room. Charles had poured the wine, Mrs. Fisk had set out salads, and it looked like a very happy party was about to take place, but Lauren had her doubts.

Max was annoyed.

Celeste was at her supercilious best.

And Gerald just simpered behind his rich-jerk tan.

Lauren sipped her wine and tried to make small talk, but her mother managed to steer the conversation toward wedding planning, a subject Lauren had wanted to stay away from.

"I had the loveliest lunch with Amanda Carlyle while I was in Rio," Celeste announced. "She told me that Paige is looking for a wedding consultant, and I suggested you might be able to help her out."

That comment seemed totally out of character for Celeste, considering how she detested Lauren being in business. Obviously Celeste hadn't yet discovered that Paige and the rest of Palm Beach weren't the least bit interested in Lauren's services. "Thank you, Mother, but Paige is interviewing other planners. She wants someone with more experience."

"Oh, yes, I know that, darling. I thought you might be able to give her some suggestions on someone else to contact, since I knew you weren't going to continue as a wedding planner after Betsy's wedding."

Lauren shoved her glass of wine to her mouth and took a healthy drink. "Paige wasn't interested in my suggestions, Mother. But that's neither here nor there any longer. Planning society weddings has become rather tedious so I thought I'd try my hand at something else. I'm just not sure what."

Max frowned, studying her eyes, which she hoped didn't reveal the sadness she felt at giving up the profession she'd thoroughly enjoyed.

Celeste merely smiled her pleasure. "You really don't have to work, darling. There are other things you can do that are far more important."

"Like volunteer work," Lauren said.

"That's a delightful idea," Celeste chirped. "I believe there's a charity auction being held at the club in a few weeks. Perhaps you could donate an item or two of clothing."

"I was thinking of something a little more hands-on." She squeezed Max's leg under the table. "Like working at the Hole in the Wall."

"And what, pray tell, is that?" Celeste asked.

Lauren smiled at Max, who was leaning back in his chair, apparently enjoying his wine, the conversation, and probably Lauren's fingers, which were inching up his thigh. "It's a place where kids—underprivileged or underloved— can go after school. They get help with their homework, play sports, hang out and talk. Max started it several years ago."

"My word, Max," Gerald said, "you're quite the hero, aren't you? Helping underprivileged kids. Taking in foster children."

"I don't consider myself a hero, just a man who likes kids."

"Do any of these children who hang out at the Hole in the Wall have criminal records?" Gerald asked.

"If a kid comes in looking for help, we help them," Max stated. "We don't ask about their background unless they volunteer the information."

Gerald steepled his index fingers in front of his lips. "So you don't know if any of them have been caught stealing?"

"Not that I'm aware of."

"But it could be possible?" Gerald's continued questioning had become annoying, and Lauren could see Max's anger building in the way his jaw continually tensed.

"Anything's possible," Max answered. "Of course, *you* could have been caught stealing before, and I wouldn't know that either."

"Why don't we change the subject?" Lauren suggested, adding more wine to her glass. "How was Rio, Mother?"

"It was lovely, darling, until Bunny realized that her necklace was missing." Celeste aimed her eyes at Max. "Had you heard about that, Mr. Wilde?"

"I can't say that I have."

"It was a beautiful necklace, worth close to a

quarter of a million, and it disappeared during Betsy Endicott's wedding."

"You *think* it disappeared then," Lauren corrected.

"All right, Bunny and I think that's when it disappeared. And now I hear that a necklace of Holly Rutherford's may have also disappeared at Betsy's wedding."

Lauren watched Max take a long swallow of his wine, keeping his fury in check.

Gerald leaned back, holding his glass to his mouth, staring at Max over the rim.

Celeste glared at Max, too.

Lauren wanted to scream.

"What do the police have to say about all of this?" Max asked, looking pointedly at Celeste.

"They've talked with numerous people but haven't come across any leads."

Max's eyebrow raised a notch. "But you have your suspicions, right?"

Celeste shrugged, suddenly looking uncomfortable. "People always have their suspicions."

"Put the wrong person in the wrong place—the people who work for *you*, for instance," Gerald added, "and people will always talk."

"That's ridiculous," Lauren blurted out. "Max's friends wouldn't be caught dead stealing."

"I'm sure that's true," Gerald said, "but gossip has a nasty habit of leaking out, and when it reaches the police, well, they could easily get suspicious. Then—"

"Then the blame gets laid in the wrong place.

You know," Max said, pushing away from the table, "I'm not in the habit of talking about other people or laying the blame on them, and I'm finding this conversation extremely dull."

"I thought it was rather stimulating, myself," Gerald stated. "It's a shame you feel the need to leave so soon, especially before we've had a chance to taste Mrs. Fisk's superlative meal."

"I've lost my appetite." Max tossed his napkin on top of his plate. "It was nice seeing you again, Lady Ashford." He looked at Lauren, a hint of a smile softening the rage in his eyes. "Are you coming with me or staying here?"

Lauren didn't hesitate in answering because there was only one thing she wanted, and that was to be with Max. She put down her napkin and reached for Max's hand. "I'm going with you."

"You have guests," Celeste said, turning her controlled fury on her daughter. "It would be better if you stayed here."

"The best thing for me is to be with Max," Lauren threw back.

"Please don't embarrass me, Lauren."

"This isn't about you, Mother. It's about me."

Lauren knew she should have felt guilty uttering those words. She should have been struck down by lightning for speaking to her mother that way. Instead, a sense of relief washed through her as she and Max left the house.

When they reached the Harley he pulled her into his arms. "Are you sure you want to go?"

She kissed him softly. "I've never been more sure of anything in my life."

"I was hoping you'd say that. Now let's get out of here." Max slung his leg over the cycle, holding Lauren's hand as she hiked her dress up to her thighs and slipped on behind him.

"I'm sorry about all the accusations," she said, snuggling close, weaving her arms tightly about his waist. "I'm sorry our evening was ruined, that we didn't have dinner—"

"I didn't want dinner anyway." Max kick-started the engine, then turned slightly on the seat, fixing Lauren with a pair of fiery brown eyes. "As for the ruined evening"—he grinned seductively—"you can make everything up to me when I have *you* for dessert."

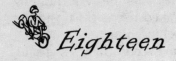 *Eighteen*

*T*he wind whipped through Lauren's hair as Max raced the motorcycle down Ocean Highway. Riding without a helmet was foolish and dangerous, but tonight was a night for thrills, for living wild and free.

When they reached a stretch of deserted beach that Lauren knew well, she tapped him on the shoulder. "Stop here."

Max swerved the Harley into the hard-packed sand at the side of the road. "Some special reason you wanted to stop?" he asked, bracing his feet on the ground when they came to a halt.

"I want to show you something," she told him, climbing off the bike. She dropped her heels on the ground and walked out onto the soft, cool sand, with Max by her side. "My grandmother—

a very frugal woman," she stated, "gave me twenty dollars for my thirteenth birthday, and my brother talked me into investing it. He said twenty dollars wouldn't buy much, but I should see what it would get me when I turned eighteen." She looked about her, at the beautiful spans of beach, and smiled. "This is what I ended up with."

"Pretty smart investing," Max said, draping his arm over her shoulder as they walked toward the water.

"I just followed Jack's advice. He made a killing in the stock market when he was in his early twenties. You'd never know it, considering the rundown ranch house he lives in, but he's happy."

"Money and happiness don't always go hand in hand."

"I've found that out more than once. Still, I'd like to have them both."

Max laughed. "Yeah, for some reason I don't picture you as a contented housewife living in suburbia."

"I'd rather be a contented housewife living on a stretch of beach like this," she admitted, and hoped she hadn't been too blatant. She was falling in love, and it was difficult to keep her feelings to herself. "I like it here because it's close enough to Palm Beach to go shopping at a moment's notice, and far enough away that you don't feel like you're being watched—and judged—all the time."

"You don't mind giving up that monstrosity you live in?"

She shook her head. "All I need is a place that's big enough for a nice-sized family, but not so big that it feels lonely and empty when you're the only one inside."

"Do you get lonely?" he asked, squeezing her arm, drawing her close. She stretched her hands around his waist.

"I think everybody gets lonely at times."

"I'm not interested in everybody, Lauren," he said, stopping in the sand and turning her to face him. "I want to know if you get lonely."

"You know what it's like to be alone—"

"We're not talking about me," he said, his fingers digging into her arms. "I asked about you."

"Yes, I get lonely. I hated being raised by a nanny, hated getting shoved off to one school after another because my mother didn't have time for me, or because she'd married someone new who didn't want a kid around. The only constant I've had in my life is Charles, and even though I love him dearly, it's not often that a butler gives you a hug. I've got a brother I love, but he lives out west and we didn't see each other all that much."

She bit her lip, trying not to cry. "But the loneliest times of my life were during my marriages. I thought my husbands would love me, I thought I'd have children . . . but I was wrong on both counts."

And then she saw the concern and warmth in Max's eyes that wiped away the torments of her past. "I don't feel lonely when I'm with you," she whispered.

He cradled her face in his hands. "I'm going to

make sure you're never lonely again," he said, and then he kissed her, and all thoughts of loneliness disappeared.

Slowly he lowered her to the sand and moved his marvelous body over hers. They were going to make love—at last—just what she'd hoped for when she'd asked him to stop at this stretch of beach.

His heated gaze raked across her mouth, a passion that made her body flame inside. She dragged in a deep breath when his hands moved over her breasts, when he kneaded them gently, and a low moan escaped through her lips when his thumbs swirled over her sensitive nipples.

Moonlight shone on his jet-black hair, and she wove her fingers into the long unruly strands, pulling him tighter, tighter, allowing her tongue to explore and taste the sweetness of his mouth.

She'd never known a thrill like this, something so exciting and blissful that she never wanted it to end.

But it did—all too soon.

"What's wrong?" Lauren stammered, trying to regain her senses, to understand what had caused such an abrupt halt to their lovemaking.

"I don't want you on the beach," Max said, pulling her up from the sand and into his arms. His hands were in her hair as if he couldn't bear to let her go, and his mouth stayed close to her as he said, "I want you behind closed doors. *Locked* doors. I want to strip away every speck of your clothing and then I want to take my time just looking at you."

That sounded so very nice, but she wanted so much more. "You will touch me, too, I hope?"

"Oh, I plan to touch you, Lauren, with my fingers, my tongue, my entire body. Before I'm through, I want to kiss every single part of you that I'm able to touch. And the last thing I want is for someone to intrude on what I'm doing."

"I've got strong locks on the doors at home. I've got a bottle of chilled champagne, and I've got chocolates."

"Going back to that monstrosity you live in and meeting up with Gerald and your mother is the last thing I want to do."

"We can't go to your place. Not with the kids there, and Jazz."

"That's not what I had in mind."

"Then what?"

His grin frightened and excited her all at the same time. "You'll see."

They dashed across the sand to the motorcycle, tugged on their shoes, and once again they were racing up the highway, angling inland at a cross street that didn't look at all familiar, toward some mysterious destination. They sped past car dealerships and bright neon signs, until they came to a stop in the parking lot of the Fantasy Inn, a gigantic structure that looked like something straight out of the Arabian Nights.

"This doesn't exactly look like the Ritz," Lauren quipped.

"It's not even close." There was a little too much humor in his voice for comfort.

"You don't really expect me to sleep in this establishment, do you?"

"Sleep's the furthest thing from my mind."

"It's not on my mind, either, but I thought we'd go someplace a little classier the first time around. It wouldn't take us all that long to get to the Breakers, we could rent a suite, we could have room service brought in."

"I don't want to go to the Breakers. I want to stay here."

"It looks . . . Goodness, Max! It looks like one of those places where people stop for a quickie."

"Looks are sometimes deceiving. A week or so ago you might have thought I was the kind of guy who only liked quickies, but I assure you, I'm not."

"I'm sure you're not that kind of guy at all, but I've got a lot of uncomfortable feelings about the inside of this place. I keep picturing vibrating beds, mirrored ceilings, porno flicks on the TV, and condom machines in the bathrooms."

"The bed's going to vibrate enough without running up the electric bill, I've got condoms in my pocket, and the closest thing we're going to get to a porno flick is you and me dancing naked."

"You neglected to comment on the mirrored ceilings."

"I've never been here before, but I'm hoping to find mirrors not only on the ceiling but on the walls." His fingers slid slowly up to her hip. "I want to see you as well as touch you, Lauren."

"Oh, dear."

He grinned, his mindset not the least bit altered by her hesitation. "Come on," he said, tugging her from the motorcycle and rushing her toward the office.

"Don't you think the proprietor will wonder why we don't have luggage?" she asked.

"No."

"I don't even have a nightgown with me."

"You don't need one."

"You're determined to drag me into this place, aren't you?"

"I'm determined to *have* you . . . period."

She felt extremely awkward walking into the lobby, a garish place where brightly colored fringed carpets had been suspended from the ceiling. An elderly gentleman in flowing robes and a turban appeared from a back room, pushing through a red velvet curtain to greet them. "How may I assist you?"

Max gripped Lauren's hand a little tighter. "We'd like a room."

He looked from Max to Lauren then back to Max again. Lauren despised the man's lascivious smirk, hated the fact that he knew what they were up to because, goodness, they'd come into this establishment without even a toothbrush—a very sinful thing indeed!

"I have several rooms to choose from," he said, opening a picture book in front of them. "Two of our favorites, Blackbeard and Jungle Fever, are already taken this evening. Some of our smaller rooms are available, such as Night Eyes and Swaying Palms. However, I believe the two of you might enjoy our ultimate fantasy room, Sheik's Delight."

"We'll take it," Max said, plunking a credit card down on the counter and filling out the paperwork shoved in front of him. The man handed Max the key and gave them directions, and a moment later Max was leading Lauren through a twisting corridor lit with fake candles sticking out of Aladdin-type lamps. The elevator was lined in burgundy crushed velvet, an ominous precursor of things to come, and it climbed slowly toward the fourth floor. When the door opened, only one room appeared on the landing before them.

Sheik's Delight.

She couldn't believe she was doing this. She believed it even less when Max opened the door and she stepped inside. "Oh, dear," Lauren murmured. "This definitely isn't the Ritz."

Max closed the door and leaned against it, arms folded across his chest, watching her as she inspected the room. The bed looked as if it were designed for an orgy. Big, round, it was laden with tasseled pillows in bright reds, blues, and yellows, and the entire thing was draped with yards and yards of sheer white fabric. The ceiling was painted midnight-blue, with large mirrors in the shapes of stars and a moon affixed overhead. She caught a quick glimpse of Max, who was eyeing the overhead mirrors, an extremely satisfied grin on his face.

Oriental carpets and even more pillows were strewn across the floors, and at one end of the room was an oasis, a rocky waterfall and pool, surrounded by palms—real ones in pots, not some tacky plastic things coated in dust.

As quirky as the place was . . . all of a sudden she couldn't think of a more perfect spot to make love.

"What do you think?" Max asked, the need to have her growing by leaps and bounds with every second that passed.

She turned slowly, the softness of her smile highlighted by the dim lights. "I think we should stop talking and get back to what we started on the beach."

He crossed the room and pulled her against him, the wait to know her, to feel her, to see all that he'd imagined finally over. There were so many things he wanted to say to her, but they had to wait. Crushing her wonderfully soft breasts against his chest, he captured her mouth.

He felt the searing heat of her fingers on his cheeks, sinking into his hair, holding him so close he could barely breathe, but that didn't seem necessary. Her kiss breathed life into him, hope, happiness, emotions he couldn't remember ever feeling with a woman.

His hands swept over her back. Tugging on the sheer fabric of her dress, he pulled it up to her waist and let his hands roam over her smooth, warm, and naked bottom. His fingers dug into her skin and her kiss deepened, her tongue swirling around his, her mouth sucking on him, and a moan escaped his throat.

"God, Lauren."

She came to a screeching halt. "I haven't done anything wrong, have I?"

He shook his head, looking at the worry, the fright in her eyes. "What makes you think that?"

"I did everything wrong with Peter. I was lousy in bed. I was too fat."

"You're perfect, and Peter was a fool." He breathed the words against her lips. "I don't want to hear about any other men. They don't exist and as far as I'm concerned, I'm the only man you've ever known." He cradled her face in his hands. "Do you understand that?"

She nodded.

"Now kiss me again."

She did, and he could feel the saltiness of her tears on his lips. They should have stopped him, made him slow down, but instead they fueled the flame inside him and made him want to give her more love than she'd ever had in her entire life.

Grasping the hem of her dress he pulled it higher, higher, tearing his mouth from the heat of her kiss to tug the silky fabric over her head. He drew in a deep breath as he looked at her. "You're beautiful," he whispered, and watched a soft smile brighten her face.

Slowly he slipped the bright red straps of her bra from her shoulders and pressed a lingering kiss to the hollow of her throat, where he could smell her perfume, taste the heat of her body, feel the blood pulsing through her veins.

Her head tilted back and a gentle purr whirred beneath her lips. Her passion, her excitement, drove him wild, making him feel powerful, but he knew the moment she touched him again, he'd fall completely under her control. She could do anything to him, anything at all.

Resting his hands on her hips, he slid his tongue along the lacy edge of her bra, listening to her moan, feeling her needful quiver. His palms skimmed lightly around her waist, up the curve of her spine until he found the catch of her bra. In a matter of seconds, he'd freed her luscious breasts.

The silk drifted from his fingers to the floor, while his mouth, his lips, his tongue grazed her nipples, nipping, teasing, until she touched him, pressing her hand to the hard, needy length of him. His body shuddered. He nearly lost his ability to hold on when he felt her fingers slide over him, felt her grasp his buckle.

Taking it slow with Lauren had become an impossibility. He gripped the backs of her thighs and pulled her legs upward, wrapping them about his waist, and carried her to a bed full of pillows.

The green of her eyes glowed like emeralds as he ripped back the covers and laid her down. She held her hands out to him, beckoning him to come to her, but first he removed his jacket, his shirt, nearly ripping off the buttons in his need to make her his. He dropped his boots to the floor, stripped off his socks, then reached into the pocket of his slacks and pulled out the foil packets, dropping them on the bedside table.

In another moment he was free of every stitch

of clothing, and his body burned as she pushed herself up on her elbows and studied him.

"I never knew a man could be so beautiful," she said, and he managed to laugh while he panted, trying to catch his breath.

The only thing between them was a skimpy piece of red silk, but he had no intention of letting it get in his way. Sliding his fingers beneath the slip of fabric, he drew her panties slowly down her legs, loving the curve of them, the velvety softness of her skin, the fact that when he let the thong drop to the floor, the only thing keeping them apart was a few feet of air. And he closed that space in a heartbeat.

"I've dreamed of you this way," he said, while his hands, his fingers, his lips, and tongue explored her curves and the very center of her where she was hot and slippery and ready to be loved.

And just as he promised, he kissed nearly every inch of her, his desire and excitement building with each of her sighs.

And when he thought he couldn't hold on any longer, he captured her mouth and kissed her tenderly. "I want you."

"I know," she whispered, and then, dear God, he felt her fingers slide between them and circle him tightly, the gentle pressure making him swell with a need that was beyond his wildest imagination.

Rolling onto his back, he carried her with him. She lay on top of him then slowly swirled her tongue down the length of his body, stopping just where he wanted her for the moment.

Her mouth was hot and wet and she did incredible things with her lips, her teeth, and her tongue, driving him mad. "Do you like that?" she asked, raising her head to look at him.

Strands of her hair had fallen over her face, turning her into a wild creature toying with her prey.

He groaned as she suckled him, as her torturous fingernails raked over his chest.

"Keep that up and you're not going to know what all I can do to you."

She laughed as she straddled him, her breasts swaying in front of his face.

He reached for them, kneading her glorious flesh, while she leaned across the bed, grabbed a foil pouch, and ripped it open. Slowly, ever so slowly, she rolled the sheath over him.

"I've never done that before," she said, smiling.

"What part of that haven't you done before?" he asked, surprised at her comment.

"I never put a condom on a man, and I never..." She licked her lips, and God, he thought he'd explode. "I never wanted to taste a man—until now."

If it was possible to grow another two or three inches in both length and diameter, Max swore it could have just happened.

"I've never done this before, either," she said, holding his hot, stiff penis and guiding him into the tightness of her sweet, blessed warmth.

"Oh, dear!" Her eyes were closed, her breathing labored, and he reached again for her breasts, loving the cry that erupted from her lips.

Slowly, tentatively, she pushed upward, then came back down again, and he watched the smile on her lips. Again and again she moved, up, down, up, down. Her hips swirled, moving around and around until she found exactly the right angle, and then she rode him hard and fast, while he watched the feverish ecstasy in her face.

Suddenly, he wanted to be above her, driving her to the brink of passion and beyond. When he rolled her beneath him, her legs found their way easily around his waist, and he slipped his hands under her hips and held her up to meet each one of his thrusts.

"Oh, Max!" His name escaped from her lips on a deep, heart-pounding moan.

Her fingers wound tightly in his hair, pulling him toward her, kissing away the perspiration on his brow, kissing his lips, loving him, as they moved together, slowly, rhythmically, touching each other's hearts, each other's souls.

"I love you," she whispered.

Those three words had never sounded so real or so right, and he knew he felt the same. "I love you, too," he breathed against her mouth, and together they exploded into heaven, then came back softly, slowly to earth.

Lauren woke in the middle of the night, wrapped in a tangle of sheets. The pillow beside her was empty, and worry sliced through her that Max had gone. She jerked up in bed, and then she saw him, standing near the oasis, water pulsing over the waterfall behind him.

She sat there for the longest time just watching him as he watched her, waiting for the frantic beat of her heart to calm. Finally she was able to ask, "Having trouble sleeping?"

"Having trouble keeping my hands off you."

"You have my permission to touch me all you want."

He smiled. "Come here then."

Obeying a man had never been so easy. Gazing at a man had never been so pleasant. He took hold of her hand and led her into the grotto, reaching behind a fern to turn a hidden knob that made the water flow lightly over them. It was warm, gentle, and Max stood in front of her, his hands softly exploring her breasts, the curves of her waist and hips.

The muscles flexed in his arms, and she watched his mermaid tattoo almost swim with each ripple of his biceps. "What's your fascination with mermaids?" she asked, swirling her fingers through the soft hair on his chest.

He turned her around and pointedly stared at the tattoo on her bottom. "You tell me what your interest is, first."

"Mine's the result of too much liquor and probably slurring the words *mermaid* and *man* together."

"What kind of tattoo did you really want?" he asked, drawing his finger over the design that covered far too much of one of her cheeks.

"A tiny orchid would have sufficed. How I ended up with this is anybody's guess."

He knelt down for closer inspection, and she was sure her face turned purple. "What's this?" he asked, and she knew he'd spotted the most humiliating aspect of the tattoo.

"It's pretty obvious, isn't it?"

"Yeah," he said, sliding his hard, slick body over hers, only to grin when they stood face to face. "Pretty nice of you to have Max tattooed on your butt."

"You think I did that on purpose?"

"What am I supposed to think?"

"That I must have cursed you in my sleep and Tattoo Annie found it funny. And if you ever breathe a word of this to anyone—"

He stilled her words with a kiss. "You could always have it removed."

She frowned as she shook her head. "I've grown attached to it. Now," she said, running her palm over his biceps, "tell me about yours."

"This?" he asked, grinning as he bent his arm and made the powerful muscle dance.

"The one on your motorcycle, too. I thought you might have been in love with a mermaid once."

"I've only been in love with you," he said, turning her around and pulling her back against his chest. Reaching for a bar of soap, he lathered his hands and caressed her breasts, her belly, and lower still.

"That feels very nice," she said on a moan, "but really, Max, I do want to know about your mermaid."

"I got it the night you married Chip."

His words were a whisper against her ear, and his soapy fingers reached between her legs, swirling around, drawing one moan after another from her, but still she managed to ask, "Why?"

"It's a long story." His fingers slipped inside her and her legs went weak. "Are you sure you want all the details?" His voice was raspy as he spoke. His lips moved over her shoulders, up the curve of her neck, while his fingers did absolutely delicious things to a part of her anatomy that was desperately in need of his attention.

"I want to know everything." She wondered how much more of the story he could possibly reveal when she felt the hard length of him pressed against her back, felt her own throbbing desire to have him inside her again. Still, she pleaded, "Tell me, Max."

"I was angry." The pressure of his swirling fingers increased and she leaned her head against his chest, unsuccessfully trying to keep her breathing calm. "I talked Bear into riding down to Miami with me."

His thumb toyed with her favorite little pulse point and her body jerked. "Oh, God, Max. Please don't stop."

"The story?" he teased, "or this?" His mouth tormented the sensitive spot beneath her ear while his hands worked their magic on most every visible and invisible place on her body.

"Don't stop any of it?" she begged. "Please."

"There was a tattoo shop in a seedy party of town, and Bear dared me to get a tattoo."

She felt his hands on her arms, turning her around, pressing her back against the smooth rock wall. "Bear had a dozen already. I didn't want even one." His lips trailed along her neck, over her chest, capturing her breast, licking, sucking, nipping lightly, and driving her almost to frenzy.

"There was a smart-aleck kid sitting in the waiting room watching *The Little Mermaid*. He was taunting me, telling me his mom had a million tattoos and I was a chicken for being afraid." Lauren heard the rip of another foil pouch as Max continued to speak, and her gaze darted toward the blessedly swollen length of him. She gasped for breath as he slid the condom slowly over his skin.

"Bear was goading me, the kid was egging me on," Max said, moving close, closer. "And I walked behind the curtain and told the man to put a mermaid on my arm, one with bright green eyes, golden brown hair, and luscious breasts."

Lauren felt the heat of Max's rock hard body between her legs, and cried out when he thrust into her.

Grasping the backs of her legs and wrapping them around his waist, he moved in and out, pressing her against the wall. "That tattoo's a reminder of what I could never have," he said, "a reminder that two different worlds could never come together. I believed that until tonight. Nothing can keep us apart, Lauren. Nothing."

She swept her arms around his neck, pulling him tight, tighter, loving the feel of him moving in and out, loving the way his body pressed her against the wall, loving the urgency, the desire, the overwhelming need in him as he carried her to places she'd never been, introduced her to a world of pleasure she never dreamed she'd find. And for the first time in her life, she felt, she was really and truly loved.

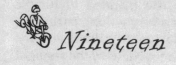

Nineteen

Lightning tore across the morning sky, drowning out the roar of the kick-started engine. A moment later the clouds opened and released a torrential downpour. It was a delightful way to start the morning, Lauren thought, as she slid her arms around Max's waist and held on tight when he tore out of the Fantasy Inn parking lot.

They cruised along the rain-slick streets for nearly half an hour, time for Lauren to reflect on all the delicious things Max had done to her during the night and the way he'd whispered sweet-nothings into her ear—sinful, erotic sweet-nothings that had made her blush. And they planned to do it all over again tomorrow morning, right after Ryan and Jamie left for school.

For once Lauren was excited about getting up at seven A.M., because she planned to tumble right back into bed with a very willing partner.

The closer she and Max got to Palm Beach, the farther away the clouds moved, until the sunlight struck the pavement and shards of bright light blinded their vision. Max slowed as they maneuvered around corners, hit a few too many impossible-to-miss puddles that splashed dirty water onto her legs and rain-soaked dress, and finally turned into her circular drive.

That's when the good times ended.

Celeste stood next to the open driver's door of the Bentley, her eyes narrowed in undisguised anger. "Good morning."

"Good morning, Mother." Lauren climbed off the motorcycle, handing Max the helmet and the leather jacket she'd been wearing. Ruffling her fingers through her hair, she tried to make herself presentable in just a few seconds, an impossible task, for sure, considering that her dress was sticking to her body and water dripped from its hem.

"I'd give you a hug," Lauren said to her mother, attempting to lighten Celeste's mood, "but I'm a mess."

Celeste didn't look amused. "Did you have a good evening?"

Lauren squeezed Max's hand. "The best time of my life."

"Are you the least concerned with my evening? Do you care at all that you humiliated me in front of Gerald?" Celeste asked, gripping the car door. "I will agree that the conversation about jewelry thefts might have been out of line, but there was no reason for you to run out on your guests simply because Mr. Wilde was offended."

"I was offended, too, Mother."

"By what?"

"By the way you treated *my* guest."

Max put a hand on her arm. "You don't have to stick up for me."

"The only one I'm sticking up for is myself," Lauren said, facing her mother again. "You've spent twenty-nine years telling me that I've humiliated you in one way or another, and I've spent twenty-nine years trying to make up for all my mistakes, but so far I haven't been able to make you happy."

She felt Max squeezing her arm, knew he wanted her to stop before she regretted what she said, but the words had been bottled up far too long. "I love you, Mother, but I can't live by your dictates any longer. Being with Max makes me happy, and I don't care what anyone else thinks."

"You feel that way now, but how will you feel when your friends talk behind your back or when they stop inviting you to parties?"

Celeste drew a deep breath, and Lauren realized she'd never seen her mother filled with so much anguish. The last thing Lauren wanted was to hurt her mother, but she was tired of standing still while her mother aimed her bitterness at the daughter who loved her.

"My so-called friends are already talking behind my back," Lauren said. "I got a hint of that yesterday when I was turned down left and right as a wedding planner."

"That won't be the end of it, either," Celeste tossed back. "And after a while you'll begin to hate the man who caused all your trouble. I know, because that's what happened between me and your father. Please, Lauren, listen to me. You may think you love Mr. Wilde, but stay with him much longer, and you'll lose everything you've ever known, everything that's ever been a part of you."

"My life's been fairly empty, Mother, so I don't understand what I'd be losing."

Celeste shook her head. "There's no reasoning with you, is there?"

"For the first time in my life, I have no doubts about what I want."

Obviously Celeste wasn't happy with that answer, and she turned to Max. "If you care for my daughter, Mr. Wilde, you should leave her alone."

"I can't do that."

"Lauren's father said the same thing once. He wouldn't leave me alone in spite of my mother's protests, and just like Lauren, I fell in love. I did everything for him. I gave up my home, my lifestyle, because I thought loving him was all I needed, and I ended up miserable." An uncharacteristic tear slipped from Celeste's eye. "Please," Celeste implored, and even Lauren could hear the torment in her mother's voice, "if you care for my daughter, leave her alone."

Without another word, Celeste climbed into the car, slammed the door behind her, and drove away.

Lauren took a deep breath as she watched the car turn out of the drive. She'd felt so sure of herself when she made all her statements about not caring what her friends and family thought of her, but she knew in her heart that that wasn't totally true. She also knew in her heart that she loved Max, that he was more important than anything else in her life.

Looking up at Max, she saw worry in his eyes and, far more frightening, she saw traces of doubt. She attempted to smile, but her fear that he was going to leave her made her lips tremble instead.

"Your mother's right," Max said, shoving his fingers through his hair. "Stick with me and you'll lose everything you've ever known. Then you'll end up resenting me, and I don't want that."

Oh, God, she didn't want to hear those words—not from Max.

"She's wrong."

He shook his head. "No, she's not. Your business is falling apart because of me."

"People were laughing at my foray into the business world long before I met you."

"Yeah, but having me cater Betsy's wedding just added fuel to their fire."

"Do you think I care?"

"I *know* you care," he said, gripping her arms.

"That's what you do, Lauren. You care about everything and you're constantly worried about what people think. There's nothing wrong with that. Hell, more people should be like you, but if you and I stick together, you'll wonder every moment what people are saying, what they're thinking, and you'll be miserable."

"So what are you going to do, Max? Walk away from me?"

"I don't see much choice. I love you, but—"

She laughed cynically. "You don't love me, Max. If you did, you'd stick by me and we'd ride this thing out together."

His fingers tightened and she could see the anguish in his eyes. "I do love you, that's why I'm going to walk out on you."

"That's the most ridiculous thing I've ever heard."

"Not to me. Do you think I care if people laugh behind my back? Do you think I care that your mother despises me? As for accusations about my friends being thieves, I've lived with that kind of crap all my life, and most of the time it bounces off of me. But, damn it, Lauren, I love you so much that I'd get hurt every time someone laughed at you, every time you argued with your mother, or lost a friend or your self-respect, because I know how important those things are to you."

Tears spilled from her eyes. "I don't want to lose you."

"I don't want to lose you, either. But we both

knew at the start that this would never work, that your world and mine were far too different."

Lauren pulled away from him, wiping endless tears from her cheeks. "I never would have pegged you as a quitter. God, Max, I was married to men who didn't care enough about our relationship to make it work. I fell in love with you because you weren't at all like those men. I thought you'd fight for me, that you'd love me no matter what. But I was wrong."

"I do love you, Lauren, but the last thing I want to do is hurt you."

She laughed and let the tears go right ahead and fall down her face. "Well, guess what, Max," she said, defeatedly walking up the steps to her big, lonely home. "You've hurt me far worse than anyone else ever has."

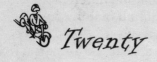 *Twenty*

Sleep, a box of Godivas, and a bottle of Dom Perignon helped Lauren make it through the first day. The second day she lay in bed trying to get over the blinding headache induced by too much champagne and chocolate.

Going shopping would have been a much easier way to run away from her troubles, but she couldn't possibly have gone out in public with swollen eyes and a constantly tearstained face. Besides, she hadn't wanted to leave home for fear of missing Max's call—the one that hadn't yet come.

How could he love her, not want to hurt her, and still walk away? Did he know how miserable she was? Did he care?

Of course not! No one seemed to care, and she was beginning to feel terribly sorry for herself.

Reaching across a bed piled high with pillows and magazines, all of which had brought her no comfort at all, she grabbed for a tissue, knocking over the half-full bottle of aspirin that, so far, hadn't helped her headache.

She blew her nose, then tossed the tissue at the trash can beside her bed, missing, just as she'd done at least fifty times before.

When the knock sounded at her door, she tightened the ties on her black silk robe and sniffed. "Come in."

Charles appeared, bearing a silver tray filled with some of Mrs. Fisk's delectable food. He walked across the room, shaking his head when he gave her a quick glance, then crossed to her dresser. "I've brought a fresh supply of food," he said, setting that tray down and picking up the one left over from lunchtime—the food still untouched.

"Pardon me for saying this, Miss Remington, but are you going to stay in this room forever?"

"I've thought about it."

"Have you thought about the fact that crying for two days is not going to make Mr. Wilde come back?"

"It doesn't appear that anything's going to make Mr. Wilde come back, but I'd hoped crying might gain me a little sympathy, at least an ounce of understanding and concern from the people I love."

"Are you finding that to be the case?"

"No, quite the contrary. You're the only visitor I've had in two days, and you've been anything but congenial."

He grinned. "I thought my attitude might get you out of bed sooner. Obviously I was wrong."

"Do you have any other thoughts that might get me out of this room? I'm particularly interested in hearing what you have to say about how I can get Max Wilde back."

"I believe there are dozens of possibilities."

"Care to share them with me?"

"No."

"And why not?"

"Because you've spent your entire life doing what everyone wanted you to do or expected you to do. I seem to recall you telling me that you were tired of that, and you planned to do things on your own from now on. Well, I believe it's high time you follow through on that."

"All I asked for was one small suggestion."

Charles walked toward the door. "And I've complied with that request." He stepped into the hallway. "Good night, Miss Remington."

Why was it that Charles was always right?

Blowing her nose again, she shot the tissue toward the trash and missed. She'd probably missed a lot of other things in the last two days—like her entire life.

Get a grip, she told herself, and think of a way to get Max back. But her brain was too muddled to think. She needed help.

Picking up the telephone, she punched in her

brother's number. It was just past seven in Wyoming and she knew she couldn't possibly be interrupting anyone's sleep. She'd done that once in the last couple of weeks and she couldn't do it again, not when she thought about Sam's delicate condition.

Her sister-in-law's voice was just the thing she needed to feel better. Trying her hardest not to sound hung over, not to sound like a woman on the brink of madness, she took a deep breath and tried to launch a calm conversation after all the hellos, how-are-yous, and how-are-you-feelings were exchanged.

"Oh, Sam," she cried, "I don't know what I'm going to do."

"The first thing you're going to do is stop crying," Sam instructed, "and then you're going to tell me what's wrong."

Grabbing a tissue from the box in the middle of her bed, Lauren blew her nose, sighed deeply, then tried again.

"I'm in love with Max Wilde."

"And that's making you cry."

"Of course not. He loves me, too."

"I don't see the problem here."

"Mother hates him."

"That's your mother's problem. Not yours."

"He's a biker. He has a big mermaid tattooed on his arm, a goatee, and he wears earrings in both ears."

"Sounds like the kind of men I was attracted to before I met your brother."

"You're not helping me a bit, Sam."

"How can I help when I don't understand the problem?"

Sam had a point. She always had a point, but she always had answers, too.

Lauren took a deep breath. "I told myself I didn't want to get involved with Max because he was all wrong for me, but goodness, Sam, he's just so gorgeous, and wonderful, and he makes me feel special and loved in a way no one else has ever done."

"Then you should be with him."

"That's the problem. He doesn't want me."

"But you said he loves you."

"He does," Lauren admitted, "or at least he says he does, and that's the reason he doesn't want to be with me."

There was a terribly long silence on the other end of the phone. "Are you there, Sam?"

"Yes, I'm still here. Could I ask you a question about Max?"

"Of course. Ask any question you want?"

"Are you sure he's sane?"

"Positive."

"Then you'd better explain to me why he walked away from you because he loves you."

Lauren spent a good ten minutes going over the situation and when she was through, Sam simply said, "I think the man's crazy."

"But he's not. He's wonderful, Sam. He's adopting a boy and a girl, and they're the greatest kids you'd ever want to meet. He spends a lot of his money on a place for underprivileged children. He donated all the money I was going to pay him for Betsy's wedding to your charity. And I can't forget the fact that he makes wonderful barbecue sauce, and well, everything else is pretty personal."

"You really do love him, don't you?"

"I never thought it was possible to love someone this much. You know," Lauren said, lying back in the pillows and thinking about her time with Max, "I've always been afraid of trying something new, of stepping outside the boundaries of what's expected, but Max made it all so easy for me. He encouraged me to ride a motorcycle, and baby-sit his kids, which I'm really pretty good at, and, goodness, Sam, he brings out the best in me."

"Sounds like he's worth fighting for, but I don't have any suggestions, Lauren. You're on your own this time."

He's definitely worth fighting for, Lauren told herself. She only hoped she could come up with the proper strategy, and that Max would be willing to get in the ring and go a round or two. Succeeding at this was far more important than planning the perfect wedding. This time, her future with Max was at stake.

"You look like hell."

Max jerked his head toward the sound of Jazz's voice and the slamming kitchen door. She was dressed in her best throw-in-an-extra-twenty-and-I'll-give-you-the-works streetwalker outfit, slinging a big floppy chartreuse plastic purse.

Max grinned, always amazed at the way Jazz dressed for work. "You look like hell, too."

"Thanks. I do my best." She dropped her bag on the kitchen counter, kicked off her five-inch heels, and climbed onto one of the barstools.

"What's for lunch?" she asked.

Max stared at the concoction in front of him. "Salmon tartare."

"You've got to be kidding."

Max shook his head. "That's the specialty of the house today."

"No fried chicken?"

"I've got leftovers in the fridge. Want me to heat it up for you?"

"I'll get it. Don't stop what you're doing." Jazz slid off the barstool, sauntered to one of the refrigerators, the same thing she did two or three times a week, pulled out a dish of cold fried chicken, and sat back down at the bar.

"So, what's with the salmon tartare?" she asked, lifting the plastic wrap off the plate in front of her and grabbing a drumstick.

Max looked up from the salmon. "I got a very discreet call from some woman who was at Betsy Endicott's wedding, asking if I could cater an intimate dinner she's having this evening. She loved the Caribbean brochettes and she's just *dying* to try some of my other specialties."

Jazz chewed on the chicken, staring at him as if he'd gone mad. "You don't sound happy about it."

"I spent years getting away from preparing this kind of stuff."

"So why'd you take the job?"

Because, damn it, he wanted the people of Palm Beach to like him. "It's my attempt to fit in."

Jazz laughed. "Is that possible?"

"Hell if I know."

"Is that what Lauren wants?"

"I haven't talked with her in a week." He slammed the broad side of the knife down on the salmon and flattened it in one whack. "I've been busy trying to figure out how the two of us can be together without starting a feud between bikers and society snobs."

Jazz grabbed a napkin from a holder, pulled the lid off the cookie jar, and dug for a fresh oatmeal pecan, not the least disturbed by his disgruntled behavior. "Does she know what you're trying to do?"

Max smacked the knife down again on the fish. "No."

"So why don't you tell her?"

"Because I might not be successful. Because she might try talking me out of what I'm doing or, worse yet, come up with an idea that's worse than mine."

"In other words, you're afraid of calling her."

"And why would I be afraid to call?"

"Because if what Bear told me is true, you walked out on Lauren with one of the most half-assed excuses I've ever heard for calling it quits, and now you're afraid she won't want you back."

"Okay, I made an ass out of myself. I'm trying to remedy the situation the best way I know how, and I don't need help from you."

Jazz bit into another cookie and glared at him from across the counter. "You know, Max, you've been ready to kill for a week now. It could be several more weeks before your remedy's ready. If I were you, I'd go see her before she decides you're not worth waiting for."

"I've got three parties to cater this week. I've got an appointment with the adoption attorney tomorrow. And I've got Harry calling every other day to report on one false lead after another. I've got two kids that need help with their homework, I've got the Hole."

"If you want her badly enough, you'll quit making excuses."

In his heart, he knew Jazz was right. But what if he went to see Lauren and found out she'd already lost interest—and turned to another man.

Lauren uncrossed and recrossed her legs for at least the fifteenth time since her friends arrived for brunch. She'd invited them over because she'd needed a break. Trying to figure out how to get Max back by bringing together two worlds that were at the opposite ends of the spectrum was not an easy task. Senseless prattle was a wonderful way to rest one's mind.

"I still can't believe it," Bunny Endicott babbled, as they sipped tea and feasted on watercress sandwiches.

"What can't you believe?" Lizzy LaFontaine asked.

"You mean you haven't heard?" Bunny asked, her hand clasped to her chest.

"Heard what?" Lizzy asked, again.

"Kitty Whitfield has hired that avant-garde caterer, the one who made all those delectable foods for Betsy's wedding, to prepare an intimate dinner for her and Guy Thrasher." Bunny's words seemed to echo through the room, and Lauren's ears perked.

"That can't be true," Lizzy gasped.

"But it is," Bunny went on. "I heard about it from my butler who heard about it from Kitty's personal maid."

"What would ever possess Kitty to do that?" Lizzy asked.

They didn't know Max, Lauren thought, or they wouldn't be so quick to judge him, to think he wasn't worthy enough to cater an intimate—or even a non-intimate—Palm Beach affair. "He really is a wonderful chef," Lauren piped in.

Bunny glared at her as if she'd lost her mind. Lizzy's perfectly plucked brows almost knit together, she was frowning so hard.

"I didn't know Guy Thrasher was a chef," Bunny said.

"Me neither," Lizzy added. "I was under the impression that he couldn't do much of anything any longer, not even with the help of Viagra. And from all the things I've heard about Guy in the past, even when he could do something, he wasn't very good at it."

"I'd heard exactly the same thing," Bunny went

on, leaving Lauren completely confused. "What just amazes me is that Kitty could fall for a man like that. He's a terrible bore, not to mention an absolute snob. Why, I tried to get him to work at that soup kitchen in West Palm Beach last Thanksgiving and he flat-out refused."

"And I couldn't get a donation from him when the last hurricane hit the coast. All I wanted was a few old clothes, and we all know Guy has plenty of those."

"Wait a minute!" Lauren interrupted. "Do you mean to tell me it doesn't bother you that Kitty's hired Max Wilde?"

"You mean the chef?" Bunny asked, looking totally perplexed.

"Yes, *that* Max Wilde."

"Of course not, Lauren. Why should that bother—" Bunny clasped a hand to her mouth. When she'd regained her composure, she smiled slyly. "I forgot. You've been seeing that man, haven't you?"

Here it goes. The inquisition. The snide remarks. "He's a friend," Lauren stated.

Lizzy grinned as she reached for a watercress sandwich. "If I were you, Lauren, I'd want him for much more than a friend. You may not be aware of this, but several of us were checking out Mr. Wilde's body at Betsy's wedding. Absolutely gorgeous! And I hear that Angie Hart made a pass at the man tending bar."

"Wasn't *he* attractive!" Bunny quipped. "And would you believe he's a dentist? Quite well-to-do, in fact. I can't believe I thought he might be a thief."

"We all make misjudgments like that from time to time," Lizzy stated. "It's just one of those things that happens."

Lauren smiled as she listened to the conversation. She'd often found these friends boring, superficial, with lives that were trivial, at best. Today she'd listened, though. Really listened, and she'd heard such incredible things.

Why didn't she know that Bunny spent Thanksgivings working in a soup kitchen? Why was it that the only things she'd known about Bunny were that she had breast implants, that she was looking for husband number four?

And Lizzy. When did she start collecting money for disaster relief?

What else didn't she know about her friends? Maybe she really had been a snob—in more ways than one.

Her life really had gotten better since Max appeared in it. Not just because he made her happy—before he'd insanely called it quits between them—but because he was helping her see the other side of the people she'd always known.

Suddenly, everything became clear. She knew exactly what she had to do to bring Max into the world she loved—she was going to take her world to him.

*   *   *

It was just past midnight when Max led a half-asleep Ryan to his bedroom and watched him collapse in bed, clothes, shoes, and all. Turning out the light, Max closed the door and carried Jamie to her room. She'd been asleep for over an hour and hadn't made a sound when he lifted her from the car.

Pulling back the covers on her bed, he laid her down, took off her sandals, then tugged the sheet up to her shoulders.

"Thanks for taking us to Disney World," she said, her voice nearly muffled by the pillows. "It was fun, but it would have been nicer if Lauren had gone with us."

Max sat on the edge of her bed. "You think so?"

Jamie nodded, then tucked her hands under her cheek. "I thought you liked her."

"I do."

"Then how come you haven't seen her in a while?"

"I've been busy."

"That's not a good excuse."

"Yeah, well, I plan on calling her tomorrow." And with all his heart, he hoped she'd take him back.

Jamie smiled, apparently satisfied with his answer, and snuggled further into the pillows.

"Good night," Max whispered, kissing her brow.

"Good night, Dad."

Max closed his eyes, enjoying the lingering sound of that word. *Dad.* It was the first time Jamie had used it since the attorney called to say Jamie and Ryan's dad had decided to give them up. There hadn't been any remorse from either kid. It had been far too long since they'd seen or heard from the man, and as far as Jamie and Ryan were concerned, their biological father had pretty much ceased to exist. Now the children Max loved were legally his.

Getting up from the bed, he headed for his office and slumped down in his desk chair. They'd been gone three days, and the recorder showed a slew of messages. He hit the rewind button, yawned, then hit play, figuring he ought to get this out of the way before going to bed.

Mrs. Fabiano had called to thank him once again for Luigi's birthday party. Bunny Endicott—of all people—wanted him to cater an intimate dinner, and if he wasn't mistaken, he could have sworn he heard Bear's laugh in the background. Two more calls were from prospective Palm Beach clients, a call from Bear, one from Jazz, and then he heard Lauren's voice, soft, sweet, sexy, maybe even a little hesitant.

"Call me. Please."

The call had come two long days ago. What a fool he'd been not calling her before going away with Jamie and Ryan. Hopefully, when he called her tomorrow, she'd still want to talk.

Surprisingly, the next message was also from Lauren.

"Sorry to bother you, Max. This is Lauren. I don't believe I left my name on the last message, so I wanted to call again, just in case you weren't sure who had asked you to call. So now that you know it's me, could you please call?"

He grinned. Her voice was definitely more encouraging.

Beep.

"This is my third call, Max. It's been three hours since my first one, and I really do need to talk with you. Please. Call me."

Beep.

"Fourth call. I really do want to talk with you, Max." This time he heard trembling in her voice. "Call me. Please."

Beep.

"All right, Max, it's Lauren again. I don't know why you're not returning my calls, but . . . but, oh, hell! I'll be at the Hole in the Wall at noon on Tuesday. You may not want to see me again but I want to see you. Please be there. If you don't show up, well . . ." She sighed deeply. "I love you, Max. *Please* be there."

He'd be there at noon no matter what, and then he'd never let Lauren out of his sight again.

Beep.

"Hey, Max, it's Harry. I might have some good news for you. Call me as soon as you can."

It wasn't quite nine-thirty in California. Max grabbed the phone, punched in Harry's number, and waited.

"Harry Crow."

"It's Max Wilde, Harry. I've been out of town and just got your call."

"I'm glad you called," Harry said. "I've got another lead."

"How good a one?" Max asked, his hopes high in spite of all the past failures.

"Promising, that's the best answer I can give you. I managed to find a retired agent who handled a few child actors nineteen, twenty years ago. He distinctly remembered a little girl named Charlotte Wilde."

"Did he have any records, any—"

"All he had was a vivid memory of the girl's mother. Loretta Wilde."

Max plowed his fingers through his hair. This was the first Charlotte Wilde Harry had ever connected to a woman with the same name as Max's mother. "What else did he tell you?"

"Not a lot. The woman was a tyrant. He couldn't place the girl in commercials or anything because of Loretta's demands on everyone. I checked a few other leads, found out Charlotte had been adopted, and finally tracked down her adoptive parents."

"Christ, Harry. What do you mean this is just a promising lead?"

"Because her adoptive parents won't give me any information."

That wasn't what Max wanted to hear. "Why not?"

"I don't have a clue. He's a retired Marine Corps chaplain. She's a housewife. They live in Barstow and that's where they lived when Charlotte was growing up. Charlotte Mattingly's the name she went by."

Max repeated the name to himself. This was the closest they'd ever come. "Is she the right age?" he asked, sure that Harry wouldn't have called if he hadn't confirmed that information first.

"Yeah. Right age. Right hair and eye color."

"What about her past?"

"That information's fairly sketchy. They traveled around from Marine base to Marine base until they hit Barstow. Charlotte was quiet, or so her few old acquaintances told me. Real religious. She led Bible study groups at school, didn't go to dances, didn't hang out."

"My sister liked to dance and sing. She was outgoing, full of life."

"Look, Max, the girl's parents seem pretty strict. A kid can change living with a family like that."

Yeah, Max knew full well the influence parents could have over their kids—good, bad, indifferent.

"So, where do we go from here?" Max asked.

"I keep looking. Something's bound to come up."

"Okay, call me when you hear something more."

"One other thing, Max. I feel good about this one. I don't say that too often, but I think I can find her."

Max hung up the phone, staring at the paper where he'd scribbled Lauren's name over and over, and under that where he'd written Charlotte Mattingly. He didn't believe in fairy godmothers or guardian angels, but he figured he must have done something awfully good in his life to deserve this new streak of fortune.

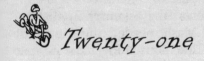

Twenty-one

*L*auren stood at the door to the Hole in the Wall at exactly twelve o'clock. She wore a knock-Max's-socks-off perforated-leather spaghetti-strap dress. Short, white, and very low cut, it looked stunning with dangling diamond earrings and a two-strand diamond tennis bracelet. She'd thought about wearing knee-high white leather boots, but that would have been overdoing the effect, so she settled on a pair of Ferragamo heels. Three-inch spikes, because nothing less would do.

She wanted Max to drool. Then she wanted him to fall into her arms because the past two weeks, although the busiest time of her life, had also been the loneliest. She needed him desperately.

But did he need her? He hadn't returned any of

her calls—but he could have been out of town or busy. She couldn't jump to conclusions, she simply had to operate on the assumption that he needed her as much as she needed him. He might have said a lot of ridiculous things, but he had said he loved her—and she believed him. And he was going to love her a lot more when he heard the details of how she planned to bring the best of their two completely opposite worlds together.

Taking a deep breath, she pushed open the heavy door and walked into the Hole in the Wall. A second later it slammed behind her, echoing through the empty warehouse.

"Hello. Anyone here?"

Silence. Yet she'd distinctly seen half a dozen motorcycles outside, including Max's.

She walked across the concrete floor, the clicking of her heels reverberating against the walls. She hated the hollow sound. Hated to be alone.

And then she heard the distinctive thud of heavy boots on the floor.

"Hello, Lauren."

She spun around when she heard Max's deep, mesmerizing voice echoing through the warehouse. He leaned against a wall, his hands shoved in his pockets. There were dark circles under his eyes and he looked worried, but in spite of that, she couldn't miss the tiny sparkle in his eyes. He looked strong, warm, and unspeakably desirable, just the kind of man she'd always needed in her life.

"Hello," she said softly.

She walked toward him, completely captivated

by the strands of black hair falling over his brow, the powerful muscles in his arms and beneath the white T-shirt he wore. She stopped maybe a foot away from him, drawing in the musky scent of his aftershave. She wanted to touch him, but she held back, still mystified by the emptiness of the Hole. "Where is everyone?"

"Gone."

"Why?"

His heated gaze strolled leisurely over the entire length of her body, and goose bumps rose on her arms. "So we could have the place to ourselves."

"At the risk of sounding crazy, why did you want to be alone?"

"Because I didn't want anyone to see me crumble if you said you loved me, and then said you didn't want to see me again."

"That would be a terribly foolish thing for me to say. It would be foolish for anyone to say, don't you think?"

"Yeah. Real foolish. I know someone who's regretted saying it to the woman he loved."

"Did he call her and say he was sorry?"

Max shook his head. "He was afraid she might have decided he wasn't worth troubling with."

"If she loved him, really and truly loved him," Lauren said, "she'd understand, and she'd forgive him."

She reached out, touching the smoothness of his cheek, brushing her thumb over his mustache and goatee, and the remarkable lips she'd grown to love. "She might have even reserved a penthouse suite for them at the Breakers—hoping they could go there to make up."

Suddenly she was in Max's arms and his mouth closed over hers, leaving no doubt at all that he wanted to make up. "I want things to work between us," he breathed against her lips. "I don't care what I have to do, Lauren, but one way or another I'll fit into your world."

She hugged him tightly, resting her cheek against his. "I heard about the intimate dinner you prepared for Kitty Whitfield. She's a bit ditzy and not easy to please, but she's raved about you to everyone." Lauren looked into his wonderful brown eyes. "I'd say you've gone over and above board to fit into my world, now I want mine to fit into yours."

"That's never going to happen, Lauren."

"But it can. I've spent nearly two weeks figuring it all out and—"

The outside door burst open, sending sunlight skittering across the floor. Two burly delivery men walked in. "Where do you want the stuff?" one of them yelled at Lauren.

"Oh, dear. They're early."

"Who's early?" Max asked, frowning when she pulled from his embrace.

"The delivery men." She smiled weakly, wishing she'd had a few more minutes to explain. "Would you excuse me a moment?"

She didn't give Max time to answer, she just twisted away from him and headed toward the biggest, burliest guy, the one who looked like he might be in charge. Through nearly clenched teeth, she said, "You weren't supposed to arrive until twelve-thirty."

"Look, lady, you get it when you get it. So where do you want it?"

"How can I possibly know where I want it when you didn't give me time to decide where it should go?"

"We could always dump it outside."

"No, that's not a good idea."

She felt a heavy hand on her shoulder. "What's going on?" Max asked, confusion narrowing his eyes.

"I need to decide where to put the plants."

"What plants?"

"The ones I ordered. The ones that are going to start flowing in here any second now."

"We don't need any plants in here!"

"Of course you do."

"The place is fine like it is."

"Pardon me for saying this, Max, but it's boring. It's got no style whatsoever."

"It's a warehouse!"

"Please don't argue with me. I've got enough on my mind just trying to decide where everything should go."

He shook his head. "You are the most—"

"Yes, I know, I'm exasperating, but you can tell me all the reasons why you love me later. I've got too much to do at the moment."

One of the men walked toward her, his arms laden with two potted plants. "Where do you want these ferns?"

"Those are dieffenbachia."

"Yeah, okay, so where do you want them?"

Lauren looked all about her, finally settling on the perfect place. "In the corners, on either side of the basketball court."

"You can't have plants over there," Max grumbled. "They'll get in the way."

"If they get in the way, they can be moved later. Now," she said, marching across the room, I want a few ferns over here." She headed for another spot. "You can put the baskets of philodendron here, and we'll arrange them when the furniture arrives."

"Furniture!"

Goodness, was Max going to stand around and bellow all day?

She spun around, thinking Max was still clear across the warehouse, but his chest was just inches away. His heated eyes were even closer. "Yes, Max," she smiled sweetly, "furniture."

"We already have furniture."

"You have *wooden* furniture. I've found something that's far better. A few sofas. They're black leather, not exactly my taste but I wanted something you'd approve of. I'm also having some occasional chairs delivered, in colors and fabrics that will complement the black leather, and I found some lovely glass-topped tables."

Max rubbed his temples. "The last thing we need around here are glass-topped tables."

"I think you're in desperate need of them, Max. This place has absolutely no atmosphere."

She heard a distinct giggle coming from the

hallway that led to the rest rooms. "Who's giggling?"

"Jamie, more than likely."

"Why's she hiding?"

"I suppose she sneaked back in here after I told her and everyone else to clear out while I talked to you. Obviously she didn't listen to me, because no one seems to listen to me anymore, especially you. I wouldn't be surprised if a dozen people were in the back, listening to the show you're putting on."

"This is not a show, Max. It's my attempt to combine the best of both worlds—yours and mine."

"With furniture? With atmosphere?"

Goodness, he could be *so* difficult. "For starters."

"Please don't tell me there's more."

"Of course there is. I want to give the kids a comfortable environment to hang out in."

"I suppose you're going to have Starbucks coffee, too."

"I hadn't considered food at this point, and really, Max, food is *your* specialty, not mine."

He shoved his fingers through his hair, and she did so love the way it just flopped right back down over his brow.

"So what else should I be expecting?" he asked, in a disgruntled tone that was becoming quite charming.

"Computers."

"And?"

"Desks and chairs."

"Who's going to teach the kids how to operate the computers? You?"

"You know that's an impossibility, Max. I'm not the least bit capable of handling anything electronic. Fortunately, Charles has volunteered his services. Dickie Stribling has, too. He's promised to start as soon as he and Betsy get back from their honeymoon. In fact, Dickie's the one donating the computers, printers, scanners, the whole works."

"You're not serious?"

She moved close, putting her fingertips on his throbbing temples, rubbing them softly. "I've never been more serious about anything in my life. I've spent the last week drumming up donations, putting together one plan after another. It might surprise you, Max, but I have an awful lot of friends who are quite interested in helping out here at the Hole. You might have known that if you'd ever bothered to ask the people of Palm Beach for help, but you didn't. You know why, Max?"

"Why?"

"Because you're just as much of a snob as I am. You don't like rich people."

His hands slid around her waist, tugging her against his chest. "I like you."

"I like you, too. I've never liked anyone more, as a matter of fact. But you're going to have to like more than just one snooty rich fashion plate if you want things to work out between us."

He kissed the tip of her nose, his beard tickling her lips. "It's going to be tough." His voice was deep, mesmerizing, something that was going to change in a matter of seconds.

"It's going to be more than tough, Max. It might be pure hell."

"Why?"

He kissed her, and she whispered her words against his delicious mouth. "Your first project will be to start liking Chip."

He jerked away. "That's impossible!"

She planted her fists firmly on her hips. "I told you before that Chip has a few good qualities. In fact, he excelled at math in school and I've never known anyone who could figure out so quickly how much they won or lost at the racetrack. *So*, he's volunteered to tutor kids in math once a week. I know it's not much, but Chip has made a commitment, which is a big step for him."

"I thought Chip had a gambling problem."

"He does, but I've given him explicit instructions that he can't teach the kids any of his betting tricks."

Max chuckled. "I imagine some of them will teach him."

"That might be a good thing. Chip loses far too much money."

Max dragged her against him again. Obviously he wasn't as angry as he pretended. "What about you, Lauren? What are you going to do at the Hole?"

"Teach."

"What? If I remember correctly, you flunked physics."

"But I'm very good in geography and history—at least Ryan thinks so. In fact, I've traveled all around the world and I can tell anybody anything they want or need to know about places like Cannes and Monte Carlo, not to mention Paris and Milan. But I strongly feel that there's a need to teach children much more than the basics."

"You mean things like pouring tea and how to set a proper table?"

She aimed a nasty glare at him. "I mean things like how to operate a cash register so they can get a job. Not the greatest job in the world, maybe, but not everybody gets to start at the top. So, I've ordered a cash register and hired an instructor."

"You accomplished all of this in a week?"

"It's not all that much when you're organized. I even found time to talk my sister-in-law into going into partnership with me on a clothing store."

Max closed his eyes and shook his head. When his eyes opened again, she could see a speck of mirth.

"Okay, I'm waiting. What's the story behind the clothing store."

"It's a thrift store called How Tacky and even though I wouldn't be caught dead shopping there, Sam has always loved the place. I got to thinking the other night that some of the girls who come here could use a job, so I plan to give them one once they learn a few rudimentary things about dress. And before you get all high and mighty and say I don't know a thing about how the girls here should dress, I've asked some of the current staff from How Tacky to come around and give classes, which includes free clothes, even if the girls choose not to work for us."

Max laughed. "What about your wedding planning business? Is that history?"

"Definitely not. Oh, I may have thought I was a failure at that for a day or two, but the wedding planning business is definitely back on. I have a lot of friends who are going to help out here, so I'll have plenty of time for my business. It may even surprise you that Bunny Endicott's going to volunteer."

"That doesn't surprise me in the least. I'm catering an intimate dinner for her."

"I heard a rumor that Bunny's got a new man in her life," Lauren said. "Do you know who he is?"

Max's glare shot toward the back room, to a laugh that unmistakably belonged to Bear. "I don't know, and I'm not too sure I want to find out."

"Well, I'll check into it. Bunny's usually pretty forthcoming about her affairs, and if she's got any thoughts at all about another wedding, I need to be the first to know. Born To Be Wild Weddings won't survive without paying customers."

Max's brows knit together. "Born To Be Wild *Weddings*?"

"The advertising will say it's for brides who want something not quite traditional."

"And you want to call it Born To Be Wild?"

"Only if you'll be my business partner."

She loved the way his lips tilted into a wry grin. "What's in it for me?"

"I was hoping you'd ask that question, because I really do think this is the best part of the entire idea."

"Hey, Lauren!" There was no mistaking Ryan's shout. "There's a phone call for you."

She turned toward the disembodied voice. "Could you ask if I could call back later? Max and I are terribly busy at the moment."

"I don't think so," came Ryan's voice from out of the darkness. "It's your butler. He sounds worried, something about the police being at your house to arrest some jewelry thief, and your mother's frantic. He said you really need to get there quick."

"Oh, dear!"

Lauren's entire body screamed with anxiety as Max whipped the motorcycle in and out of traffic. She hugged him close, never more thankful to have him near.

The police car was just pulling onto the street when Max zoomed into the circular drive, and Lauren did a double-take at the person she saw through the back window. "Oh, dear."

She wasted no time at all getting off the bike, rushing through the house with Max not far behind. She found her mother sitting quietly on a sofa in the library, her hands folded in her lap.

"Are you all right, Mother?" Lauren asked, sitting at her side.

"Charles is bringing me some tea. I'm sure I'll be better after that."

Max leaned against the library door, not coming fully into the room. He smiled at Lauren, and she knew he'd be there for her if she needed him. Always.

"I saw the police leaving," Lauren said. "Was that really Gerald I saw in the back?"

Celeste nodded, her eyes glazed, as if in shock. "He's been stealing jewelry for years."

"That's impossible! I've never cared for him all that much, but a jewel thief?"

"I'm afraid so."

Charles walked into the room, setting down the silver tea service. "Shall I pour for you?" he asked, directing his words to Lauren.

"I'll take care of it," Lauren said. "Thank you."

"Is there anything else I can do?"

"The tea will be enough, Charles," Celeste added, smiling at the man she'd rarely noticed over the years. "You've always remembered exactly how I like it. I don't think I've ever thanked you for that."

Lauren couldn't miss the slight sparkle in Charles's eyes. "I'm happy to serve you, any time you'd like."

Charles was gone in a moment, probably as perplexed by Celeste's sudden—but very lovely—change as Lauren was.

She watched her mother as she poured the tea. Celeste's hands trembled and her eyes were rimmed with red. This was not the always-sure-of-herself mother Lauren knew. She was different, vulnerable, and Lauren's heart warmed to her more than ever before.

"What happened?" Lauren asked, stirring in the little bit of cream her mother indulged in, and handing her the cup.

Celeste blew lightly on the tea and took a sip. "Gerald and I spent the past few days sailing, talking about you, how he wanted to marry again. It was all so idyllic and then we came back here . . . not more than an hour ago." Celeste drew in a deep breath. "I was all prepared to talk you into going with us to his island in Fiji when the police came. It was awful, absolutely dreadful."

"Why did they come *here*, Mother? Why not his yacht?"

"I don't know. I suppose I should have asked, but it all happened so quickly. They had a warrant to search Gerald's car and luggage and they found things that completely surprised me. Bunny's necklace. That ruby and diamond necklace of yours that I love so much. I don't know when he took it. Probably the night he was here for dinner. I was so stunned, so amazed that he'd take jewelry from his friends."

"What made the police suspect him?"

"His ex-wife, Jessica, turned him in. You know how he always loved to give her jewelry. Apparently he made a mistake and gave her a piece that belonged to an acquaintance of hers. They searched his home in Martha's Vineyard and found artwork, jewelry, it was staggering." She laughed nervously. "I should have known."

"He fooled everyone, Mother."

Celeste reached out and clasped Lauren's

hands. "I wanted you to marry him. I'm so sorry, darling."

"You just wanted me to be happy, that's all."

"No, you were right when we had that argument a few weeks ago. I've meddled too much in your life. First Chip, then Leland and Peter. I made wrong choices for you, and criticized you when you couldn't make the relationships work."

"I could have said no. Please, Mother, don't worry about it."

Celeste looked across the room, toward Max. "I owe you an apology, too."

"You don't owe me anything," Max said.

"But I do. I've been very judgmental, and I'm sorry."

There was a moment of silence between them, Max studying Celeste, Celeste analyzing him, and finally a small smile touched Max's lips. "It's not a problem."

"Thank you."

Max walked toward Lauren and cupped her cheek in his warm, gentle palm. "I'll be outside on the patio if you need me."

Drawing his hand to her lips, she kissed it. "I'll be outside soon."

"Take all the time you need. I'm not going anywhere."

She watched him leave, knowing over the years she'd see him walking away from her many times, knowing, too, that he'd never be far away, that they'd always be there for each other.

"Do you really love him?" Celeste asked.

Lauren turned back to her mother, her heart bursting with all that she felt for Max. "He brings out the best in me."

A slow smile touched Celeste's face. "Then I'm happy for you."

"Do you mean that?"

"I had a very rude awakening this afternoon when Gerald was arrested. I thought people like you and me were above all that." She shook her head. "Now I realize we're no different from anyone else."

"There will always be differences," Lauren added, "but it's amazing how much we can learn from each other. I can't begin to tell you how much I've learned being with Max."

Celeste laughed. "I can well imagine what Max has taught you. Probably things I would never approve of, but that's between the two of you."

Celeste rose from the sofa, smoothing her hands over her apricot linen skirt. "I've got a flight in a few hours, so I'd better go pack."

"Where are you going to go now?" Lauren asked. "Aspen? Back to Rio?"

"I'm going home. I have a husband I love very much, a husband I never should have run away from." She laughed lightly. "I have an awful lot of apologizing to do."

"I have the feeling Andrew will forgive everything the moment you walk through the door."

"I certainly hope so." Celeste smiled. "I bought a lovely Carolina Herrera dress right before going sailing. I can't wait for Andrew to see it. He has such wonderful taste in clothing, and . . . goodness, I shouldn't be rambling so. You've got a young man waiting outside for you, and I've got a distinguished gentleman waiting at home for me. I think I'll call him. Let him know I'm on my way."

Celeste wrapped her arms around Lauren and hugged her closely. It lasted only a moment, but it was a memory Lauren would keep for a lifetime.

"Run along, darling," Celeste said, as she breezed out of the library. "I'll call you when I get home."

Lauren watched her mother until she disappeared, listened until she no longer heard Celeste's heels on the marble stairway, and then she walked toward the open French doors, toward the man she loved.

He leaned against the balustrade, his wild black hair blowing about, as he gazed toward the ocean. She stood at his side, loving the feel of his hand as it slipped around her waist, pulling her close, the place she always wanted to be.

"I've been thinking," Max said.

"About what?"

"This partnership you want me to get involved in."

"You mean Born To Be Wild Weddings?"

"Yeah. I'm not too sure a business partnership is going to work."

He was teasing, of course. She could hear it in his tone of voice, could feel it in the way his fingers gently massaged her side, the way he kept inching her body closer and closer to his.

"It *will* work, Max. I've got the entire thing

planned out. We'll hold the weddings here because, really, this pink marble monstrosity isn't fit for much of anything but parties, engagement balls, or a gala here and there."

He tilted his head to look at her, and the twinkle in his eyes made her weak. "I take it you're moving out?"

"That's another plan I've been working on this past week. Do you remember that piece of beach property I showed you, the one I bought with money from my very first investment?"

"I remember."

"Well, I was thinking that would be the perfect place for a home—a real home. Of course, I don't want to live there on my own."

"Do you have someone in mind to live there with you?"

"Charles, naturally, because I couldn't possibly go anywhere without him. And Mrs. Fisk, because she knows all my culinary likes and dislikes."

"Anyone else?"

She wove her arms around his neck and pressed her body against his, loving the feel, wanting to hold him and be held by him forever. "I might let you live there, too, and Jamie and Ryan, of course."

"You'll already have one chef."

Smiling, she kissed his lips. "But no one can cook quite like you."

"Is that so?" he asked, the twitch of his mustache tickling her mouth.

"Oh, most definitely. In fact, I've got this fantasy of you cooking in bed, feeding me all sorts of delectable treats."

"Is there something you particularly enjoy?"

"Mmmm," she murmured, pressing a kiss to his scrumptious lips. "Anything Wilde will do."

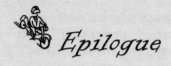

Epilogue

*L*auren Remington's wedding to Max Wilde would not go down in Palm Beach history as a highlight of the season. It would, however, be remembered as the only wedding where the groom wore a black leather tux while the bride wore a shimmering silver Oscar de la Renta original, where champagne flowed at the same rate as beer from kegs, and where pigs-in-a-blanket were arranged on silver platters right next to Caribbean brochettes.

The groom and his friends arrived in a thundering motorcade of choppers that contrasted sharply with the bride's entourage, which came in a dignified procession of Bentleys, Mercedes, and Rolls. And then, of course, there was the highly unconventional entertainment.

"Oh, dear!" Lauren clasped a hand against her chest. "I know Bear's been doing odd things since Bunny dumped him. I know he meant well hiring a band of ex-cons to play at our reception and I've accepted the fact that most of them feel they got a bad rap. But *please* tell me he didn't hire a stripper to round out the evening."

Max chuckled at his wife's anxiety. "Not a stripper, Lauren. A Las Vegas showgirl."

"You might see a difference between the two, but I don't. Goodness, Max! She's not going to be topless, is she?"

"The only one who's going to be topless is you." Max pulled his frantic bride behind a secluded palm and took advantage of the privacy, trailing his fingers over her soft round shoulders, along the curve of her neck, at last tracing the silky skin edging the satiny fabric of her dangerously low-cut gown. "The topless part comes later, of course . . . when we're alone, and I have the pleasure of slowly peeling off every stitch of clothing you're wearing."

She leaned into him, her heavenly breasts pressing against his chest as she kissed the base of his neck and made his body shudder. "There's not going to be much to peel off," she said, her words a mesmerizing purr against his ear. "Beneath this gown are a thong, a skimpy bra, and nothing else. I was afraid I wouldn't have the patience for a slow striptease. Not tonight."

"I don't have the patience, either," Max admitted, a definite understatement given his current state of anxiety. "So why don't we ditch the rest of this reception and start the honeymoon ahead of schedule?"

"That's such a lovely thought, Max, but we can't leave until we've had our first dance together." Her words whispered warmly over his mouth, making him want her even more. "After that, we have to cut the cake, toss the bouquet, and let the guests throw birdseed at us."

"That could take hours."

A seductive smile touched her lips. "So could a lot of very pleasant things I have planned in the days to come."

"Ladies and gentlemen." The squealing microphone and Bear's booming voice tore Max's attention away from paradise. Getting a grip on his senses, he tugged Lauren from behind the palm to face the laughter and questioning stares of the guests.

"Now that I've got the bride and groom's attention—" Bear's voice burst through the amplifiers, "I want to tell you about the special treat we've got for you this evening, straight from the Las Vegas strip."

"Please don't let her be topless," Lauren chanted, as Max led her toward the bandstand.

"The little lady I'm about to introduce you to can belt out a song better than anyone I've ever heard," Bear continued. "So, without any further ado, may we have a big round of applause for Charity."

Max and every guest watched in awe as the long-legged, black-haired knockout stepped from her hiding place behind the band and strolled toward Bear wearing the shortest, tightest, reddest mini-dress Max had ever seen.

Applause erupted through the crowd. Well . . . the men were applauding. The women were far more subdued, except for Lauren, whose eyes fixed on the stunner from Las Vegas. Even Pastor Flynn was caught in her trance. Max didn't know the man, but Lauren had told him time and again that Mike Flynn wasn't interested in women. Apparently she didn't know the stalwart minister all that well, because it was more than obvious he found the showgirl intriguing.

Maybe it was her longer-than-long legs Mike found fascinating. Maybe it was her wild black hair. Hell, Max didn't care what attracted Mike to the woman, he just wished she'd sing so he could dance with his wife.

Charity took the microphone from Bear. "Thank you," she said, her voice soft and low as she faced the gathering, hitting Mike with a killer smile that could have knocked a lesser man off his feet. Slowly she turned her focus on the other guests. "I've always loved the song Lauren picked for her first dance with Max." Her voice was melodic, and Pastor Flynn looked completely mesmerized, Max thought. "I don't think anyone can sing 'Could I Have This Dance' quite like Anne Murray, but the words are beautiful and perfect for two people beginning a life together."

Charity's dark brown eyes sparkled as she looked across the dance floor. Her gaze rested momentarily on Lauren, then trailed toward Max. He saw something familiar in the tilt of her smile, but the remembrance was fleeting, chased away by the tinkling of the piano and by the nearness of his wife, who swayed with him when he pulled her into his arms.

"I'll always remember . . ." Charity began, and the beautiful lilt of her voice filled the air.

Max pressed his cheek to Lauren's, tuning out the music, listening only to the rhythm of his heart beating in time with his wife's. They circled the pool and their guests, but Max saw only his bride. She was lovely and warm and he lowered his mouth over hers, kissing her tenderly, feeling as if his heart would burst with happiness.

"I love you," he whispered.

"I love you, too," Lauren said, her smile and the trace of tears in her eyes charming him as nothing ever had.

Suddenly their song ended and another began. A blur of family and friends began to dance, a male voice sang into the microphone, and the cool night breeze whispered around them as Max led Lauren away from the crowd, needing to have her all to himself.

Stars and thousands of miniature lights twinkled around them. Lauren had master-minded this whole incredible event, yet all Max wanted was to spirit his wife away from the festivities, to leave the reception and begin the honeymoon. But a gentle hand touched his shoulder, drawing him to a stop. The showgirl stood at his side, smiling with question-filled eyes.

"I think you might be looking for me."

Max frowned, shaking his head. "You must have me confused with someone else."

Her dark brown eyes sparkled. "I'm sorry. I was under the impression you were looking for your sister."

Lauren's fingers dug into his arm as he stared at the woman in red.

"Charlotte?" he asked, the word nearly sticking in his throat.

"I haven't gone by Charlotte in years. I'm Charity now."

All Max could do was stare, trying to match this woman with the four-year-old who'd waved goodbye to him twenty years ago. She had the same black hair, the same brown eyes, but he was afraid to get his hopes up.

"How did you know I was looking for my sister?" he asked, his words short, to the point.

"Your investigator told my parents, for starters."

"Harry never said anything about looking for a Las Vegas showgirl."

"I'm afraid my parents would never divulge my current occupation to anyone. I imagine your investigator was looking for a shy young girl with her nose in her Bible." Charity smiled. "That was me in a former life."

Max wasn't buying it. "How do I know you're my sister."

"Goodness, Max!" Lauren glared at him as if he'd lost his mind. "Can't you see the similarities? You've got the same eyes, the same smile."

Lauren made it sound so easy, but he'd seen too many other women over the years who had his eyes, his smile. Too many other women claiming to be his sister, when they weren't.

"Do you remember where we lived?" he asked, ignoring Lauren's protests, needing some kind of confirmation from Charity.

But she shook her head at his question. "My parents wouldn't tell me much about my life before they adopted me—only that my name was Charlotte Wilde. I don't have an original birth certificate. I don't have any old photos, and it was just a week ago that my parents told me I might have a brother. I had to persuade them to give me Harry Crow's phone number, and I had to beg him not to tell you I'd be coming today. I wanted time to try and remember the early years of my life before seeing you."

"And did you remember anything?" Max asked, some of his skepticism easing away.

"Only this." She pulled a lock of hair away from her forehead to reveal a scar not more than an inch long. "I remembered an accident and my head hurting. I remembered crying, and someone holding me, making me feel better until the ambulance came. But that's all."

Max touched the scar lightly, remembering the accident, remembering the way he'd pulled Charlotte into his arms and pressed his T-shirt to the gash on her forehead, telling her everything would be all right.

But everything had gone all wrong. Charlotte

had disappeared, leaving a hole in his heart for twenty years.

Now—finally—she was back.

Max felt tears welling in his eyes, felt his wife squeezing his hand, felt as if the best day of his entire life had suddenly gotten even better.

He pulled his sister into his arms, holding her close, letting the reality of the moment sink in. "There's so much to talk about, so much to tell you."

"And I've got at least a million questions—but they'll have to wait till later."

"Why later?" Max asked, holding on to her hands when she tried to pull away. "What's wrong with now?"

"Because this is your wedding day. Because you've got a honeymoon to go on and I've never come between a husband and wife and I don't intend to start now. Besides, I flew in just for the day. I've got a plane to catch in less than two hours—"

"Please stay longer," Lauren urged. "We can postpone the honeymoon a day or two."

"That's the craziest thing I've ever heard, and let me tell you, I hear a lot of crazy things in Vegas. No," Charity stated, "I'm not interrupting your honeymoon. In fact, I'm not going to take up even one more minute of your time."

"We'll come to Las Vegas," Max said, studying the beauty of her face, soaking up a few new memories to hold on to.

"I'd love that," Charity said. "I start a new show

in a few weeks and I'll get you the best seats in the house."

All too soon she was out of his arms, telling him where she could be reached, and doling out kisses and smiles before she walked toward the other guests. She stopped not ten feet away and flashed a bright smile over her shoulder. "By the way, who was the tall, good-looking guy who was watching me sing?"

"The one all in black?" Lauren asked.

"That's the one."

"Oh, dear," Lauren answered. "That's Mike Flynn—the minister."

Charity rolled her eyes. "Well, I'll scratch him from my list of dance partners. There's just something about me and ministers that doesn't quite compute."

Charity didn't say another word. Instead, she headed straight for the guy standing next to Pastor Flynn and tugged the reluctant gentleman to the dance floor. Max drew his wife to his side and watched his sister until she disappeared into the crowd.

"We can go to Las Vegas tonight," Lauren said, curling her fingers over his cheek, kissing him lightly.

"Is that what you really want?"

She smiled. "Not exactly, but I love you, Max. I want you to be happy, and if that means spending time with Charity, well . . . I can wait a little while for our honeymoon."

"I don't want to wait," he said, smoothing a lock of wind-tossed hair from her cheek. "Not for a week, not for a day, not even till this reception's over."

"The plane to Tahiti doesn't leave until morning."

"But the Fantasy Inn's open all night."

Lauren's eyes darted toward the patio where over two hundred guests had congregated, two hundred guests who were eating, drinking, dancing, and didn't seem to miss the bride and groom.

A soft, slow smile touched her lips as she gripped his fingers, lifted the hem of her silver gown, and beat a hasty retreat through the pink marble monstrosity to the sleek black motorcycle parked in the circular drive.

Max swung his leg over the Harley, and Lauren did the same, her delectable body snuggling close to his. "I love you," she whispered against his ear.

Max twisted in the seat, sweeping his fingers through her hair. "I love you, too." Then he kissed her. Softly. Tenderly.

And Max knew, without a doubt, that this was just the beginning of the sweetest, wildest ride of their lives.

Look for Charity Wilde's story coming soon from Avon Books.

*"I'm Tess Redding, and I know everyone in
Mount Circe, Georgia—there's my three best,
life-long friends, the Sweethearts—we've stuck
by each other through thick and thin waist-lines,
half-hearted boyfriends . . . and everything else.
But now, Mount Circe's very own prodigal son,
Flynn Garvey's, returned . . . and the Sweethearts
don't know it, but they'd better stick by me
till I get him out of my system!"*

Meet Tess, Flynn and the Sweethearts of Mount Circe
in a fresh, sexy, unforgettable debut romance . . .
only from Avon Books!

Sweethearts of the Twilight Lanes
by
Luanne Jones

And don't miss these other Avon romances available next month
A Breath of Scandal by Connie Mason
The Lawman's Surrender by Debra Mullins
His Forbidden Kiss by Margaret Moore